# A Brand New Saint

Stories by Mary Renzi

# A Brand New Saint

stories by

## Mary Renzi

Ellis Press     2021

Published by Ellis Press, David Pichaske, editor; P.O. Box 6, Granite Falls, Minnesota 56241. Web site: ellispress.com.
Cover design by Marcy Olson.
Printed by Sheridan Books, Inc., Chelsea, Michigan.

ISBN: 978-0-944024-77-5
Price: $20

01    02    03    04    05          2021    2022    2023    2024    2025

# Contents

# Acknowledgments

Several stories in this collection have been previously published online or in print. Ellis Press gratefully acknowledges the following previous publishers (and their editors) for their permission to reprint stories here: *One Throne Magazine* for "Everything Is More Beautiful Here" (fall 2014); *The Newer York* for "Cliff's Edge" (September 2014); *decomP magazine* for "City Burn" (October 2014); *Jersey Devil Press* for "The Dog with the Rhinestone Eyes" (May 2014); *Pantheon Magazine* for "The Crows Followed You Here" (January 2014); *The Molotov Cocktail* for "School Busses"; *Hypnos* for "post Trauma Robotics"; *Swamp Biscuits & Tea* for "Oya" (published as "The Message in the Sound"); *Aphotic Realm Magazine* for "A Brand New Saint." Thanks also to Kristen Neumann and Michelle Pichaske for proofreading help.

# About the Author

Mary Renzi was a born reader and story-teller. As a child, she loved being read to, especially the *Wizard of Oz* and *Peter Pan*. After hearing numerous readings of the Oz story, she walked around saying, "The wizard gave the scarecrow brains! I have brains, too!" to everyone she met. After hearing infinite readings of *Peter Pan*, she would repeat the phrase, "John Michael Darling by name!" over and over.

Eventually, her tastes in reading matured. In middle school and high school, she developed a love of science fiction and horror. A visit to hear Stephen King reading from his latest novel at the National Press Club in Washington, D. C. was something of an epochal event for her. Soon, she was devoting endless hours to reading the Beat Generation writers—Jack Kerouac, William Burroughs, and the like—as well as Edward Abbey, Kurt Vonnegut, Henry Miller, and more.

As an English major at Arizona State University and in the years following, her tastes continued to expand. Her bookshelves filled with the likes of John Steinbeck, and Thomas Pynchon, Douglas Adams and Terrance McKenna, Dostoevsky and Tolstoy, the Illuminatus Trilogy and HP Lovecraft. Meanwhile, she took creative writing classes, and made her first forays into short story-writing.

What also blossomed in Arizona was Mary's love of the outdoors. She had grown up in Maryland, but the mostly tame and tamed East Coast was not for her. A two-week road trip to the Southwest during her teenage years had opened Mary's eyes and her imagination to the vivid spaces of the wild west. After her college years, she would never live anywhere else, although she returned to Maryland often to visit her family.

Her passion for the west and for the outdoors convinced Mary to pursue a career as a wild-land firefighter. She was not a big woman, though she had always been fit and fearless; as a pre-teen, she had been youngest person on her youth soccer team but also the quickest and feistiest. As a firefighter, she welcomed the challenge of a demanding profession. She more than kept up with the big boys and won the respect of every crew she ever worked with, many of whom became lifelong friends. Over the course of a couple of decades, she fought fires from Oregon and California to Colorado and New Mexico, at one point winning a prized slot on a Hotshot crew, elite firefighters who are often the first line of defense in major wildfires.

Through it all, Mary wrote. Her stories evolved into the surreal, grim, sometimes horrific. One of her stories, "A Brand New Saint," is in the form of a prisoner's letter to his mother. The prisoner describes his mistreatment at the hands of a sadistic guard, his long hunger struck and his eventual evolution into what he calls, in the final phrase, "a brand new kind of monstrous saint." In another, "Tolstoy and G-Man," a woman blames Anna Karenina and her "sensual and vigorous world" for her unhappy marriage and proclaims that she "didn't want perfection but wanted her soul broken open."

In an email to her parents, she attached a story and the half-joking apology that the story had "no sentimental humor" to make them happy, and added: "This is about as dark as it comes. No use fighting my natural tendencies as a writer."

In another email with another story attached, she wrote, "It's bizarre. Enjoy."

Mary honed her craft through her reading and with the help and support of a variety of friends and relatives, some readers, some not, but all impressed with and often astonished by her talent. Increasingly, editors were impressed as well: over the years, her stories appeared in a variety of magazines and journals, both print and on-line. The success encouraged her to keep writing. But even her failures could be a source of inspiration for Mary: Until the end, she treasured a personally written rejection letter from the *New Yorker*.

Cancer derailed Mary's firefighting career, the disease and a months-long round of treatment leaving her exhausted and often in pain, unable to meet the demands of the job. It also ended her life in the Southwest, eventually convincing her to return home to Maryland to live with her family.

Cancer derailed her writing as well, although not immediately. Even as she battled pain and exhaustion, operations and therapies, Mary wrote. During her last months, she was working on two short stories. She was reluctant to talk about either and left behind only pages of half-legible notes, but her enthusiasm for the work was obvious.

And then, as the cancer advanced, the writing stopped, leaving only her reading as the last vestige of a life-long love of words and stories. In the final several weeks of her life, Mary read fiction by authors as varied as Herman Hesse, Flannery O'Connor, Larry Brown and Joe

Hill—the son of one of her first loves, Stephen King. And soon, that was gone as well. The day after Christmas, 2020, Mary entered hospice. The drugs relieved her pain but left her too tired even to read. For more than two weeks, she was barely conscious and read nothing—certainly the longest such stint of her life since middle school.

If her mind had given up, Mary's body did not. Her battle with cancer, which had prompted her to research and undertake a wide variety of treatments and kept her going far longer than the medical experts had predicted, continued.

In the end, cancer did what it so often does. On Jan. 11, 2021, Mary died.

She never finished those last two stories. But she left behind this trove of well-crafted pieces—children of a relentless love of literature, an imaginative, creative mind and a devotion to the craft of writing.

Peter Pichaske

# A Brief Note from the Publisher

Back in 2016, I first suggested to my niece Mary Renzi that we publish a book of her stories. She had been sending me stories to read, critique, and edit since before 2010. I kept a folder of printed stories (the fact that I have "Jackson James Is DEAD" only as a printed story suggests a date before 2010), and as word files attached to her e-mails. After 2016, Mary was busy working and editing other people's writing, but in an e-mail of July 2019 she accepted the idea of a book: "It would be a short collection, a couple hundred pages, but maybe that's okay." She listed candidates for the book, including "In the Blood and the Bone" with the note "unpublished—that's a really old one that I've always liked, but some of the old writing makes me cringe now." She added, "I'd really like to include some original stories I haven't written yet, but as long as my health is good, I'd have them done by the new year or maybe sooner." Alas, her health did not remain good, and those stories never got written . . . or never got finished.

Her phrase "some of the writing makes me cringe now" rang through my head as I assembled this book. I've heard the words before from other authors, and I feel that way about some of my own work. But as a famous Roman politician once said, "What I have written, I have written." And as I tell students in my literature classes, even a weak or badly structured work often contains great lines, memorable passages. This book contains all the Mary Renzi stories I could find . . . attached to old e-mails, in her computer (forwarded by her mother Marie), as printed texts in my manila folder. Admittedly, some are better than others, but collectively they memorialize an impressive writer (and person), someone whom I and many others will miss.

David Pichaske

# Jackson James is Dead

*Jackson James Is <u>DEAD</u>.* "Dead" was written in all capital letters and was underlined twice. It was an advertisement for him.

He could not stop staring at it from where he sat in his Theory of Knowledge class—the only class Jackson could actually stand at Capital High School.

It was not even a threat, exactly. A threat would have been, "I Will Kill You, Jackson James." He almost thought it would have been better for him if they had worded it that way. Better than this declarative statement. A statement that was simple, direct, and sure of itself. A statement that left absolutely no room for debate.

Mr. Lyons stood in the front of the classroom, holding up a sheet of newspaper for everyone to see. Jackson was not sure why Mr. Lyons held the newspaper, or what Mr. Lyons might be saying. He seemed extremely far away, like someone on a stage in a large amphitheater, when you were sitting alone in the back row. Jackson felt nauseous.

*Jackson James is <u>DEAD.</u>*

It had a life of its own, out there next to Falcon home field, more prominent, in Jackson's mind, than the giant, broken-down scoreboard that towered several hundred feet above it. It was a cocky, homicidal statement, loaded with all the barracuda viciousness of an angry teenager eager to assert himself in the weird social pecking order of a public high school.

Mr. Lyons was ripping the sheet of newspaper in one quick motion, from top to bottom. It struck Jackson as strange, a little grandiose, but he could not be interested. Not right now.

*Jackson James is <u>DEAD.</u>*

Although it was too far away to make out clearly from where he sat, Jackson knew what it said, knew it as intimately as the Rorschach birthmark on his inner thigh that looked like a half-eaten apple. It was spray-painted in sprawling, juvenile letters across the trunk of a large Silver Maple tree, a tree he had seen every day when he looked out the window, but never really paid much attention to . . . until recently.

1

"Now tell me what is different," Mr. Lyons was saying. He ripped the newspaper again, this time horizontally. The suggestion of a smile played on his lips. Mr. Lyons had the half-smile of a stroke victim, perfectly in keeping with his pock-marked, asymmetrical face.

*Jackson James is <u>DEAD.</u>*

It was spray-painted using bright, cherry red touch-up paint, no doubt lifted from the garage of some unsuspecting father, who was probably a lot like Jackson's own father—reading the *Times* in the mornings, commenting snidely on someone or other's political agenda, congratulating Jackson on his report card, making corny, outdated comments about girls, and giving Jackson a hard time about his haircut. In other words, as Jackson would put it, totally fucking oblivious to the harsh realities of life.

Facing confused silence, Mr. Lyons demonstrated again, first ripping vertically, and then immediately ripping horizontally. Someone snickered in the back of the classroom, thinking that maybe Mr. Lyons was putting them on. "Come on," he said to the class. "Come on. Look closely."

*Jackson James is <u>DEAD.</u>*

They must have done it over the weekend, because it was Monday morning when Jackson had been called into the office. Mr. Bentley, the school principle, had looked at Jackson, and then asked him with a benign smile to please have a seat. He had rubbed the bald spot on the back of his head contemplatively. Then he smiled, sighed, and rubbed his bald spot again. Finally, he had asked him, "Have you been having, ah, problems, Jackson?"

Jackson had shrugged but said nothing. Could he be referring to the incident in Mr. White's class? Had he heard about the book?

But Jackson had been having problems. He was always having problems, really. Jackson never ceased to be amazed at the ability of adults, and in this case a bureaucratic adult, to think he would actually trust and confide in them. As if they could actually be of any real, practical help, with their lackluster philosophies of life, their trite advice for overcoming "obstacles," their completely uncreative, step-by-step guide to becoming just like them, their heavy-handed approach to solving the delicate problems of youth. And Mr. Bentley, especially, who really didn't like Jackson at all. He had sent him home just last week for wearing a *Napalm Death* T-shirt, a shirt he called "disgustingly morbid" and "morally and aesthetically offensive."

2

"Well," Erin Falcon was saying, sounding somewhat unsure of herself, "when you rip it from top to bottom, the rip is more jagged?" It had started as a statement but had ended as a question.

Excited, Mr. Lyons slapped down on his desk hard. A few of the students jumped.

"That's exactly right, Erin," he said, with a slightly insane grin that suggested that they were getting much warmer, but had not hit the mark yet.

The sound jolted Jackson, even got his attention momentarily. It was Jackson who held the record for figuring out most of Mr. Lyons' signature riddles. But not today. Today he had much more important things to focus on.

*Jackson James is* <u>DEAD</u>.

Finally, Mr. Bentley had taken Jackson outside. On their way around back he had said, "I don't want you to be too upset about this, Jackson. Kids like to talk, that's all, because it makes them look big and bad." He was trying to sound casual, not overly concerned—on the level. "I need to know if you know who might have done this, so we can help you. Your parents and every single administrator at this school are here for you. We won't let anything happen to you."

There was almost as much comfort in that, Jackson considered, as running naked through stinging nettle.

By lunchtime that Monday—which seemed impossibly remote from where Jackson sat now, two days later—a small crowd had gathered next to the tree, made up of both students and teachers. Mr. Bentley was back outside among them, giving his deft analysis like an experienced tour-guide, saying something about video games and cable television. Shaking his head at how sad it all was, the state of kids today.

And maybe the real tragedy was, this particular tree happened to be very special to the staff of Capital High School. It really was a beautiful tree. It had a leafy canopy that was formed tightly and perfectly, like an umbrella. It turned brilliant shades of red and yellow in the fall. This tree was older than the school, in fact. There had been two of them, equally beautiful, but the root system of the sibling had started to upset the school track, and, unfortunately, had to be taken down two years ago. This was the only one left, and now it was defaced. It was a shame, they all agreed.

"Anyone?" Mr. Lyons was asking, "Anyone?"

"Okay," he said finally, "I'll throw you a bone. *Against* the grain," he said and ripped the sheet of newsprint horizontally. The tear was, as Erin had pointed out, very jagged. "Now watch when the tear is *with* the grain," he said, and ripped it vertically. The tear was smooth and even. Mr. Lyons paused, letting it sink in. He had dramatic silences down to an art.

"I want you to go home and think about this," he said. "Your homework is to write an opinion piece. Write about a time in your life when you went against the grain, doing something that maybe your parents, teachers or friends did not agree with." As he talked, Mr. Lyons sketched a rough outline of the assignment on the chalk board. "And then I want you to write about a time in your life when you went *with* the grain, when you did something that pleased your peers, teachers or parents. Which situation, in retrospect, had more of an impact on you? And why? Just think about it. There is no right or wrong answer, of course.

"Tomorrow," he said, giving the class a campy look that made a few of the students giggle, *"dah dah dah dum* . . . we will relate this concept to history."

When the bell rang, Jackson was the last student to get up from his seat. It was as if an extra dose of gravity was holding him there. Mr. Lyons came over to him. "I expect a thoughtful essay out of you Jackson," he told him. "Of course, that's because I've never gotten anything less than that so far." He quickly squeezed Jackson's shoulder, and then went back to erasing the chalk board.

Jackson made his way down the cramped hallways of Capital High School. During the five-minute breaks between bells, they were filled to capacity with students, like a clogged drain.

"These hallways already have the feeling of a bad childhood memory," Jackson thought to himself, looking around him. It did not seem too far-fetched that he could be killed in a place like this. The floors were pea green colored and flecked with little smidgens of red and white but were, on the whole, definitely green, and they were lined with clashing military green lockers that looked as if they had been salvaged from the set of a 1960s after-school special.

Jackson had the passing thought that he should borrow his father's old Forest Service uniform and camouflage himself for protection. His dad's uniform, and these hallways, were almost ugly enough to deserve each other. Yet there was some amount of safety, he

4

considered, if not comfort, in being surrounded by so many students and by Capital's innocuous, if out-of-touch, teaching staff, who were standing outside of their classrooms now, ushering their pupils in like feckless sheep.

Without his father's uniform, Jackson was somewhat less than a chameleon, wearing black Levis (tapered up past his ankles just enough to reveal his black dress socks), black low topped Doctor Martins (impeccably polished), a black silk dress shirt with an (even blacker) Kyoto dragon on the breast, an equally black silk tie, a set of six-gauge, coiled, animal-bone earrings (dyed black), and a jet black head of hair with cobalt blue highlights for contrast. Jackson was reasonably tall and skinny, some might even call him lanky. He had an iron-deficient pallor that helped to accentuate the whole *black* motif, and when you noticed Jackson walking down the halls—as many students at Capital High School did—he always seemed just slightly off balance.

A lot of the girls at Capital agreed: Jackson was almost cute. He would be cute, if he didn't act like such an alien all the time. And try to look like such an alien on top of it.

"Hey, Jackson," someone called to him from down the hall. It was Keisha Pope, one of Capital's many highly attractive black girls, who was adept at pushing the envelope of the dress code with her provocative outfits. Just last week, while he was carrying his big wooden bathroom pass that looked like a paddle, Jackson had seen Keisha and Andre Holmes slipping out of the utility closet—a rendezvous that Jackson had imagined in vivid detail later that night.

"Hey, Jackson . . . *Jackson James is DEEAAD,*" came the voice again, in a malicious sing-song. Then a giggle, and a *"No she Didn't."* from one of Keisha's girlfriends.

Jackson turned, gave her the finger, a polite smile, and said "Fuck You."

"You Wanna what?" Keisha asked, her hand cupped around her ear like she was straining to hear him. And then, "Sorry Jackson, but I don't do white boys."

"No she don't," her friend said again.

Jackson laughed and said, "Fuck off, Keisha." It was a laugh designed to sound unconcerned, and contemptuous in a superior way. Jackson kept moving towards his classroom. Why did it always burn even more to be insulted by a girl?

5

Until recently, Jackson found that he was able to stay out of fights at Capital, a school that had something of a reputation for violence even by King County standards, by cultivating what he considered to be a very balanced approach to responding to harassment. He couldn't really explain it, except to say that he had a way of standing up for himself, without stepping up to anybody. It was its own art form, really. Jackson imagined that he was able to keep his self-respect this way. And at the same time, as an added bonus, he did not have to come home with a busted head. But now the situation had, well, escalated, to say the very least. Because a healthy portion of the student body at Capital High School believed that Jackson James was a Neo-Nazi.

Of course, Jackson was not a Nazi. He could say this with even more certainty than he could say that he was not queer. In Jackson's value system, Nazi was the lowest form of life, right under plankton, single celled amoeba, and cops. Jackson considered himself socially progressive. He even attended anti-racist conventions in the city. He listened to punk bands that lyrically trashed racism. And he was definitely attracted to black girls, even though he found that most of them would not, in a million years, give him the time of day. This particularly ironic rumor was started when Jackson was, as usual, reading his own book during lecture in Mr. White's U. S. History class, third period. When Mr. White came and took the book away from Jackson, he had read the title of the book out loud to the entire class.

"Talk Radio," he said, looking over his glasses. And next he read the subtitle: "Rise of the American Neo-Nazi Movement." Mr. White had paused significantly before asking him, "Are you a Nazi, Jackson?"

Realizing his infraction many seconds too late, Mr. White patted Jackson on the shoulder and responded to his own question with, "Of course you're not."

But the damage had already been done.

Jackson walked past the school library. Stacy was working behind the check-out counter. She worked at the library for the last two periods of each school day as part of a work-oriented program called "After Graduation." She was the only girl Jackson knew who aspired to be a librarian, and who already dressed like one at age sixteen, with her long skirts, her extra-thick white stockings, and her pastel colored cardigans. There was something about her bookish naivety and her complete indifference to sex appeal that Jackson found highly comforting.

6

Stacy noticed Jackson, smiled, waved, and then pantomimed for Jackson to call her on the telephone. "Just come over," Jackson mouthed, exaggerated so she could understand him. Stacy started to shake her head "no" but Jackson brought his hands together like he was praying, and stuck his bottom lip out with what he imagined was charming impetuousness.

He mouthed, "Pleeeease."

Stacy gave Jackson the look of a disapproving mother, but nodded okay, she would be over. Jackson needed Stacy, needed her to help him relax tonight.

Ten seconds later, Jackson's head was being slammed into a locker. And then Montel Eliot was skipping backwards away from Jackson in a cocky Muhammad Ali-esque two-step.

"You gotta problem with black folk, Jackson?" Montel's voice was a high-ranged falsetto whine, designed to attract attention. And it worked, because several students were now milling around them, like corralled animals anxiously waiting to be let out.

Jackson's head was spinning but he managed to get out a weak, "Naw, man." Then, leaning into the lockers to keep his balance, he looked straight at Montel uttering a more earnest, "NO."

" 'Cause it's alright if you do, as long as you a man about it and admit that shit." Then Montel thumbed his nose, a bit of flair he probably picked up from a Bruce Lee movie. He was still hopping around and seemed to be enjoying himself.

Jackson was recovering, reorienting after the shock, and already he understood that Montel was not a real threat to him. Montel had already played his part, had made himself look good, had taken care of his bragging rights for the day, and now it was over. Montel was not exactly a *dangerous* person. Jackson understood this instinctively with a simple intuition related to survival. Mantel was the type to try to show off for his friends. He was the type of kid, Jackson knew firsthand, who you would find playing a game of H.O.R.S.E. during open gym, instead of lifting weights or playing a more competitive game of ball. The type of kid who was always surrounded by girls who considered him "just a friend." A cocky bastard, Jackson thought. But not dangerous.

Jackson was just considering that he could probably take Montel in a fight, when Mr. Fulton, one of Capital's administrators, marched towards them, looking extremely serious. All of the students in the hallway seemed to part for him like the Red Sea.

7

"Montel. Office. Now," he commanded. Mr. Fulton grabbed Montel by the shoulder and spun him around like a child who was playing pin the tail on the donkey.

"You lucky, Jackson," Montel was saying as he walked away, "There's always Mr. Fulton to help out little bitches like you."

"Jackson, are you okay, son?" Mr. Fulton asked him.

"Just great, actually, Mr. Fulton. It's a beautiful day out, sir. "With a gesture Jackson indicated the sunny courtyard. He was feeling sarcastic. Defiant. He had to be. Or he would look weak. He qualified that in his mind to even weaker. It occurred to Jackson that God was fucking with him. Was he having fun doing it?

"Okay, son. Why don't you get to class?" Mr. Fulton asked. "We might be calling you down to the office later."

"Sure thing," Jackson said. "Did I mention it's a beautiful day out, sir?" he asked, and with that, walked out of the front door of Capital High School into the sun and made his way toward the Addison Road metro station.

When Stacy came over that evening to see Jackson, his mother was baking in the kitchen. She told her that Jackson was downstairs in his bedroom listening to his records. As her granola baked, Jackson's mom kept rearranging random items in the kitchen in a nervous fashion, and picking at tiny pieces of uncooked granola that were littered over the counter top, instead of just wiping them off with a rag. She asked Stacy if she would like anything to drink and with a quick, self-conscious look, communicated that she *wanted* her to accept the drink. So Stacy said, "Well, do you have any orange juice, Terry?"

When she came back with the drink, Jackson's mother asked in a softly deliberate voice, "Stacy, how bad is it for Jackson at school?" Terry James had anxious, over-sensitive eyes that always looked to be on the verge of tearing, and slender arms and hands that hinted at gestures as she talked.

Stacy quickly decided on a balanced mixture of half-honesty, half-consolation. "It's pretty bad for Jackson right now, but he's handling it well," Stacy told her. "This will probably all be over in a few weeks. That's how it always is at our school." And as she said this, Stacy realized that she believed it. She could not imagine it any other way. Capital High School was not Baghdad, after all. Next year, she imagined, this would just be a very unpleasant memory for Jackson, a bygone era.

Jackson's mom played distractedly with the comer of the tablecloth. She had gotten a phone call this afternoon from Jackson's principle, Mr. Bentley, about the incident in the hallway and about Jackson's truancy. She knew that things must be bad for her son. And the hard thing to accept was there was absolutely nothing she could do for him, short of pulling Jackson out of school, which of course he would never agree to. On top of that, she certainly was not able to console him. Any attempt at consolation only served to anger Jackson. She remembered how he had once told her, after failing to place in a photography competition, that her sympathy was "as pointless as a fart in a hurricane." And to "go waste your energy somewhere else, mom."

"I really appreciate what a good friend you've been to Jackson," Jackson's mom told Stacy. "I'm sure he heard you come in. He can hear everything from down there. Even with his music. In fact, I bet he's already suspicious that you haven't come down yet." Jackson's mom smiled—Stacy thought courageously—and got up from the table.

When Stacy walked into Jackson's bedroom, he was busy studying a record sleeve. "Thanks for coming over," he said to her, but did not look up from what he was doing.

The sleeve, Stacy assumed, belonged to whatever record happened to be blasting through his stereo at the moment. It was something fast, with bleating guitar riffs and driving drumbeats. At moments like these Jackson seemed the most content and at ease, as if he were some strange mutation of a bodhisattva who was able to center himself most effectively amid the machine gun blast beats, the low tuned guitars, the alternating slow and then violent tempos, and the shrill demon screams of the music that left Stacy dizzy.

"Just so you know, I need to leave by seven so I can work on my Parthenon presentation. I just wanted to stop by, since you asked me," she said. Stacy walked over to Jackson, squatted down on her haunches, and hugged him from behind. Still reading his liner notes Indian-style, Jackson leaned back against her in acknowledgement. Stacy lost her balance, and they both fell backwards. Stacy started to crack up. She was the only girl Jackson had ever met who actually honked when she laughed. Jackson had the suspicion that she cultivated it for some reason.

Setting the record sleeve aside and turning himself over so that he was lying on top of her, Jackson told Stacy, "That's okay if you have to go. Because I have to leave in about a half hour anyway. I forgot about

9

this Darkest Hour show when I asked you to come over." Stacy flinched slightly at his comment so he asked her, "You're not pissed at me are you?"

"No, not pissed," Stacy said, lying just a little bit. "You can do whatever makes you happy. I just wanted to see you for a minute, since you asked."

"Whatever makes me happy? Really?" Jackson asked, lifting her sweater just barely, and then looking her up and down.

"Jackson, stop it," Stacy told him, blushing.

Jackson laughed and rolled off of her. "Come on Stacy. That's not how it goes. You were supposed to say, 'Whatever makes you happy, Jackson' in this throaty, sexy voice, and that's when we start fucking like animals." He paused, "It would help me temporarily forget all of my bullshit problems, anyway," he told her, cocking an eyebrow and delivering this last line like a sales pitch.

"Okay, that's really me," Stacy said, managing to turn even redder.

"I'm just kidding, silly. Relax. I know your M.O." Jackson reached over Stacy to turn down his stereo, then lay back down. He put his arms around her.

After a moment, Stacy told him, "You know, your mom's pretty worried about you." Jackson shifted slightly at her comment, and he was not holding her as closely anymore. "Why are you annoyed by that?" Stacy asked him.

"Stacy," Jackson started tersely, "My mom is a lesser form of tyrant who stunts me with her protectiveness. And so is yours, by the way, but that doesn't seem to bother you for some reason. Probably because you enjoy being controlled. Like everyone else."

Now it was Stacy's turn to move away. "Jackson, you always make these harsh statements that are so. . . ."

"Absolute," Jackson finished. "I'm sorry. I don't know shit, really. I'm sorry," he repeated, pulling Stacy back into him. "I'm stressed out. You are so good in comparison to me," he said, kissing her neck. "I'm just an asshole."

Stacy relaxed. "Well, you're very difficult," she told him.

"Talk," Jackson told her, "I just want you to talk to me and I can just lie here."

"That's too much pressure," she said. "What am I supposed to say?"

10

Jackson sighed, and they lay there quietly for some time.

When Stacy did start talking, it was about little things that were unimportant and incidental. Jackson was grateful.

Stacy told Jackson how she had been using the laser pointer he gave her to play with her cats, how they chased that little dot of red endlessly, and would pounce on it like skilled stalkers, only to find that it had disappeared, never tiring of the game. And she told him about the guy sitting at the table next to her at Tully's coffee shop after school where she was studying, who would not stop clearing his throat, and who would go into these convulsive fits of coughing every so often, how when the man talked on his cell phone it sounded so coarse and phlegmy, like he was talking under water. (Jackson kept clearing his throat as Stacy told him about this, making her laugh.) She told Jackson about the Library Science program she was looking into at King Community College, about how much she liked the new Death Cab for Cutie album (and please spare me your diatribe against popular music), about her mother's boyfriend, Alex, who had a weight loss infomercial, about how she was going to sit around in her pajamas and eat brownies tonight while she worked on her Parthenon presentation.

Jackson rested his hand lightly on Stacy's midsection, tracing her contours with his fingers. They were still in the exact same spot they had started out in a half an hour ago. Jackson did not want to get up. Not for the show tonight, and not for school tomorrow. He just wanted to lie here with his girlfriend. He realized that he was absolutely exhausted. There was a heaviness in his limbs made up of lack of sleep, lack of food, and a vicious cycle of thought that had gotten him nowhere tonight.

But the pane of glass in Jackson's bay window started to rattle and the rain started to come down. It was fast and heavy when the wind picked up, making little pressurized tapping sounds on his window glass, and there was a relatively slower, dull, pattering noise when the wind would die down. It was about to storm. If he was going to borrow his parent's Honda, he needed to leave before the weather got any worse outside.

Jackson was hardly able to see or hear anything on the way to the show. He could just see the glare of streetlights reflecting off the water, and the sound of rain was like white noise drowning out all the auxiliary sounds of the city, and the wiper blades on his Civic could not move fast enough. *Jackson James is <u>DEAD</u>* was imprinted on his mind visually as if by some morbidly effective initiation ritual, and he should have kicked Montel's punk ass, he thought. And then the paranoid thought that he should not have left Stacy, that he was in some kind of danger, that his parents weren't so bad. Then lightning combusted louder than a gas-powered lawn mower coming to life, and Jackson was inside the club in his wet hoodie and jeans, smoking cigarette after cigarette, and it was not warm enough inside, very dimly lit but still light enough so that he could make out tons of muddy tread prints on the concrete floor, converging into little puddles here and there, breathing in the humidity of rain and sweat, and he was standing with his friend Adam near the sound stage and he could feel the bass moving all through him, and he had the thought that there was something completely false about them standing there together like pals, that Adam was full of shit, and Adam asking Jackson if he was going to get in the pit tonight, or if that was just too *physical* for him, not intellectual enough you arty fagot, and punching Jackson in the shoulder. And then Adam was in the pit, but Jackson had stayed back. And Darkest Hour was on stage starting up; their gritty heaviness was like a soundtrack to his thoughts tonight, the crowd screaming out lyrics desperately, a surreal call and response, and then Jackson was up front yelling "And to reflect is to regret throwing it all away And apathy my one-way street it took so much from me" and the double bass was like an accelerated heartbeat, and then this restless energy and the definite and lucid realization that he needed to learn how to be hit, how to take a punch, and then Jackson was in the center of it, all these flailing bodies and Jackson was just letting himself be hit, to be thrown around according to the currents of the pit, not even trying to direct himself, just feeling the painful stinging in his face and the throbbing of his muscles, and letting himself be terrified as fists and boots connected and battered him, but finally adapting to the pain, no longer scared, accepting of the throbbing in his muscles, of the salty taste of blood on his lip, of the hoarseness in his lungs as he screamed, "So let's go out west and bask in the overcast, and walking through the rain we'll see the beauty in life again." And then Jackson was back by the sound stage, but he was feeling thrilled, unable to wipe the smile off of his face, and Adam came up behind him and massaged his shoulders tersely like a prizefighter. Jackson could see that Adam thought of him differently now, but it didn't matter. The bright red was like new paint as Jackson pulled his hand away from his mouth, and staring at it, he realized that he had accomplished something tonight, that he was fucking amazing, the sheer force of his being, and he smoked a cigarette that he had earned, that tasted better than any cigarette before it, and that would taste better than any cigarette after.

# Trilobites

Jake Callahan hadn't slept through the night since the first week of September. Each workday stunned him with the blue glare of endless computer monitors. When he returned home, his blood hummed with kilowatts. His eyes were dry husks. When he closed them he only saw tattooed squares of light. He drugged himself into uneasy slumber with Benadryl and whiskey, but awoke each morning during the witching hour and stared zap-eyed at the ceiling until the sun rose.

After work he wandered the streets in an insomniac daze. Downtown, Jake portaged through a dank alleyway between restaurants. It was there—muddled by the spent ash of his exhausted mind—that he discovered his fourth grade teacher, Mrs. Birch. The woman sat among fish heads, trash and dishwater, sucking on a can of condensed milk which dribbled thickly down her chin. There was no mistaking her cleft lip, or her gunmetal eyes.

"Mrs. Birch, it's Jake Callahan." He squatted down beside her. "I had you for fourth grade"—he did the math—"in 1990."

She didn't answer him. Her eyes were inert as taxidermy.

"Trilobites," he told her. "I wrote the paper on trilobites."

The word—*trilobite*—was loaded with power for him, an incantation which awoke something subcortical and deep in his fragmented psyche. It brought a rush of visceral memory. The die-cut image of the ancient trilobites emerged sharply from his addled brain: bizarre, dark-armored creatures without faces.

He was struck next by the memory of the white, acetone schoolroom, policed by a much younger Mrs. Birch, whose deep-lined face broadcast the gray seriousness of the world to all of them. She had been provoked to anger by odd stimuli: the too-fast tempo of a ceiling fan, the slatted blinds which jammed each time, a fat fly buzzing her cola. She was despotic, and although Jake had worked desperately for her approval, he had not been one of her favorites.

When she handed the science papers back, he was left empty-handed. She had called him into the hallway for a *tête á tête*.

"These creatures, trilobites"—the word seemed to disgust her—"are a product of your imagination."

She snapped the paper into his hand.

Jake, overcome with shame, looked down at it, red-faced.

He had taken time while the other children played to draw a detailed oceanscape, which he had stapled to the back of the paper. The drawing showed, very accurately, the trilobites' lobed and elliptical bodies. Jake had articulated each jointed segment of exo-skeleton with a black pen and his patient hand.

The creatures did indeed look very bizarre, almost Lovecraftian. He had drawn them ranging in a mighty herd over a tumultuous ocean, their epic wakes producing murderous and titanic swells. This is how he imagined them—as alien ocean kings. Or else he pictured them swimming through nebulas in space, because their bodies were shaped like the hull of the Starship *Enterprise*.

In his paper he had written how trilobites ruled the earth many million years ago, until the volcanic oceans boiled, which ended their mighty and unparalleled reign with all the sentiment of crabs boiled in a pot.

"They were real," he told her, simply.

"No," Mrs. Birch had decreed. "They were not real. I would have heard of them."

While the other kids were at recess, Jake had gone to the library. Then he visited Mrs. Birch at her desk with the correct encyclopedia.

"You see," he said. His arms quivered under the weight of the volume.

Although his integrity was vindicated, tears flowed freely and he ran into the bathroom to hide.

\* \* \*

Jake looked around him in the darkening alleyway. Everything in space was drunkenly abstracted by his muddled mind, fractured by waterfall. Frenzied, he emptied his wallet of twenties into the old woman's lap. The image of trilobites was more insistent, however, than the molted shell of his former teacher in pigeon shit. Trilobites seemed very important, the key to . . . *something*. He did not know what. He rushed home, his mind a confused weather pattern.

Jake poured a stiff drink and lit a cigarette. "Trilobites," he muttered. "How did I forget them?" He smiled.

15

As a child he had created paracosms. He had absorbed everything, which in turn became fodder for his detailed worlds and gigantic curiosity. If it wasn't trilobites, it was black holes, ice ages, or Ernest Shackleton.

Today, in the alleyway, he had momentarily regained that natural, absorbed order—the intense wonder of childhood which had been so easy, brilliant and non-compulsory.

But his heart sank as he looked at the impoverished room and considered the threadbare night. He thought of the technical manual and his latest deadline, and of the sleepless, crackpot nights ahead.

Fuck it, work could wait. Jake opened the laptop and ran a search on "trilobite." He clicked the hyperlink. He studied fossil records. He read about the great die-off at the end of the Permian age. But it was no good. He could not will fascination. He saw blueprints and diagrams, and an ugly insect-like creature with no face. He was grateful one would not greet him if he took a dip in the ocean. He no longer saw starships or ocean kings.

He poured another drink.

He thought of the vagrant Mrs. Birch, and her malnourished body and empty, crustaceous eyes.

They had both fallen.

# Snow-Eater

The Chinook thrashes at the young man's window. Residents of his town call the wind *Snow-Eater*. He knows that when it passes he will be much warmer. In the meantime, it is important that it does not shatter his window glass on its way there, which is clanging wildly now within its frame, as if rattled by a pissed-off and frenetic god.

Today he stays in his bed instead of getting into the wheelchair, where he keeps his body cocooned in an electric blanket and his heavy down comforter. At night, when the lights in the room are turned off, all of the heaters in the space will glow like a garden of furnaces. The young man never seems to get enough heat—his ailing body craves it continuously. On the shortest days of winter, he thinks that the blood in his veins will thicken like custard from lack of it, and then make it only so far from his heart.

Even with the heaters working, it is difficult to operate the bed controls, and he calls the nurse in to help him. The two have learned to communicate in a type of pidgin made up of wild facial expressions, her dramatic hand gestures, and a very basic vocabulary. There is a short but important list of things that he needs, and the nurse has learned them quickly. She is easily his favorite aide. He can remember her first day of work, and how she had shrieked happily at his cobalt-blue Mohawk, and at the many piercings on his face glinting like shrapnel lodged there. To her it seemed a wonder that only America had to offer. She is different from the good residents of Carson who visit him dutifully at Christmas and tolerate his eccentricities due to a Hallmark piety that excuses you, if you are dying, from certain obligations such as social dress codes.

The young man has the nurse open his curtains and through the glass he watches the massive sycamore outside sway unbelievably, like an upset monolith. His panorama is made up of the black walls surrounding him, his silent LCD screen waiting to open like a portal with the next Criterion film, his Cam de Leon acrylic, the walk-in closet with the sliding doors that always come off track, and this one small window front and center. These things are such a permanent part of his

17

field of vision that they are images burned onto screens or retinas. On difficult days, the young man feels that he is sitting with the slow movement of time just watching them erode. The small changes in the room emerge like in a series of time lapse photographs: the fading paint on the walls, the dust accumulating on the window sill, the cricket setting up in the corner of the place, and finally moving on. There are many days like that when time crawls.

But today he only has a calm, charged feeling. He knows that it has to do with the chaos of the wind around him. It seems that something is happening. He is in the eye of the hurricane, and his bed is the still point around which everything else spins dangerously. The young man understands that if the wind brings down a transformer or power line, he could lose electricity in this place. He also knows that his health depends on the power grid. He is jacked into it: his thermal pump, his pulse generator, his suction unit, his oxygen delivery system. Today his mother will call him every hour from work to check up and he will need to reassure her. She will read weather updates on her computer screen.

The insanity of the winds and the danger involved catalyze his creativity, syncing it with the devastating weather outside. The nurse sets the computer up on the bed when he asks her, removes his arms from the cavern of blankets, and places both his hands in their proper position on the mouse. When she is done, his arms sit heavy on his lap with dead weight like two stone troughs. The young man still has some movement in his fingers—his illness has not taken that from him yet—which allows him to type by means of an on-screen keyboard:

> The wind plants images.
> New wisdom
> advises healthy terror
> while simple compliments
> only impress
> on the backs of slave laborers.
> Singing voices will never want
> your one-beat poems.

He reads it over and over to himself when he is done. He has started working on poetry recently and thinks that he has a talent for it. It is teaching him the power of words on a page. He finds it mysterious that he can create an atmosphere from careful language, and cultivate rhythm through articulate pauses. He sends the writing to his friend because he sends all of his poems her way. When he forwarded her profile, none of his other friends online thought that the girl is beautiful, but he knows that she is, and he is quickly falling in love with her. He has tried his hand at many tenuous and romantic poems also. He always hits *send* before he has the time to reconsider. He is experimenting, reaching, attempting to make the close connection that he has in the past witnessed only from a distance, like an inmate locked out of it. The girl always responds to his words without aversion, but without reciprocity.

Her picture on Facebook is her senior photo from high school, and the young man stares at it now. In this particular photo she is wearing very dark eyeliner fully surrounding both eyes, and like a picture frame, the liner suggests a weariness for which she seems too young. Her smile is a slight rise at the corners of her lips. The girl's auburn hair is dyed black at the tips and is fastened by a single barrette in the portrait, keeping her bangs just to one side; her skin is as pale as his skin, except for the small red tracks of dilation flushing her heavy cheeks. The young man imagines the picture planted in some yearbook among shiny faces with straight teeth and carefully done hair. He knows that hers is the photo most students will skip over. He also knows that she is more beautiful than any of them. He waits several minutes before refreshing the Facebook page, and when he does he clicks on the hyper-link to navigate to her response. What he reads there is very important. It might be the most important thing that he will ever read: "I am leaving home, Tucker. And I am taking the dog with me. Can I come there to Carson and stay with you?"

She adds kindly at the end of her message, "Your poems are so amazing. One day I think you will be famous."

The young man reads over the message again to be sure that he has it right, that it is not just some mistake, or a trick of his mind. The girl wants to come to Carson and stay with *him*. The request is brilliant medicine, and its effect on him is instantaneous. The simple message supplies him with the possibility of a life involving true romance, and he can sense the isolation—always over his head, locked into the walls, streaming in his oxygen supply, saturated into the pleural lining of his lungs—begin to crumble and break away slowly like an old mud house.

He writes her back immediately: "Yes you can stay with me." It is the only possible answer to the girl's question.

He does not ask *why* she is leaving, because he understands that much already. They have been talking for several months, and the words in her e-mails have painted a picture of nightmare domesticity as stark and true and undecorated as a police narrative. He knows how, when she was a young child, her mother shut her up in their garret for days at a time when she left for whatever debauch, leaving the toddler trays of jelly sandwiches and boxes of apple juice so that she would not starve. The mother no longer used the razor strap on her (a razor strap that has been passed down through the generations), but he suspects that is just because she is just too gone now. Two nights ago the girl found her on their back porch, staring down into an empty paper cup, and urging it quietly, "Breathe. Breathe."

It is the father who keeps the tradition of physical abuse alive in the house now, with the mother out of that role. She explains that on lucky nights, he is impotent from too much whiskey. The young man has often fantasized about killing him to save the girl.

"I have money put away from my disability checks," he writes her; "I will buy your ticket."

She sends back, "I will leave here Monday. What is your address? I can take a taxi from the airport to your house."

Monday. That is just four squares on the calendar. He thinks that all of the time that he has spent from birth until now has been a detour to arrive there. He understands very well that the girl is only nineteen. He understands that she is still frivolous and undisciplined, and he knows that tomorrow she could lose her nerve, or come up with a very different plan for her escape. But for now the air in his room is so thick with the possibility of next week that he could slice through it with a knife. He imagines the girl talking to him privately in the dark of his bedroom. He already smells her eucalyptus shampoo and body soap like a palliative when she lies down beside him, wrapped up in his comforter, her toes curled right there by his calves. He will remind her how amazing she is, and she will believe him. His sincerity will be enough to convince her. They will share things with each other that they have never been able to give to anyone else. The young man has often fantasized about this type of closeness. Now he thinks he will truly know it.

The current running inside of him is incredibly strong—it is a stepped-up feeling much like a race horse being held back at the starting line. He knows somehow that writing will not solve it this time. Not at all. This feeling is much too physical, and it requires a response that is solid. It requires a response that is substantial and corporeal and impressive. This is the most important day of his life, and the young man needs a monument.

He calls the nurse back into his bedroom, and when she answers, he explains to her very patiently what has to be done. She understands. She takes the shears and the dog clippers from out of his bathroom closet, and then raises the front of his bed with the control so that he is sitting upright. He keeps his eyes closed while the nurse clips the gelled spikes, one by one, from off of his head, and places them carefully at the foot of his bed on a dark bath towel. She follows the shears with the dog clippers in order to get the longer hair, and then lathers his head gently with shaving cream before performing her final strokes with a disposable razor. Now his whole dome is smooth and clean. The cobalt spikes are still whole and mostly together from the glue-like gel that he uses, and they rest at his feet like strange hirsute sculptures. The nurse holds the mirror for him when she is done working, and the young man stares forward at his reflection, moving his head from side to side to check out the different angles on his new cut. He likes what he sees.

When the nurse leaves, he looks out through his closed window. From the bed he can still hear the wind cracking trees outside like balsa wood, and he hears the neighbor's Aussie dog barking wildly at the violence. He can see that much of the snow has already melted off from the heat and velocity of the Chinooks, and the powdery eaves of the past several weeks have been replaced by a wet sheen of dark green foliage. The sun is a goldenrod disk articulating a large blue sky. The chaos of Snow-Eater screaming at his window seems very surreal laid over that benign winter backdrop. The young man thinks that it is so beautiful outside, but he knows it is still only one view from a small window. Now he has much bigger things to inspire him.

# Post-Trauma Robotics

My sister used to paint these amazing canvasses—glossy explosions of oil that made your eyes pop, that belted-out color so you could hear it. After the accident, her work took a strange, technical turn. She began drawing insects with armored skeletons, which she plotted out proportionally on thin graphing paper: tree roaches and beetles with clock-gear eyes, and hinged, mechanical limbs.

She started to depict cyborgs after that. They had alloyed arms, legs and torsos, were drawn as schematically as engineering diagrams, except that their faces were tragic and sick with emotion. Their faces looked too human for their iron bodies. Lindsay withdrew into her art, didn't talk much after the hospital. There hadn't been much in the way of easy conversation or laughter. It was rare that any light broke out.

The accident that killed our parents happened over a year ago. They were driving to Aunt Kathy's for a long winter weekend and Lindsay was with them. I had an all-state hockey game coming up. As left winger and team captain, I couldn't take a vacation. So I was sleeping soundly as my family sputtered along the slick and lonely North Dakota highway.

There was an elk, Lindsay told the police, or maybe a buck, she couldn't be sure. My mother swerved to miss it, impacting a candled spruce at 60 miles per hour, and starring the windshield with her skull as her sternum shattered on the wheel. My father was ejected from the vehicle, dead on impact from a broken neck. Lindsay arrived at the trauma center with relatively minor injuries: several cracked ribs, a bruised heart muscle, something called a coup-counter-coup where your brain is rattled in your skull like Yahtzee die. A few weeks of bed-rest and hyperbaric treatments later, and Lindsay's brain was back to normal, medically speaking. Her heart was healed, in the physical sense.

We lived with Aunt Kathy, but it felt like boarding.

All the furniture was white with small lavender flowers and covered in plastic. The walls were white, the carpet was white, little dust motes hung in the air, generic landscapes decorated the walls. The vibe of Kathy's place was retro unaesthetic—a grandmothers' den.

Lindsay chewed her fingernails to nubs on Kathy's chaise lounge. "Everything's different since the accident," she confided. "Like something was re-wired up here." She knocked her knuckles against her skull. "Every thought I have affects my body; I think remote"—she picked up the television control and juggled its heft in her hand—"and I feel a chemical reaction of remote. It rockets down my spine like an express train, diffuses into my blood, moves through my limbs and out the soles of my feet. It's different than the thought 'white doily.' " She picked up a white doily from Kathy's coffee table. I laughed at the word "doily," and she did too. "Most thoughts carry a light voltage, I can ignore them. They aren't emotional thoughts. But when I think of certain things," she said, trailing off when she caught the worry in my eyes. "It's just harder."

My sister had blazing green snake eyes and black hair that flooded the dull room with a kind of crushed beauty. She was a sensitive, artistic soul who had once danced and painted and salved the hurts of others with kindness. It doubled me over to see her suffer. It felt like watching the beating wings of a rare bird nailed to a board.

I sat at the foot of her bed one afternoon. She was looking over my pre-calc homework, and I was looking at her walls papered in those careful diagrams. They had recently become anatomical: a panel was removed from one robot exoskeleton, revealing a cross section of living heart beneath the metal, arteries and veins groping down like vines, framing each steel rib of thorax in blue and red channels.

* * *

She had recently told me, "I don't feel math thoughts like I feel other thoughts. Math doesn't hurt." But I knew it was also that she liked helping me. I could tell by the way she was patient. Took her time. Really explained things.

"Here," she said. "Number three is wrong. Look over my work. You missed a step."

I looked it over, was going to ask about the slope on the first tangent line, when she said, "I remember something new about the night mom and dad died." She was standing up now, vacantly tracing the outline of a sharp edged robot with a crushing gaze.

23

"Right before mom drove off the road, she looked at me in the back seat, directly at me, as if to say, I know exactly, what I'm doing." Lindsay's once bright eyes were ruined, darkened by half-moons, broken and red from frozen days and insomniac nights.

"The elk," I reminded her. "Mom swerved to miss the elk."

Lindsay waved this away.

She had recently started adding details, constructing a new and grisly narrative of the night of my parent's deaths. I didn't know what it meant. I just knew it wasn't good.

\* \* \*

Aunt Kathy's neighbor, George Shaftoe, worked for the North Dakota state police. He had a hulking lumberjack body and hands the size of Andre the Giant's, but his china-blue eyes were kind, and he had a knack for listening. My sister began to show up on his porch in the evenings with "new information" about that fateful night. George slurped black coffee from a camp mug, furrowed his brow, had the habit of running his finger around the rim of his cup when he focused.

Lindsay gave him every detail that flooded back to her: the hitch-hiker at the elbow in the highway, dressed in an orange wind breaker and duck cap (suspicious looking), the pungent smell of a grilled cattle truck they passed on a straightaway (incidental), the meteorite stamped above them in the night sky all blazing, green and sulfurous (some kind of harbinger from god). There were darker details: my mother pumping the brakes futilely as they failed (foul play, she suspected now), my father planted in the snow, his spine angulated like a snapped twig, his blood bright red as anemone against a white, steaming floor.

Her narratives were overwrought, contradictory, bizarre, disturbing. And the blood seemed to drain from her face when she spoke. Her eyes looked like screaming into a vacuum. You could see her stories literally torment her. I was slowly coming to understand the full scope of my sister's condition. Through a combination of genetics, accident and repair, Lindsay had come into possession of a cursed psychic talent: she was able to feel a million different hues of pain distinctly, each cell in her body sensitized and reprogrammed to receive suffering instead of nutrients.

"You do know, Ryan," George told me one night while my sister was in the bathroom, "that as time passes, witnesses to traumas tend to lose details. They don't gain them."

"I didn't realize," I said, although I wasn't sure what he expected me to do with the information.

We were over at George's one night when I got angry as hell with her. "Lindsay, do you really think we want to see that? Why would you want me to see what you see, your fucking horrors?" I was shouting, livid. She didn't say anything, just studied me silently for some time. Her delicate feet barely impressed the carpet as she shuffled away, shutting the door quietly behind her.

Just two sentences to alienate my sister. Efficient. Bravo.

But the resentment had been building. I hardly realized its foothold until the anger exploded from my words. I wanted to knock her on her ass and say, "*Reality.* Come back to *reality.* Look at *me*, I'm right *here.*"

* * *

Shortly after that, Lindsay began building her machines. Like math, the enterprise seemed to calm her. Her first machine was modeled after a cockroach. It had a solar panel body with a small vibrating motor attached underneath, and soldered transistor wire for legs and antennae. At any time there might have been four or five of these set loose in our house, shimmying coarsely around on the thin carpet, some knocked helplessly onto their backs like Kafka's bug. She moved on from insects to larger robots made out of acrylic and plastic. They were dull-looking things made from condiment jars but sped around more impressively on wheels. Metal was the last medium Lindsay came to and it was the one she loved. She'd wax poetic at junkyards and RadioShacks.

"The organic decays," she'd say, studying her reflection in a car window or display case. "Metal is closer to the eternal, to the divine. Steel joists, struts, skyscrapers—think of their beauty! The wings of bats should be flexible alloy, one carbon layer thick. They should wrap their bodies and hang from trees like sleeping golden statues. Bodhisattvas would be wiser if their veins channeled molten ore. . . ."

Despite her fire, the machines she built remained simple: sheet metal rolled into cylindrical arms that moved back and forth on clunky servo-motors, a metal garbage bin fashioned into a kind of torso, an animatronic head with a jaw like a rake and these goofy eyes she glued on—many steps down from a slick C3PO, or the terrifying robot terminators of film. She named her first humanoid Lovejoy, and you could see she was proud, although Lovejoy resembled her schematics in the crude way a triangle resembles a mountain peak. You saw nothing of the complex, articulated limbs of the graceful, sturdy cores, of the eyes heavy with blood, tragedy and wonder that you could see in her art. My sister was an artist, but not an artisan. A very bright girl, but a novice engineer.

One night we were watching television when she set one of her roach bots marching across the end table. She'd spin it each time before it dropped over the edge like Wile E Coyote. Then she picked it up, cupped it in the palm of her hand, pet its solar panel body affectionately.

"Machines don't feel pain," she whispered, intrigued by the simple revelation.

Strangely enough, Lindsay's focus on the mechanical returned the blood to her cheeks and the skip to her step. One night she told me, "Building machines is turning your thoughts three-dimensional. It's more magical wine into blood." Then she turned to me and said, "I'm sorry, Ryan. I don't want you to feel what I felt, to see what I saw. I shouldn't have shared that with you."

The feeling of dread I'd been harboring for the last several months slowly pushed back, making just enough room for a careful optimism to slink in.

\* \* \*

George Shaftoe's son, Martin, had developed a nine-year-old's crush on my sister. He was this serious little guy with a crew cut and chubby, wind-burned cheeks. He was already walking in his father's footsteps, his heart set on lieutenant detective. Martin's school-boy innocence was good medicine, I thought, and Lindsay nurtured the crush by sneaking him sodas and Sour Patch Kids, by whispering secrets in his ear which made him look pensive. He really liked her art, called her drawings cool, had no inkling of any dark psychology behind their design.

One night Martin brought over this tackle box full of finger-printing equipment, rolls of crime scene tape, and a jumbled mess of junior officer badges. He called it his "kit for catching criminals." There was this little key chain breathalyzer, too, and we all blew into it, zero point zeros.

Lindsay got an idea, smuggled peppermint schnapps from the kitchen in a Big Gulp cup. She put Tom Waits on her record player, and we got to drinking, letting Martin test and retest us, until our blood alcohol reached .1 percent.

"I think you're drunk now," Martin said, staring at the display. "I can't remember." Which was funny as hell, at the time. It was toasty warm in the room and "Kentucky Avenue" played like a siren's song.

So see, there were some good days. Some easy nights. But it wasn't over. My sister was still sinking.

I noticed that the "secrets" she told Martin were becoming longer, more involved. Inappropriately long, I thought. Like, what can you whisper in a nine year-old's ear for five minutes straight? At times I'd catch little snippets, words like *coroner, suspect, murder*. Whatever narrative she spun held the young boy spell-bound.

One evening after their *tête á tête*, Martin went all pale, said that he needed to go home now. I knew it wasn't right, feeding him such details. And I was partly to blame. I had cut Lindsay off, so she had found a darker avenue—another means to break her silence. I knew that in a convoluted manner it was to maintain sanity. Sometimes you had to speak. Sometimes the silence could kill you.

\* \* \*

One day after school I paid Rachel Harris twenty-five dollars to invite my sister out with her and her friends. It went down beside the lockers, like a drug deal. I somehow believed through the fierceness of my will I could help rearrange her life back to some pattern of normal. Lindsay needed friends, I reasoned, which was logical enough.

We were sitting at home when the phone rang. Kathy called out, and Lindsay gripped the handset to her ear. The phone was pink with a heart-shaped cradle. It fit her personality better prior to the accident.

"Hello," my sister said. Then, "Okay." (long pause) "Okay." (very long pause) "Yes, yes thank you." She hung it up.

"That was Rachel from chemistry class. There's a sauna, on the shore of Clear Lake." Her voice trailed off but then she added, "I'm going with them Friday night."

"That will be great for you," I said. But hot little butterflies of worry were already pinballing inside.

I guess I imagined they'd all go for a movie, perhaps to an open mic at some cafe with frothy drinks and warm music. I hadn't banked on ice, wilderness and fire. It seemed like dangerous chemistry. I wanted to kick Rachel's ass. There was nothing to do but invite myself along.

\* \* \*

Lindsay was quiet as our convoy of teenagers skidded along a frozen dirt road toward an oxbow lake in the night. During the silence between Kelly Clarkson tracks, I could hear pockets of ice crunching beneath the tires. After we parked we all walked with flashlights and headlamps. The group was a spritely mob phubbing on their phones, skating on patches of frozen ground.

The night was brutally cold, and the wind knifed through our jackets like icy claws. The frozen stars spread out in a horizontal infinity above us. I rested my hand on Lindsay's shoulder. "You're limping," I said.

"It's nothing. I hit my shin on the . . . never mind. Let's just have fun tonight. It's what you wanted, isn't it?"

"Yes," I told her. "And I am having fun."

She was holding something back but I didn't push it. It was a delicate balance with my sister. I knew that my anxiety—if I wasn't careful—could be just the emotional contagion to send her spiraling inward.

We came up on our abode for the evening—a hewn, one-room cabin with little yellow squares of light gazing out onto Clear Lake. There was a low inversion of smoke which clung like a stubborn mist, but the smoke smelled sweet and promising. Kevin Jones was already inside, feeding birch into the wood stove.

"Where's Jason and Kara?"

"They're wifi-ing it at home."

"Kara's scared of the lake," someone offered.

"And Jason's her bitch."

"Scared of everything."

"Like a maniac hiding in the cedar, waiting to ax murder us."

Laughter.

28

"What about Ellie?"

"Didn't invite her. She made that app and now she thinks she's queen of the world. Thinks Google might recruit her." Laughter.

"She's beautiful though. Damn. Do-able."

"Not as beautiful as Lindsay." This from Kevin Jones, with an impetuous grin.

Lindsay pulled some hair in front of her eyes, flattened it against her face.

Kevin opened the door and pulled a bottle of liquor from the snow. He cracked it, swigged, passed to Lindsay.

"Thanks," she said, and drank.

Kevin threw water onto the stove rocks, putting up a marine layer of steam.

Everyone heaped their parkas in the corner as the room heated up, and we spread out along the thick wooden benches built into the walls.

The night kicked off with plenty of drinking, flirting, talking shit—typical teenage stuff. The tinny sounds of hip-hop played from someone's phone speaker, swirling around the cabin with the steam, and I kept my eyes on Lindsay. She had this look like the noose was tightening. But she kept putting beers back until something flipped, and she was hypnotized by the strangeness of it all, like listening to music alone late at night when you don't hear the lyrics, exactly, but the sounds are clues that point to something. I knew she was in her world of tin men, that this sauna was her dream. Still, she managed to lift her beer to her lips, scanned the room every so often, smiled.

Kevin Jones had started the night sitting beside her, so close that their legs were touching. But now Lindsay's knees were pulled into her chest, like a child refusing something, and Kevin had long since edged away. There was an alarm in his jock brain that sensed a pariah and stayed the fuck back because death might be preferable to humiliation.

When the heat in the room had ratcheted up high enough, everyone stripped down to just bathing suits. Except for Lindsay, who kept her wool pants on. It was a detail people noticed.

"Maybe someone forgot to shave their legs" (snickering).

"You want me to keep these on," Lindsay said, which was a bizarre enough comment that there was a collective, unvoiced decision to ignore her for the rest of the night.

As kids moved in and out to cool off, Lindsay stayed glued to her bench. Her hair was slicked to her face. She was sweating rivers, never toweling dry. She looked pale and drenched with a touch of septic. I knew her thoughts, whatever they happened to be at the moment, were sickening her. That she was feeling all the proteins, the hormones, the invisible processes of the blood, bone and nerves, wrack her body with a kind of vicious quantum suffering. I hated to watch it.

I sat down beside her.

"The first person who takes off, we'll leave with them. Don't worry," I said.

"I'm not worried."

"What are you thinking about?"

"The place I'm going to live."

"You're 18 in January. You should move somewhere warm."

But her mind was on a different track.

"We'll be angels there. Machines. Perfect," Lindsay said. "Machines don't suffer. They are simple. In the present. Suffering comes down on humans like the Roman legions. It's because we create the chemical signals for it in our bodies, through our thought—about the past or future. See? It is a deadly magical gift we have. We can conjure pain from thin air. But in the land of machines, no one hurts. We'll roam the open range glinting like jewels and recharging from sun and wind."

It sounded as though another voice was speaking through her.

"We'll have the endurance of mountains," she said, "and the strength of steel wreckers. We'll be more beautiful than steel orchids. And no . . . one . . . hurts."

Listening to my sister's words gave me this narcotic feeling inside. I was already sleepy and sticky from the steam and beer. When I looked at her, I expected to see dark engine oil sweating through her pores. Her delusion had gained momentum; her neurosis was thorough. I cracked the door of the cabin and pulled two more beers from the snow. The beer felt final. It felt like I was saying goodbye.

"Time to jump in the goddamn lake!" someone shouted.

I just followed the mob out like the damned. Lindsay was behind me. The night was progressing like a die-cut dream.

The cold air woke me up some. It was dark enough to see the Milky Way like a brush stroke of light bleeding from space. The moon lit up the white ground spectrally, and past the dark silhouettes of tottering teenage bodies, past the flats and frozen lake, you could see this immense, snowy desert.

We followed a path of boot prints to the lake's edge. There was a squarish opening drilled through the ice, about five feet by five feet. Everyone was shouting and laughing and Rachel was the first to jump in. When she surfaced she started breathing these shrill little breaths of shock and cold, these *who hoo hoos*, until she was pulled out, and bee lined it back to the hellish hot of the sauna. It was what was called a Finnish Sauna Bath.

Everyone jumped in, one by one, and were helped out in quick succession by the next-in-line. Finally it was just me and Lindsay standing by the lake.

"Do you want to try it?" I asked her.

She nodded.

"Just hunch down by the edge, and I'll lower you."

"Stop worrying," she said, and looked at me coolly. Then she stepped over the ice and sunk as smooth and straight as a lead line.

She didn't gasp like the others when she emerged, but I could see it was taking will. She was holding it in, treading water, testing something. I squatted down, reached in to pull her out, but she swam away from me.

"Not Yet," she said.

"This isn't a swim, Lindsay," I said, my voice rising shrilly. "It's meant to be a quick in and out.

"I'm fine," she said.

I skated around to the other side, slipping on the ice, but she just moved away again.

We played this cat and mouse for I'm not sure how long. I was starting to go numb in just my swim trunks and tennis shoes.

"You'll kill yourself," I finally yelled.

"Machines don't die." She announced it calmly from the water like some remote oracle.

I was going insane with cold and distress. An ear-worm from an old film rose in my throat: "Bad machine," I yelled violently; "Bad fucking machine."

Her shocked body finally overpowered her robot dreams, and Lindsay began thrashing around. I bellied out over the edge, and when she flailed to the surface again I managed to hook her, to pull her up and out.

She was shivering. Couldn't walk at all. I wasn't doing much better. I could see someone standing in the doorway of the cabin, watching.

"Need help," I screamed. A figure started trotting our direction as several others filled the doorway.

We got Lindsay inside. Her exposed skin was waxy and mottled. Her lips and nail beds were as blue as desert sky.

"Call 911," I commanded.

"Fuck you and your twenty-five dollars," Rachel shouted, dialing. "We're all fucked now."

"Shit, Lindsay, Fuck. You're frozen."

"But I don't feel cold." She whispered it up at the ceiling with this little smile on her face.

The sauna was buzzing now, everyone narrating the night like they'd tell it at school Monday morning.

"We need to get these *off*," I said, reaching underneath to unhook her bra. But my fingers were too numb for dexterity. "You do it," I said, pulling the closest warm body down.

When her top was off I dried her, wrapping her mid-section with toasty towels and parkas. As we slid her pants down all the yammering in the place just stopped like the hush in a midnight cathedral.

My sister's surgery was exposed. It glinted fiercely: a twelve-inch-long metal shim inlaid into her calf—a biomechanical checkering of metal/skin, metal/skin, metal/skin. The piece was exactly proportioned and carefully measured—her first strut of exoskeleton.

The clots were shorn open. Her blood was thick gel. Wet gauze clung like trash. I'm not sure how she had walked on it. I dried her legs as delicately as I could, a sob frozen within my chest. My body began to thaw and burn as the blood returned to my skin, and along with the burning I felt this new, intense loneliness snaking through my body, engulfing me, just as the inflamed veins of infection moved in vicious rivers towards my sister's heart.

I realized then that I had lost Lindsay the night I lost my parents. It's just that I'd been watching it for months like a slow crash, believing that if I kept my eyes on her, she couldn't disappear, couldn't leave me here alone. But it didn't work like that.

I heard the sirens approaching slowly along the icy roads, and I hugged Lindsay to me.

32

If you saw your parents die, maybe you'd go all Bruce Wayne, turn it into a mission, a purpose, or some kind of motivation for greatness. Or perhaps the irrational would take over. Maybe through a brutal alchemy of mind, body and metal, you would attempt to restructure yourself into something stronger, something better, something purer, so that you could see through the blood to the sunlight again.

# The Crows Followed You Here

Every year right around the holidays, there were always a lot of stabbings on the rez. The violence was so reliable that I could mark my calendar. Frank was driving that night, I was sitting shotgun handling the radio and dispatch, and Tim was in the back. Even with the hour drive and the empty roads, Frank turned the light bar on, and our sirens screamed out through long stretches of painted desert.

"You ever notice it's always our crew that gets sent to these transports?" I asked him.

"Yeah," Frank said, not interested.

It was always Cardiac 7. Every single time. When we got those calls I couldn't help thinking there was some relationship between that fact and my own brutal history. That there was some deeper order working.

When we hit the fringes of the reservation, we started to see broken-down pickup trucks and white roadside crosses. Trailers dotted the landscape, and clapboard shacks with tires holding down corrugated metal rooftops. Christ in his manger did not come from more humble beginnings. There were also Nativity sets arranged with half-sized barn animals, and tiny white lights strung out on paloverde trees in square dirt lots, carving sweet illumination through the harsh landscape.

The door was open when we pulled up. Joe Ironcloud's indomitable figure filled the doorway. He moved aside just enough to let us through. A muscular dog at his feet showed its teeth at us, its body tensed in knots of hard restraint. Joe had it by the collar, and his feet were planted firmly in an effort to keep it.

It was not our first trip to the property. This time it was Joe's wife LuLu, collapsed on the floor of the front room, leaning on a wooden milk crate that was also a television stand. She held a bundled undershirt tightly to her side. A young officer stood next to her.

"This is where I found her," he told us, perspiring. "I figured it was better not to move her."

"Good," I told him. "You did fine."

It was only a single stab wound, but it was hard to tell how deep it actually went. There was not much fresh blood at all, although we couldn't rule out internal bleeding. But LuLu's pulse was regular. Her face was strong and russet colored. In fact, it looked like something carved from the bedrock—iconic as a totem. I thought I would see it again that night in my dreams, carved into the side of a mountain.

When we had finished the examination we loaded her onto the Stryker. Frank took the front end of the gurney and Tim handled the back. The officer said to me, "Let us know if she talks, Aiden. I haven't had any luck. It could be Joe, but I don't think so. Could be Joe's brother. Lulu broke his nose once with a leather belt."

Joe Ironcloud was still standing at the door when we went out.

"*KoKo. Shh. Shh,*" he whispered.

He looked at his wife with disinterest when she went by, and grabbed my shoulder before I was past.

"What do you need, Joe?"

He didn't say anything. He just pinned me with his look. Finally he spoke. "The crows followed you here, doctor."

He pointed up at a power line which cut in front of his yard. I could see several shapes on the insulation. They might have been crows. They stood out to me only as deeper black. Then one jumped up lightly, resettled.

"They are messengers to you from the Creator." His voice was warm on my face and it smelled like Thunderbird. He nodded gravely. His eyes were swimming with drink but there was a hardness underneath that was still intact. I thought the hardness was a thuggish spiritual certainty. I thought it was a self-importance made stronger by a three-day drunk of cheap wine.

"They are here for your wife maybe, Joe." I said; "not for me."

"No," he said. "You." He tapped his finger above his eye, meaning to indicate that he knew about such things. "Your life," he told me, "is about to knock you right on your ass." Then he laughed, showing me his yellow teeth.

"Okay," I said, walking away. "Thanks."

I didn't need anyone to convince me that Joe Ironcloud was no shaman. Still, the crows were in my mind now. They were lined up above me on the wire like dark figurines. They were as still as sentinels. One fowl called into the frozen air, and the sound cut through it like chalk.

I needed to drive. I took the wheel while they finished with LuLu in the back.

When Frank got in, he was smiling dumbly at me. "Fucking Indians," he said. "My family might be fucked up, but at least we don't *stab* each other."

I just gripped the steering wheel and kept quiet. What Frank didn't know was that the Ironclouds had nothing on my old man. And tomorrow I was heading home for the holidays.

My uncle had been calling every weekend since October to tell me the old house needed repair. I had to do my part, he said. There was rotten siding, and now they were expecting heavy rain and hail. The storm doors needed to be put on for the season. There were a million small things. If I was expecting some payoff, I had to work for it. He was already caring for my father, traditionally the role of the offspring. Wasn't he right about that?

It had been ten years since my mother's funeral in Hagerstown. That was my last trip to Maryland. It wasn't guilt or obligation that was pulling me home. Not this time. There was some larger pay-off that I just couldn't see yet. So the crows stayed with me.

I had been having the same dream of my father for the last five nights. In the dream he was lying inside of a large hot air balloon in his command shirt and quarter boots, with his badge reflecting the sunlight brutally like a weapon. The balloon was caught up in a tangle of wires high above an electric city. He was on his back in the basket, waving his arms and legs wildly in the air above him like an insect that could not flip over. Blinking lights in the city below changed his skin alternately blue, then pink. It was hard for me to guess what that dream might mean. My mother had always been so proud of my dreams. She called them "my visions." I could have done without them. They left me unhinged every time.

We were still driving, and I heard Frank say, "Don't forget the river."

The short bridge at the crossing had a 14-ton limit, and I brought the ambulance to a stop at the center. The stars above us were icy and brilliant, but the moon was hidden. It was still too dark to see the water underneath us, although we could hear it. Frank turned and peered into the back of the vehicle and said, "River."

Many natives required this stop for their prayer. They believed it was more powerful medicine than what we could give to them.

Maybe they were right.

After a moment Tim yelled up to us, "She's too drunk, Aiden. Just keep driving."

* * *

My plane touched down at BWI late the next night. My frozen fingers burned as they warmed in the cab. Baltimore winters were brutal cold. The heat ducts of the vehicle clicked and choked as we passed giant neon candy-canes and waving snowmen two stories high. Pedestrians walked beneath the huge pieces of holiday cheer, miniaturized by them, their heads turned against the wind and their hands thrust deep into black wool pockets.

The driver dropped me off on the corner of Mason and 13th street.

"Hello Ken," I said, when he answered the door.

"'Lo Aiden. Well you made it." At age sixty, my uncle had the body mass of a grizzly bear. His eyes were bruised blue, almost sheepish among his logger's features. He extended his hand, and I took it. Then he moved aside to let me through.

"Kathy and Ashley have a thing for critters," he said. "I might have told you."

I followed him zigzagging through a maze of metal animal hutches and two-story rat manors decorated with tinsel and bells for the season. He tripped over a hollowed sphere like a child's ball on the way to the dining room, setting off a scuttling of nails on the inside plastic.

"Aiden Army," Kathy said loudly; "Come give me a hug."

I had met Kathy once, ten years ago, at my mother's funeral in Hagerstown. Familiarity was just her style. Her feet were propped on the dining table, and iridescent polish was drying on her toes. She swung her feet down then stood up to hug me.

"You look more like Ken than anybody," she said, pulling back.

Kathy was almost twenty years younger than Ken, and I thought it showed in the vitamin luster of her hair and skin.

"You'll meet your cousin tomorrow," she said. "She's up much earlier than the rest of us, but she's quiet."

Ken brought beer from the kitchen, and the three of us talked at the table. No one mentioned my father. That censorship affected my nerves. Every creak and buckle coming from the second story drew my attention. My whole consciousness was directed at the ceiling.

37

"You have Ashley's room while you're here," Ken told me. He held up his hand. "Already sleepin', Aiden, so just take it."

I hadn't planned to argue. I just grabbed my duffel bag and swung it over my shoulder.

"Your Dad has the room at the end of the hall," Ken called at my back. Then he walked into the living room and began flipping through channels for late-night television.

I followed Kathy up to the girl's room and set my bag down on the pink-sheeted mattress. Pictures of frogs and does and manatees were taped to the walls. A small fish tank sat in the corner of the room on a riveted metal stand. Three yellow fish swam in and out of orange coral tunnels in the water. A label stuck to the glass read, **BOB HEIDI AND HESTER.**

"You can see your father now," Kathy said, "if you want. Before I get him into bed. I'm not sure how much Ken told you."

"Ken doesn't say much," I said, "and I don't ask. I know he's not well." I paused. "Well, let's do it then," I told her. Then I followed her down the hall.

A blue beaded curtain covered the entryway to his bedroom. I could hear Burt Bacharach playing lowly on the other side.

"Your father broke the door down when he first moved in," Kathy explained, "like we had locked him in. Of course we hadn't. He was different then."

She parted the curtain with a swim stroke and I followed her through.

My father was sitting in the back corner of the room in a dirty green armchair. I recognized the diamond pattern of the chair from the old house. He didn't move at all. He was petrified and catatonic, poised strangely under a banker's lamp. He held one hand up to the side of his face, like blocking intense light coming through the window, but it was deep dark out. His head was turned from the glass towards us and his features were clenched hard like a reaction to a recent blow.

He just sat there in place, not moving a muscle. He might have been cursed to stone by some chthonic monster.

"Your son's here John," Kathy told him. "Aiden's here."

She turned back to me. "The doctors call it *Glyphic Catatonia*. There are only two other cases on record. In each case it is associated with late-onset schizophrenia." She paused a moment. "I guess what that means is, they don't know crap about it." She laughed.

My father was dressed in his old police blues. His aged body looked starved beneath the fabric. The worsted wool of the uniform was chalky blue almost gray from a thousand cycles in the wash, and it hung on him like a sack.

"He changes his position," Kathy went on. "Sometimes once a day. Sometimes once a week. He relaxes when he sleeps, and sometimes when he eats."

I moved closer to my father, and I motioned my finger in front of his eyes. They didn't respond at all. They were as inert as fish eyes. They were the cooled iron cores of dead stars. The skin around the eyes was thin and delicate, and I could see purplish vessels underneath. I felt nauseous suddenly, thrown out of joint by the un-reality of the whole scene.

Photographs of my mother were pinned up all over the walls of the bedroom. Some photos were bleached and cracked; others were repaired with scotch tape. My father wore her portraits around his neck as well. They were attached with copper wire to anchor-like necklaces of thick cable and bicycle chain. My mother stared out from a gilt frame at his solar plexus, her jade eyes tempting the photographer, conscious of their beauty.

"He made those," Kathy said pointing, "When he was normal."

I knew *normal* wasn't the right word. I knew it was too innocuous for the old man in any state.

"You can stay with him if you want," Kathy told me, "after I get him into bed. Grab him under the arm like this."

He was lighter than kindling when we carried him over. I thought if it wasn't for the photographs like anchors, he might float away in the night.

He relaxed on the mattress almost immediately. Then he was just a sick old man lying there. Kathy sat him up on the bed and removed his shirt over his head and threw it into the corner. I could see where the weight of the chains had bruised his clavicle deep purple. She laid him back down carefully, planking his back with her extended arm. She rolled him to one side then the other to get his pants down past his hips.

"He shakes if I take the photographs away," she explained, undressing him. Then she went for a towel and washbasin from the linen closet.

When I was alone with my father, the impulse came to shake him awake. Violently. Some of his heat was in my blood. I didn't come to

Baltimore to confront him, but now I felt he had found a remote amnesty in his coma that he didn't deserve after all he had done. I stared at his prone body, mealy and slight on the bed sheets, his savage chemistry cured after all these years by age and disease.

I couldn't look at him any longer. I left the room before Kathy was back, and I tried to sleep on my cousin's small mattress. When I turned the lights off, the walls and ceiling smoldered greenly with a hundred glow-in-the-dark stars.

\* \* \*

Ashley came with me the next day to the old house. Her small legs hovered inches above the floorboard of Ken's F-150. She swung them non-stop.

"Did you check on Bob, Heidi and Hester before we left?" I asked her.

"Yes," she told me. Then, "They cry when I leave."

"How do you know?"

She thought for a moment. "Because I hide and I watch them. Their tears look like drops of lemon juice, sinking in a cup of water."

I turned down Glasgow Street. As soon as I turned, I saw the solitary Dutch colonial at the far end of the cul-de-sac. From a block away it sent chills through my blood. I pulled up and just stared at the house with the engine idling.

A *For Sale By Owner* sign was planted there in the frozen ground. Ken's number was written across the bottom in red marker. Spoiled weeds black from freeze carpeted huge sections of the gravel driveway. They would need to be pulled after the thaw.

The girl was out before I shut the motor off. She jumped up and down on the frozen ground, and she skated the thin ice on the sidewalk. She ran up to the porch, her plaited hair swinging like a pendulum. She took the stairs two at a time in bunny hops, excited for the treasures of the abandoned house.

The lock had some play in it. I had to work the key. I told myself, I would just walk through assessing damage. I told myself that I would keep the technical mindset of a carpenter.

But the air inside was thick and still as a crocodile, waiting with its jaws open in the reeds.

40

The girl skipped through the living room, and she slapped her open palms on the covered furniture, sending up ashy clouds. She left small footprints in the dust on the floor.

"Can I go anywhere, Aiden?"

"Not the basement. Or the garage," I told her, "but anywhere else."

She skipped to the first floor bedroom. She swung the door open, and I followed her in. There was an explosion of colored pillows on the guest bed, and a thick white comforter that was gray now from dust. There was a television and a dresser in the room, and a framed landscape of the Catoctin Mountains hung from the wall.

I remembered it clearly. My mother had worked so hard to keep the room empty. Visitors might become attuned if they slept here. They might feel the violence reeled in just for company, kept in check thinly like a lid placed over a volcano. They might sense the decay beneath the warm Indian Reds and semi-sweet chocolate colors my mother had painted the walls with. The whole house was the same—infused with my father's bad blood. The festooned banisters, the impeccably cared for polished floors were meticulous decoys, meant to draw attention in another direction.

I stared out through the bedroom window. A gang of blue-black crows drank from the cistern in the back. If the birds were messengers, they were keeping it to themselves for now.

The girl came over and she stood beside me. She pressed her face against the glass and gasped, impressed by the large silver maple tree rooted at the center of the yard. Its naked limbs struck up at the sky like wooded stalks of lightning.

"No swing, though."

"No," I agreed.

"You didn't swing much?"

"Sometimes," I said. "At school," I told her.

We just stood there looking out.

"Be careful while you're working," the girl told me. She was trying on skins, mimicking the concern that adults showed her. Then she ran outdoors, spontaneous again. I thought the yellow rain jacket she wore was much too thin for the brutal cold.

But the girl was right. I had to be careful. This house was full of ghosts. I could see my mother in every room. I could feel her impulses in my blood. She had left a record.

I walked through room by room. I wanted to check for damages and scribble notes in my composition book. But in the living room I could see her on the bench of the covered piano. Her legs were crossed, and she wore the white gabardine pantsuit that she always wore in my memories, drinking her iced tea in small sips from a crystal tumbler. The ice in the glass whistled and popped as it melted, and I could see traces of mauve lipstick on the rim.

My mother had always fantasized grace and aristocracy. She had built her image piece by piece to match her fine tastes. She built it brilliantly with the style and determination of an artist. I thought it was her rebellion against the ugliness of life with my father. She had always wanted fine beauty.

When I walked through the dining room, I noticed that the china cabinet was emptied out. Ken had struck his claim on the heirlooms. He was welcome to it. I didn't want reminders.

I walked up to the sideboard and I stared into the Venetian mirror that hung over it. My face was as severe as my father's: the wide jaw of a linebacker. Gray eyes. Militant, almost. At work they always said, "built like a brick shithouse and cold as ice." Somehow they meant it as a compliment. What it was, I kept things below the surface. I had become a genius at holding it in.

I wiped a stripe of dust from the glass; then I chipped a flake of gold paint from the frame with my fingernail. I could see my mother staring into the mirror. She touched up a blue contusion on her cheekbone with foundation from a small bottle that she held. The busted capillaries showed through as red as fresh paint in her half-closed eye.

"I'm not beautiful," she said to her reflection.

And I stood behind her, twelve years old, caving. I would have taken the worst beating to make those words go away.

I flipped the lights on at the top of the basement stairs, shaky now. The moldering smell was strong when I climbed down. An inch of standing ground water covered the basement floor, and the mortar was brownish down low where water had crawled up the walls. There was an acrid smell in the space of dissolved minerals.

I went outside, switched the right fuses off, and climbed the stairs to the kitchen for a flashlight from the drawer. I walked down again with my light, and I examined what I could. There was water in the crawl space as well. It was cold and humid in the basement, with just the shallow slapping sound of water as I tromped through in my boots.

42

I stood at my old spot by the water heater. I hung the light on the knob at the top of the stairs. I had sat here like a stone for hours, sometimes days, waiting in the darkness. The confinement had been worse than the beatings, I think.

Back then, I could tell who it was by the sound of their footfalls. If it was the old man, the door swung open, and the light from the upstairs blinded me like a sun. That meant time to come up. That meant time served. But if it was my mother, the door barely started, a stripe of light there and gone again just as quickly. She left contraband—a can of white beans or a jar of sliced pears, and a glass of water with the food, the residual smell of cocoa butter, and a phantom trail of white lace.

I knew that she would save us, eventually. She whispered she would when my father was not close by. I loved her the way you might love a god or an angel—with naive trust from an unimaginable distance.

It was quiet in the basement. There was just darkness and the drip of water and an anxiety that kept me glued in place with my toes wooden inside of my snow boots. The memories seemed intensified by the darkness the way that sound is. All the objects here were talismans: the laundry basin where I drank the metallic water left in the tap—just one or two mouthfuls because the old man wrenched the shut off valve before he locked me down. Then the punching bag he had used for his workouts and the bench against the far wall—the sound of him muttering "bitch" when he dropped the bar back into the rack, his brutality calmed by exertion and the coolness of the space into a smolder of fantasy violence.

Many years later I had stood here again, and the roles were different. My father was wiping the blood from his mouth like bright red paint. I told him, "Never again, or I'll kill you."

I had slept with a shotgun after that. I stowed it between the foot of the mattress and the wall, thinking that he would retaliate. But he never did. I had left two weeks after that for the Great Basin desert, and I never looked back east until my mother's funeral three years later. I had left her alone with him.

This place was a gravity well. I felt that the ghosts here wanted to pull me through the standing water and into their underworld.

I made it to the upstairs deck sucking in large lung-fulls of cold air. I thought my heart would push through my ribcage. The cold air stung my face, and I felt better.

I saw the girl building an emaciated snowman below me in the yard. There wasn't much snow to work with.

"Help me find a good stick," she called up.

The sun was going down when we arrived back to Baltimore, and I could hear dinner popping and sizzling on the stove. I went straight to Ashley's bedroom and I didn't look down the hall. I collapsed on the small pink bed in my clothes and my shoes, and I slept there until morning.

\* \* \*

The week before Christmas Baltimore was purple grey. The violet tints of the low clouds looked charged, like the sky was on the verge of something, but the weather didn't come.

The girl read to my father every night. It was *The Sneetches* or *Baker's Dozen* or *Cat in the Hat*. I listened from her bedroom down the hallway. The girl's reading level was much higher, but she read only picture books to the old man. Sometimes in the morning on my way to the bathroom the curtains would be drawn open, and I could see Kathy feeding my father scrambled eggs, or dipping a pocket comb into a cup of water, then parting and smoothing his thin hair.

I stayed away. Still, I saw him in my dreams most nights. In one dream he hung from the ceiling rafters by his extended leg. The other leg was bent at the knee and tucked behind him, and his arms were folded in an X pattern over his chest. His eyes were dark circles with luminous crosses at the center. His eyes were just buttons stitched with light.

The dream was like veils falling away, and I knew what the posture meant. The knowledge was instant and deep but also tenuous. When I woke up, that understanding was gone, but I held onto the feeling that his poses were part of some ceremonial language that I couldn't decrypt.

My father was not a flesh and blood monster any longer. He loomed larger than that now. He was a picture of all the monsters in the world. He was an example of what they would become if they stuck around long enough.

At the old house I repaired siding, replaced roofing, and then pumped water from the basement and the crawlspace. I used a sander and plaster to restore the walls in the upstairs bedrooms, but I avoided the garage. Ken would have to find another way. I'd take the basement over the garage. That's where he had found her. One detail was all I would need. The pennies that had fallen from her pocket, or some bright yellow remnant of forensic tape. I had too many phantoms to deal with already. I didn't want to see her lying there, cyanotic from car exhaust.

When I worked, I wished I had the girl with me. Her presence was an antidote to this place. She played, and carried light with her. She wore green and red sweatshirts with iron-on giraffes and manatees. But she had tired of the house after her first visit. She stayed home instead and read in her bedroom while I worked, and she talked to her fish so they wouldn't forget her. That's how she put it.

I had finished working for the day. I figured I'd need another week to finish what could be done here, without professional help. I would call my boss in Arizona and ask for more time. I didn't mind so much. It was getting easier, being home. I liked hanging around with Kathy and Ken and especially the girl.

Outside, the houses on the street were dark and foreclosed. The songbirds had left for the winter, and the resident crows were not at the fountain. I stood under the denuded maple tree and smoked, and the rings drifted easily across the slate sky.

\* \* \*

On Christmas Eve the sky opened and new snow came down. The house on Mason Street filled up with the coarse, sweet smell of cured ham. I could almost taste it from the upstairs bedroom.

I heard Ken calling me from down the hall.

"Aiden, I could use a hand in here," he yelled.

He wanted to carry the old man down before the guests arrived. There was a method he had used before. I helped move my father from the chair to the bed, and arranged a blanket underneath him so that it supported the length of his frail body like a hammock. I grabbed two corners and Ken grabbed the other two and we carried him down swaddled in the comforter. We sat him up in an armchair by the dining room table and we left the blanket underneath him for the return trip. He sat straight-backed in his uniform. His elbows were cocked and his hands were tipped, like he held two chalices and was spilling their contents onto the ground below him.

45

The guests arrived shortly after that: Kathy's sister Lindsay from Hagerstown, their childhood friend Sandi, and Sandi's teenaged daughter. The women carried the night. Their silver voices were the rhythm of the evening. Each topic at the table eased into the next, woven by laughter which was the polar connection and the common thread, bringing the end of one story into the rise of the next. I had missed the company of older women deeply.

Ken carved the ham and kept the beer coming. He smiled at the stories he was a part of, and he kept his eyes on his wife. You could see that he followed her signals, that he went by her book. He relied on her as a guide for almost everything. Even when Ashley jumped up to hug him at the table, Ken's eyes sought his wife over the girl's shoulder, as if she was a delicate-winged angel whom he was scared of crushing with the primal strength that coursed through his blood.

Kathy paused to feed my father green-bean casserole, but he wasn't eating. "Oh he's being so stubborn," she joked, and she threw his fork down in mock exasperation.

The other women laughed politely, dabbing the corners of their mouths with the company napkins, as if the frozen figure in police uniform was just fine at a Christmas dinner.

"He's not hungry tonight," Ashley said, keeping her eyes on her plate. "He has things on his mind." She seemed certain.

Throughout the evening the girl whispered secrets into my father's ear. When she did, I thought I saw a softening over his body like the start of a reaction, or a wave-like voltage moving through. It was too hallucinatory to trust. She set a dancing elf doll in front of him on the table. It had spiral-toed shoes that chimed little bells as she moved it sporadically. But the old man stayed closed, just a strange piece of furniture.

I couldn't ignore him sitting there, full plate of food in front of him, untouched like a window display. I felt he had absorbed the nutrients through a kind of demonic inhalation. If I reached over with my fork and stole a mouthful, the food would have the texture of Styrofoam or iceberg lettuce and would taste like nothing.

"Aiden," Ken said. He set another Budweiser in front of me. He pulled the tab for me and it hissed. He clapped his hand on my shoulder before he walked away. Maybe he had an idea how I was feeling that night.

I gulped down four beers while the others finished their meals. It was almost enough to take the edge off.

When we were through eating, I helped the girl clear the table. Ken turned off the overhead lights, and Kathy lit votive candles, brought a carafe of steaming coffee into the living room, and poured the coffee into porcelain mugs. Then we carried my father in, and Ken turned the tree lights on while drummer boy played. Even with the caffeine we all became lethargic except for the girl. She squirmed with delight, in love with the sights sounds and smells of Christmas Eve. She wanted to run outside in the snow.

"It's dark out," Kathy protested. But the curtains were open and we could all see that the moon was up. It reflected off of the white ground lighting the empty streets and the snowdrifts. Kathy relented and the girl put on her jacket and whirled out into the yard.

We finished our coffee and the buttermilk parsnip pie, and when the guests left for the evening, Ken turned the overhead lights back on. He handed me another beer and opened his own. I stared at the old family photographs in a multi frame near the bottom of the stairwell. A picture of a sharp blue lake dominated the center.

"Where is that?" I asked him.

"Quarter mile from the house where we lived in Damascus," he told me. "It's smaller than it looks in the picture. Hunters set up their blinds there." He nodded at my father, asleep now on the armchair. "We coulda walked there."

"Beautiful," I said.

"Never even knew it was there 'til after our father died. I moved back for a year after the funeral and went to the lake every week. I don't think any of us ever saw it. Not back then." He stopped and gulped his beer, sensing my question.

"You never really look at anything around you," he told me. "Your life is pure Hell."

* * *

The girl woke me up early. It was still dark out.

"Everyone needs to be down," she said, "to open gifts."

I found my jacket in the dark room and I bundled it over my sweatshirt. The girl led me down the stairwell by the hand. When we reached the bottom she ran away to the kitchen in her padded feet. She

47

was back seconds later, spilling a tall glass of milk. Ken smiled and yawned at the girl's electricity, at her pre-dawn excitement. My old man sat beside him on the chaise lounge, a red Santa Claus hat stuck crookedly onto his head.

The girl put a CD into the player, then ran over to her mother, who was in place by the tree. Kathy was reading gift tags and organizing the glowing boxes into piles.

Ashley made sure we were watching before she ripped the first box open wildly.

We all took turns, but it was the girl's gifts we paid attention to. She squealed with joy at the red Converse high tops she had pointed out in a shop window one week earlier, and she put the shoes on under her flannel gown.

"Aiden," the girl whispered later, pulling a fuzzy, orange sweater over her head, "You like my outfit?" Then she lay back and cut her feet through the air, admiring the bright red.

"Those are great shoes," Ken said from the couch.

I stood up from my spot on the floor and grabbed a small box wrapped in golden paper that hung from the tree. I handed it to the girl. It was my gift to her. There was a piece of petrified wood inside. I had found it in Monument Valley, Arizona. I wrapped necklace wire around the top of the stone into a clasp the night before, and attached it to a chain for the girl. I explained to her how the wood had mixed with quartz and turned to stone. Ashley put the necklace on. It was the finishing touch to her misfit outfit.

"This is the so cool," she said.

"It's a lucky charm," I revealed to her.

The floor was a wreckage of paper and boxes when we were through. Kathy rubbed the dark crescents of mascara from under her eyes, and surveyed the mess. Ken slept sitting up on the couch while the girl rested her head on his shoulder, stretching her red feet onto my father's lap.

But I wasn't tired at all. I was alert and sensitized. I was on the edge of something. I went to the kitchen and heated a mug of black coffee in the microwave. When I came back in, I sat on the armchair and stared at the Christmas tree snow, and at the red cinders that breathed and burned in the fireplace. A car skimmed the wet pavement outside, carving the water and trailing away. The sun started to show through the window, throwing light into the room, and even the old man's stoniness was overcome by its tones, no longer volcanic, penetrated somehow by the softness of this scene. There was a contagion of calm joy in the room, and my body swam with it. The air of the place resonated on my skin and inside of my ears.

I thought about my mother and about Joe Ironcloud and about the sharp blue lake. The elements all worked together. They clicked like tumblers and interlocked into a strange formula that worked inside of me. I sensed constellations of meaning almost coming together, pointing to deeper things. I could not tell what it meant—I just apprehended a depth of meaning to all the events of the past week in Maryland like a dye that saturated completely. The smell of the fir tree and the charcoaled timber from the fire combined with my mood. It called vague genetic memories in my blood of colonial winters, and of much older fires burning in front of rawhide couches. Then, even deeper, of wild meat roasted on spits in frozen granite caves.

I saw the girl get up from her spot on the couch. She stumbled across the floor, rubbing the sleep from her eyes, and she stood on her toes to reach a small cage on the mantel place. She grabbed the gerbil from the cage off a bed of woodchips. She petted it for a moment, and when she was through, she walked to the stereo and picked a CD from the tower of disks. When the music started, the girl began a drowsy dance to the quiet rhythms of the choir.

She danced swaying at first, and then in loose circles tightening into twirls as she came awake. She danced in front of my father as her parents slept. The tall fir tree behind her washed calm colored lights over her skin and her gown. I thought that the innocent dance might wake him. I thought the girl's stepping and sliding was a ritual of some kind that could release his jailed light.

I looked at my father, still rooted on the couch, his eyes as empty as crab's eyes. He couldn't see the girl's vital dance. He couldn't receive her love, or give it back to her. That was the story of his life. He had brutalized any chance of tenderness, and then turned to stone.

I sank back into my armchair, doubled over with a shattering sorrow for the frozen figure in front of me and for the failure of his life.

# Virgil Fly Away

I loved Virgil Coates ever since the tenth grade, when he first moved to Horse Canyon from some town in Ohio. His green eyes were shaded by dark brows, and his sandy blonde hair stuck out every which way, like he had crawled through bushes to get here. But he was hot and brooding as a young Christian Bale. I knew I didn't have a chance in hell. I saw the way he looked at girls, not boys. By tenth grade I was already used to unrequited love.

Mrs. Birch made Virgil stand up front and introduce himself to homeroom. He told us how they moved to four corners for his father's job at the Mogollon power plant. His father was Irish-German, but he had *Dineh* blood coursing through his veins, too, from his grandfather on his mother's side. It was this grandfather, Virgil revealed, who had passed on to him the shamanic powers of precognition and spiritual projection.

This revelation elicited waves of laughter, coming as it did from a blonde boy in a classroom of mixed Zuni, Hopi and Navajo students. Mrs. Birch hushed everyone up, but even she had an amused smile on her face.

Virgil often sat by himself during breaks, reading from books of philosophy, or books of native lore. When he did join us, he regaled us with dark tales of skinwalkers, who could possess animals by locking eyes, or of witches skulking the canyon bottoms near Bluff with two hearts and a lust for blood. Virgil liked to paint the world as a dangerous place full of magic. I was mesmerized by his tales. I didn't much care if they were true. Still, I had to wonder if Virgil really believed what he said, or if he was putting us all on.

Before long, Virgil's stories edged from improbable to insane, like he was just testing the water with skinwalkers. He once told us, during chemistry lab, that he had missed the day before, not due to sickness, as his forged letter would have admin believe, but because he had shape-shifted into a gigantic crow, and spent the sunlight hours flying atop a mesa and riding thermal columns, finally coasting in the wake of a government helicopter that was mapping out our uranium mines. Virgil called the shift a *major achievement*.

"Yeah, fucking right," Jack Chee said, measuring sodium bicarbonate into a glass tube, where it quickly bubbled over the top. Virgil replied calmly that he had no reason to lie, because he didn't give a damn what Jack Chee or Lindsay Pete or anyone else thought of him. And did anyone calling him a liar want to go outside and settle this? Nobody did. Maybe because Virgil had arms like ironwood trunks. That, coupled with a slight aura of institutional madness.

"Crazy white boy," Jack Chee whispered. But in his voice there was a hint of demure respect for such a bold self-image.

It was the day of assembly that Virgil came into homeroom with skinned knuckles, swollen fists, and two black eyes. The cops collared him during open gym, took him away in handcuffs and basketball shorts. We learned that Virgil had sent his father to the emergency room that morning. Put him into intensive care. None of the kids were too surprised to see Virgil taken away in cuffs, although they didn't know, as I did, what home was like for him.

I won't ever forget our night at the Turquoise Inn. Me and Virgil stuffing our faces with 99-cent tacos and listening to Johnny Cash wail on the jukebox, not paying attention to our phones' dinging notifications. When Virgil finally looked, they were all messages from his dad, saying Virgil should kill himself. That if Virgil was dead it would be better for everyone. He listed different ways he might do so—by drinking lye, by soaking himself in gasoline and lighting a match, by hanging himself from a high tree branch . . . or why not all three, to be thorough?

When he passed me his phone to read, my heart thrashed in my chest like a fish dying on sand. The only upside was, it was the one time my boyhood love let me really hold him. I hugged Virgil desperately, like I was shielding him from bullets.

Days after sending his dad to the ER, his pops returned the favor and sent Virgil to the Starr Institute—a boarding school in Phoenix for *troubled teens*, a phrase which, I had to admit, fit Virgil pretty well, even if the prick had gotten exactly what he deserved. I didn't see Virgil again until the following summer, on the day he took me out with him to the shale cliffs.

We hiked for miles in unfamiliar country. Virgil sometimes checked a map he had folded to the right spot. My feet, housed in inappropriate footwear, bled and blistered through my cotton socks. We followed the rocky, parched washes that were waiting for summer monsoon. We passed stock tanks and a stranded sedan that bled black oil from a busted pan out there along a badly chosen line.

Virgil finally said, "I am being so quiet because I am preparing myself for the task ahead. I've become a very powerful *brujo* since you last saw me. I brought you with me today because I want to show you something special."

My whole body buzzed with excitement. That day I believed him—believed there was some kind of great magic in store for us. That Virgil would show me something truly unforgettable. Maybe it was a faith you can only have when you are a romantic sixteen, blinded by love.

We came to the edge of a mesa that dived off several hundred feet into a wide ravine. It was here that we ate our turkey sandwiches under the shade of a large mesquite tree, chasing them down with blue Powerade. I asked Virgil if this was the spot. He nodded, said his grandfather had cured the rug-weaver's throat cancer on this exact mesa. Danced a power dance right there under the nuclear desert sun.

My legs and feet were aching and I was slothful from turkey sandwich, so I began to doze off, but Virgil started speaking again.

"Energy," Virgil said, "is all there really is. That's the secret to shapeshifting. There is no matter. When you look close enough at a tree or a chair, it's just patterns of dancing energy. It's waves of probability. When you look even closer, there is nothing there at all. A shaman uses this. A shapeshifter is just someone who decides what form his energy will take.

"Crows and wolves are the easiest," Virgil went on. "Don't ask me why. I'd rather be a crow than a wolf. I'm meant to fly, must be." He spoke dreamily.

"The hardest thing about turning into a crow is coming back," Virgil said. "Everything is so different when you are a bird in the sky: the color, the wind, gravity. Everything is better. To come back to human is like waking up from a beautiful dream, only now you're choking on dirt. Nothing is worse."

Virgil looked at me, his eyes bright and serious. "Thing is, I've figured out how to do it. How to stay a bird forever. It's all I really care about."

Virgil sprung from our spot in the dirt and he sprinted to the cliffs edge, arcing his body in the parabola of an Olympic diver. I didn't see the fall, but I heard the thud against the rocks below, which caused a family of corvids to explode like an inky starburst from the bottom. And for a moment, just a moment, before it all sank in, I thought, "Virgil has done it! He's done it!" I watched him fly away, a black bird squawking freedom in the huge desert sky.

# The Dog with the Rhinestone Eyes

An old woman sat along the banks of the river in the high cane. Her dog, Breaker, lay beside her, his belly caked with the nutrient green mud. The moon was full and the woman stared at its fat reflection on the water. A gang of wild pigs sauntered to the banks for a nighttime drink. Breaker tensed, and the old woman lay her hand on him gently. He was old, and would never withstand a fight.

Many creatures came and went from the river, but they never saw the old woman unless she wanted it that way. She could materialize her desire into stone, dirt and bone through a combination of will and catastrophic alignment. The old woman was a sorceress, and understood invisibility.

She heard the hum of a motor and the screeching of belts. Headlights rocked up and down in the deep ruts above them and stopped just downstream of the pair. The pigs scampered at the vehicle's approach, and when the engine shut off, a young woman stepped out.

The witch knew the girl. She often stood on the river banks and stared out at the muscular peaks on the horizon. The girl was sad and intense, with dairy cream skin and grain colored hair. Her eyes were the calm green wash of a lazy river, but her beautiful face was cleft violently, as if some jealous surgeon had destroyed it under the knife.

There was something constrained and electric about this one. She gave the old witch the feeling that she might explode out of her skin at any moment. The old woman—being wise—understood that the girl felt too much and too deeply, and could not make sense of the weather pattern that tore her apart.

Tonight, she had a young man with her. He was rangy, with a cruel face inflamed by acne. The old woman recognized this one as well. He liked to stand in the mud and clip sparrows with sharp rocks.

The cruel boy pointed up at the moon with his long simian finger.

He said, "That don't shine its own light, Katie. It ain't nothing but a reflection," and spat.

As if this knowledge was seduction enough, he began to undress himself and the girl who huddled close to him to protect against the cold breeze coming off the water.

"Don't try to kiss me," he told her.

They lay down in the sand, and the girl stared up at the sky as a parcel of birds flew in strict formation above them.

"Shit," the boy said. "I can't look at yer face."

* * *

The old woman busied herself setting lines of bait from the trusses of the long stone bridge. "Trout for dinner tonight," she thought. Breaker lumbered in the shoal, chomping at water-bugs. It had rained two days earlier, and the river was a wide, quiet sheet of brown.

The girl had come back to the river alone. She wore a green shirt with an ironed-on clover and a leprechaun. She always picked giddy clothing, which contrasted with the tired circles beneath her eyes. She stared at the brown horizon and skipped a rock across the water.

The old woman finished at the bridge and walked up on shore, calling Breaker who followed her. She stopped and watched the girl, who was used to people staring at her face, and never liked it.

"What is it?" Katie asked. Her bottom lip trembled with some fine seizure of feeling. She had come here to be alone.

"I see into the blood of things," the old woman told her, "and you are caught between the fangs of the world."

The hag smelt of algae and pond scum and Thunderbird, and her eyes were milky with cataracts. She was old and wasted, and the girl felt sorry for her, and embarrassed by her condition.

"Well, I like your dog," Katie said. She bent down to pet Breaker. The salt in the dog's hair glistened like mica. The girl reached into her satchel and made an offering of roasted almonds, and Breaker took them from her palm with a gentle mouth. He licked the girl's face, his soft tongue threading the cleft in her lip, washing over her sunken nose and her soft eyelids. The girl laughed.

"Good boy," she said.

She turned to the woman. "I've seen you on the river, trolling for fish. I've seen you weaving baskets from river cane, and cooking meat on your fire. Do you live here?"

The old woman nodded.

"Alone?" the girl asked.

The witch nodded again.

"Are you ever scared?"

"No one will hurt me," she said. "I am too old and poor."

"Do you have shelter?"

The witch pointed. "Near those rocks," she said. "And it is almost time to eat. You can join us. We have plenty."

The young woman followed her. They wove through the high cane and arrived at a stockade. A grey squirrel was impaled near the entrance on a palisade. The girl's stomach turned at the sight of it.

At the center of the enclosure was a tamarisk tree surrounded by odd, discarded items. A single-speaker radio played a scratchy Streisand tune from somewhere among the heap.

"So much washes up on shore," the witch said. "I keep what glows."

Amid the rubble was a children's caned rocking chair. There was a gyroscope the size of a desk-globe. There was an eyeglass repair kit, a pink pocket mirror shaped like a trapezoid, so many odds and ends. And between the tailings, glazed pottery shards reflected the sun like jewels. Each item was strange and resonant, but, outside of an implied personal context, somehow alien and harsh. The girl felt as though civilization had collapsed, and these were the plastic ruins.

The witch rooted through her heap, muttering to herself as she searched, and when she came up she clutched an old stuffed dog in one hand. Weather and time had faded its hide to a dull liver-color, but it had green, rhinestone eyes that shone. She handed it to the girl.

"German?" Katie asked. "But how?"

She held the toy out in front of her and studied it. Small rips in the fabric had been repaired with joining stitches. The eyes were polished and clean. The toy had been cared for. Now it was hers again, and she hugged German close to her chest.

It was the alchemy the witch needed, and she went to work with heat, carving helixes in the dirt with a sharpened elk bone.

She drew in the base pairs—the nucleotides connecting the graceful curves like ladder rungs. The witch pulled a small bottle from the trough of the tamarisk and pigmented the helixes—one red, one blue. The girl recognized the pattern that was emerging—it was the simple abstraction of a DNA molecule.

When the witch was done, a deep seismic shudder disrupted the ground beneath them. It was violent, threatening to bring down the stockade, and the young woman thought the earth was opening up to swallow her. She closed her eyes. Her terrified body contracted violently.

When it was calm again, she felt a hand grasp hers, and the girl found herself staring into the face of a young child. The child had a cleft lip. Her nose was slightly collapsed, like Katie's own. And the beautiful child beamed at her—her entire condition was light. The recognition between them was instantaneous.

"Where should we go next?" the child asked.

The young girl trusted Katie implicitly, because she could not conceive of a future, of *her* future, without goodness and joy and grand strokes. The child knew she was made from the stars.

Katie handed the dog to her younger self. They walked along the river bank as the child sieved dirt between her naked toes, singing and stomping with levity. "Do you have a cup," she asked. "And we can carry the river with us?"

Katie knew that she would protect and love the girl always.

They passed by the stone fisherman's bridge. An old woman was cooking trout over a small fire on the bank, a black dog resting at her feet. The thick scent of menudo steamed up from a blue cook pot.

Katie was suddenly ravenous.

"Eat with us," the stranger invited. "We have plenty."

The pair walked over to the fire. Katie felt wonderful. Everything had such dimension. "Thank you," she said to the woman. She felt the good hygiene of the fire's flames. She stared out at the iron mountains on the horizon and pointed to the highest peak. "That's the one I'm going to climb," she said.

The child broad-jumped through the sand, but she sprinted back to where Katie stood and looked on to where she pointed. She gasped, barely containing her excitement. "Okay," she agreed.

Naturally.

# Dogs of Light

When he returned home to Area 6, Hunter Martin barricaded himself into the south-facing bedroom of his father's unit. He wore the same threadbare, faded-red suit he had worn one year earlier when he first left for the Celerion Medical Compound in Area 3. He threw the curtains open, bathing in the broad pool of sunlight which washed through the filter-glass. He wanted—no *deserved*—all the south-facing rooms to himself. He felt his year of darkness at the compound had earned him the proprietary right to all the sunlight in the place. And his father, he decided somewhat incongruously and with bravado, could suck his cock.

The window of the bedroom gave Hunter a clear view of the 1968 Ford Mustang parked across Myrtle Street, a "For Sale" sign stickered to its windshield. Hunter's heart raced as he gazed down at it. The Mustang was the only thing which still roused adrenaline in his wasted body. He saw magical potential in the rust-eaten, once bright yellow frame, a project he could throw himself into, heart and soul. A project that would transform him, somehow.

The muscled chassis of the Mustang—its heavy metal bulk—imparted to Hunter its iron steadiness and equine power. Gazing at it, Hunter felt focused, grounded, strong. He was able to forget, momentarily, the heavy footsteps in the adjoining room, and the psychic tyranny of the man they belonged to. Thoughts of the powerful 429 engine, which Hunter would rebuild shiny-new and perfect, allowed a gentle amnesia to wash over him, and for a short time, visions of hemispherical pistons and MIG welds displaced the deep-seeded fear which ensnared him so easily beneath his father's twisted rule. In fact, the whole damn crucible of the past year at Celerion washed away on the muscle car's powerful tide.

The way they had quarantined Hunter from sunlight. The way the darkness was lifted only by *hallucinations* of light. He had a recurring vision in his pitch-black quarters of dogs made from light. A whole pack of lumbering canines with stilty legs licked Hunter's face with firework tongues like Roman candles. He had named them:

58

Sheriff, Buster, Beastie. The dogs of light helped Hunter survive in the darkness. Their radiance kept him alive.

"This research will help our descendants become invulnerable to a spectrum of possible disasters," the scientists assured him, pep-talking on his importance in their grand experiments . . . grand experiments which would allow the human body to, among other things, produce vitamin D without sunlight, and function on close to zero nutrients. It was about *survival of the species*. In addition, the lab-coats reminded Hunter, he would be paid handsomely for his contribution. By handsomely they meant fifty grand for one year of his life. Now that he was home, with his father's significant debts paid off, Hunter had $1700 left to his name. He prayed it would be enough.

He watched as two kids ran along the cracked asphalt, playing in temp-controlled UV suits, winding figure eights around the Mustang and a broken-down jalopy. Even in the bulky suits, on the dead street, the children seemed so carefree.

\* \* \*

With the sun safely set, Hunter could leave without donning his bulky Ultra V. He decided it was time to head outside for a look at the yellow beauty under moonlight. Just the thought of being near the car soothed him, sent a clean buzz of joy throughout his tanked, lab-rat body. He would dial the number on the sign and *haggle*, as they called it. Hadn't his stepmother told him just that morning the car had been gathering dust for months? The owner would probably take the first offer given him. Hunter would start low.

Radio music eddied from the lightened living area as Hunter passed the archway. It almost felt inviting—the soft light, the music, the smell of food—but Hunter knew better.

When he turned the front door-handle, a woman's voice called him hoarsely back. His stepmother stood at the kitchen-pass, beating flies from hunks of meat, throwing the large pieces into a bucket of marinade. Her skin had the same red sheen as always. Salt crystals glistened in the dark hairs above her lip. She handed Hunter his bowl of beef broth, which scorched his hand as it sloshed over the rim.

His father sat by the clock-radio, erect in his favorite green armchair—somehow able to sleep like that—but he awoke suddenly, and appraised Hunter with feral eyes.

"Eat," he said, then softened the edict with, "You earned it, son."

His father's visage had unsettled Hunter ever since he was a small boy: the wild, yellow sclera of his eyes, the iridescent shimmer of his hydrophobic skin, and the charred, scaly honeycomb of his defective cyborg arms. The father's most terrifying feature, however, couldn't be seen with the naked eye.

"You're doing a crack job . . . a bang-up job, Hunter," the father said, combing his thinning hair with long, simian fingers. "I'm proud of you, son." As he appraised Hunter's pale face, the translucent feelers covering the patriarch's body modulated like nerve-endings. He was probing—distrustful—trying to unearth some filial conspiracy against him.

"Clinical trials are a fine way, a respectable way to earn a living," the father went on. "It's how I met your sainted mother. It's how I was able to feed you and your dear departed sister, and now that you're a man, you're doing your part, Hunter, and taking your place in our proud family legacy.

"Not everyone is fortunate enough to be able-bodied," the father continued, sparking the flint of his lighter repeatedly, a gleam in his jaundiced eye. "Not everyone is blessed with the genetic superiority to use their bodies as currency. We Martins come from hardy pioneer stock. True Americans, strong as oxen, and don't forget it."

The father grabbed a news sheet from the coffee table and handed it to Hunter. The sheet advertised the next clinical trial at Celerion. It would implement a bio-hack designed to cut the subject's need for sleep in half. They needed healthy males, aged 18 to 40.

"Thirty grand for three months," the father said. "I know someone on the board. I'll get you in, Hunter." When he spoke, the tip of his tongue shot out, licking the delicate mesh of spittle from between his purple lips.

Hunter tried not to think the words: *Pimp. Salesman. Thug.*

He smiled at his father.

The thought of returning to the lab put Hunter's heart in a vice grip, and roped his gut into tight knots. Every molecule in his body contracted against the offense. Hunter folded the advertisement and stuck it in his back pocket.

"Looks like a good one, father. I'll jack in tomorrow. Register."

The patriarch nodded. Then he fell asleep in the armchair as quickly as he had woken.

Once outside, Hunter drank the night air desperately. He counted, "one, two, three, *IN*," then "one, two, three, *OUT*," until his breathing normalized.

He would never go back to Celerion.

He looked down Myrtle Street.

The broken arm of a dim streetlight cantilevered above the Mustang, swinging idly. Its moody bulb gave the vehicle a flickering, supernatural aura. An army of large tree roaches marched towards the yellow beast, scurrying in a dark pilgrimage from beneath the rotting foundations of the building. They were an inky, armored river moving under a calm, silver moon. The roaches snaked around the Mustang's heat-cracked tires, and when Hunter opened the driver's door, they scattered all directions like a startled flock: some into the storm drain, some into patches of dead grass, some into rotting balks of timber.

Hunter admired them, perhaps even envied them. They were simple, strong survivors.

He took a deep breath, and ran his hand along the Mustang's cracked dashboard. It was rough and uneven . . . perfect. He checked the visor. No keys. Hunter took the driver's seat and placed his hands on the wheel. It gave him such a sense of freedom! He imagined the open roads of less than a century ago, what they must have been like. Hunter had seen the impressive thoroughfares in books and film: wide asphalt veins crisscrossing the land, vehicles speeding along in their lanes like glinting jewels, taking everyone and anyone to all corners of the continent. Nothing had been off limits! Rich or poor, exploration was at everyone's beck and call.

Those same interstates had fallen into tectonic disrepair decades ago, when the affluent citizens took to the air, and the public funds had disappeared. But Hunter knew that a few choice by-ways were still kept open, bankrolled by rich hobbyists, some even given the lauded title *National Highway* to honor the history of the once-prosperous land.

Hunter felt good as he sat in the car. He felt somehow in accord. Without thinking, he gave the horn an exploratory push. Its cry screamed out through the quiet streets, shocking him from his reverie. After a few moments, he relaxed again into the womb of the Mustang, seduced by the magic of its moth-eaten upholstery, pulled into hypnotic imaginings of a great future: A vanilla scented tree hung from the rear view, and Lila napped in the passenger seat—frail, lithe Lila from Area 5, with her grain colored skin, and soft, amber lips. The radio played twentieth-century rock music as they drove the open highway, exploring the great ruins of the west. It was—Hunter knew—somehow meant to be. He studied his reflection in the car mirror—his dark eyes, full lips, and thick, raven hair. A handsome guy, he thought, certainly worthy of a beauty such as Lila. And with this car. . . .

But Hunter's dream ground to a halt. He saw his father's dark figure look on from the porch, a quiet silhouette rooted there like a black and stunted tree.

Hunter's heart pumped mining sludge. His blood crawled like lava flow. He recognized a certain complex feeling, as an epileptic recognizes the aura before a seizure.

The patriarch's malformed figure came forward into the flickering light and rested against the car's frame.

"Everything okay, Hunter? Why are you sitting here, in this yellow car?"

"I have some money left," Hunter said. "I've always liked autos, father, as you know."

Hunter understood his words were pointless, but they came automatic, had a mind of their own, ignored reason. His father's eyes flashed at him in the dark like raccoon eyes.

"Ever since you were four," the father agreed, "obsessed with collecting those little cars, those antique hot wheels, which your mother hunted down in junk shops, God rest her soul."

"I miss her," Hunter said, gritting his teeth, preparing for the storm.

The father nodded, grunted softly, acknowledging this small piece of his son's hurt, then began, as always, with the paralysis. Hunter imagined the hemispheres of the tyrant's brain lighting up like a pinball machine—an enhanced corpus callosum gave his father the dreaded psychic ability. Hunter was a beetle, pinned to a board.

"Before you leave for Celerion," the father said, "there's a burnt-out motor on the ceiling fan. I'll need your help with that, son. . . ."

There was a certain familiarity to this dark script, a predictability that was almost comfortable. The way his father spoke of trivial things as he roughly entered Hunter's mind, like they were catching up, civilized. It was taboo—a highly punishable offense—for Hunter to acknowledge the invasion.

"Motor," Hunter agreed. "Fan," he muttered, as the words caught in his throat like goatheads.

"I'd like all the hangars on the gutters replaced, too. You'll need hardware for that, of course."

As his father spoke dully, he sent images with teeth: Hunter's mother consumed by wood rats, lying in a trashed canal. A shimmer of heat. Beetle food. Garbage. Hunter's body beside her, eyes wide, starting to turn.

A not so subtle threat.

She smuggled him the can of white beans, Hunter locked in the wine cellar, leaving behind her trace of perfume and white lace, diaphanous as a ghost. His mother. Ghost. Only the father had ever been real. Just the father. Always the father.

A titan. A mountain. A god.

"Good," the patriarch whispered as Hunter buckled, his mind coming to accept his place in the patriarch's cosmos.

And his sister's revolution—shooting blue-magic as ragged track marks crawled up her neck. Strangling vines. Inches of height, gone. Her thin, hungry bones snapping like twigs. Hunter felt it. She looked like someone's grandmother in the box. No escape.

For a moment the father lost his focus, and the nightmare vibrations broke loose from Hunter's skull, burned off like an insubstantial fog. He could see, at his core, the dense, diamond energy which was his true strength.

Not long enough. The father came back, stronger.

He showed Hunter the Mustang swallowed by wild grass, showed him the early days of his fervor decomposed into lassitude. Hadn't that always been the case? Hadn't Hunter failed every project, broken every commitment he had ever made to himself? Fluorescent snakes nested in the dark wheel wells, and paint-scrawled graffiti covered the doors. The Mustang went to seed. Never meant to be. Swallowed by a piss-colored horizon. But the Celerion compound raked the sky, imposed like a steel mountain. Celerion had been there since the earth had been loose rock hurtling through space. Since before the sun. Since before the galaxies had spun out from an unimaginable pinpoint of density.

Destiny.

The compound waiting for his body like a hungry beast.

The father was gone.

Hunter sat in the Mustang, panting.

He crawled into the empty street and lay on his back, staring into the sky as the lighted squares of window in his building became shuttered eyes.

It might have been hours before the dogs of light raced past him. There were so many more than Hunter remembered, flooding Myrtle Street, clogging it with radiance. And just when it seemed as though they had forgotten him, would leave him lying there in the street, they turned back in recognition, stampeding their starlight. Tears streamed down Hunter's cheeks. He was happy, so happy, for this reunion. The dogs pawed Hunter with large, clumsy feet. They licked him with firework tongues like Roman candles. Their ecstatic tails could never hide the immense love they felt for him.

# In the Blood and the Bone

He called her Tuesday night, right before *Big Love* came on. Joanne Farmer had a large salad bowl full of salted potato chips balanced on her lap. She heard the ringing and she reached her hand in between the sofa cushions, feeling for the phone with her salty fingers. The bowl rocked from side to side with her shifting, and her small, bloated feet, covered in a favorite pair of fuzzy pink socks, slipped from off of the coffee table.

Jo knew who it was. His ring was Joan Osborne.

She answered and Abbot told her. "Jo. She's dead. Last night." His voice sounded removed and deliberately blanked, like he was betting on a hand of poker. It was enough to stone her. He had not returned her calls for several weeks. Now his efficient narrative came across the lines in beating waves through the earpiece. Joanne felt as though she were deep under water. When she lay down, the springs below her reacted with the stiff noise of a cheap mattress.

She whispered, "Abbot, I am so sorry." But her words were automatic and barely audible, directed at the stuccoed ceiling.

Abbot exhaled heavily. He wanted to let her know that he was bored by such platitudes. But after a few moments, Joanne could not help but think to herself, "Abbot has called me so soon afterwards," and then she was able to breathe again. The choked feeling was replaced by a blood heat that started in her chest and was pumped outwards in a wave, spreading warmly to her limbs, and ending at the tips of her fingers with their drug store press on nails and their little geometric decals of circles, squares and triangles.

She would focus, she decided, on this small victory, and she would work out the other implications later. She sat up.

"Would you like to . . . meet?" she asked him. Joanne hated to hear her own voice, the way it wavered just like a young child who was lying to her parents.

"I'll be over," Abbot told her. Then he hung up the phone before she could say to him, "Wonderful. Absolutely Wonderful."

* * *

65

Joanne was barely able to contain herself. She did not move from the couch, and she felt a ticklish kind of excitement inside, as though little silver fish were swimming quickly through her blood-stream. He would be here soon. She could forget everything else and focus on this instead. She let her mind wander, imagining the night that lay ahead of them. Even as her eyes glazed over, they were drawn to the bowl on her coffee table. It was the muted blue color of a Robin's egg with a small gray chip near the rim of it. Her eyes were often drawn to colorful objects as a focal point. Her father called her habit "leaving ground," and he often teased her when she went away calling, "Earth to Joanne Farmer."

Jo generally saw things through to their most positive and unlikely conclusions. Her fantasies were varied in nature, but they always ended with an outdoor wedding of some sort in a great meadow, blanketed with lupine and tiny red flowers. The reception was held under the sprawling canopy of a giant Chestnut tree.

"You are stupid to imagine these things," she chided, calling herself out.

She knew from Mr. Paul at the Arizona Clinic that her fantasies were counter-productive and often harmful. He told her they were holding her back. She saw the wisdom in his philosophy and she was attempting to turn over a new leaf, to move forward—as Mr. Paul would put it—rather than inward.

Joanne added to herself, "And perhaps a little respect for the dead is in order."

She stood up, walked into her kitchen, found a clean glass, and poured the last of her wine into it. She said, "To Jennifer Knight," and then turned to the large magnetic crucifix that was fixed to her gun-metal refrigerator. It was inscribed, "Saint Mary of the Assumption Catholic Church." Its heavy, metallic presence looked admittedly severe amid the bone-white kitchen. She kept her eyes closed, crossed herself, and took quiet drinks from the cup until it was empty.

It was private ceremonies such as these that Joanne felt gave her life some amount of authenticity. It was what made her think it possible to remove yourself from the noise and the mud and to become quiet and beautiful. She remembered when her father told her that an act could be pure only when it was done without witness, with no thought of self-display.

Joanne drank the good wine and she honored the dead woman to the best of her ability with a strong, meditative silence in the empty kitchen.

* * *

As Joanne showered, thin moonlight came in through a thick square of bottle-glass above her tub. The little window was distorted so that you could not see in or out clearly, but Joanne could still make out the dark movements of silhouettes as neighbors walked back and forth to their cars for small, forgotten items. When she turned in the shower to rinse herself, Joanne knocked the shampoo, then her liquid body soap, from their places along the small sill. Mr. Paul would not have to worry. Even in her most creative moods, she could not stand here in her narrow bath, looking down at her large body like a mountain of pallid baking dough, and imagine an outdoor wedding.

Sometimes Joanne showered in candlelight. Candlelight was more forgiving.

But she had forgotten the lights this evening, and now she fixated on beads of water as they made their descent in little chaotic runs down her body's misshapen topography. She grew fascinated watching them. Every movement seemed perfect to her; surely there must be some fine mechanism of control behind each drop, too fine for her rough comprehension. The way that they would start forward with a beautiful and balanced momentum down the heavy incline of her chest, then mysteriously slow as if a delicate brake had been pushed softly, and finally they would stop completely (but only momentarily) before moving on and crisscrossing in fluid diamond patterns, following invisible channels down her stretched stomach, and finally disappearing into a fatty crevasse of skin at her waist.

But when Jo noticed her veins in her nakedness, she forgot this game. Once she noticed them, she could not look away. They were as audaciously blue as the large Stellar Jay that sang at her feeder every morning. They would pick up and disappear on the surface of her enormous thighs like short and incomplete roads.

Slowly, Joanne Farmer was carving out the shape of a woman. This was how she thought of it. But it was a geologically slow process; she had lost only four pounds, down from two hundred and eighteen in the three months since meeting Abbot. She knew that rivers carved out

67

canyons with greater efficiency. Still, she would do it. She *had* to do it. It was necessary that he be able to look at her without revulsion.

* * *

Joanne had met Abbot for the first time at the Trophy Room on Fifty-Second Street. It was nestled among vacant dirt lots and old saguaros that were marked with rifle shot. The bartender there did not smile at you, and filth covered the floors and the countertops like its own thin topsoil. People did not come there to drink Budweiser on a Wednesday night. But it was four blocks from Manzanita Apartments where she lived, and Joanne had been feeling bold that night. She had reached a quiet climax that was internal and subdued in the way that grinding your teeth is subdued. When she remembered that feeling now, it was as a low, galvanized buzzing throughout her entire body, but there had been a thickness to it that would not allow her to think, that would not allow her to examine it or name it as it smothered her. Emotion had always manifested itself as a physical pain in her blood and in her bones.

The thing was this: she had been alone for too long.

Joanne knew how ridiculous she looked walking in. She knew because she had seen it reflected in all of the different floating faces. The faces were hostile and disembodied, like white masks without expression on a dark stage. She was larger than they were used to, and who wore a pink cardigan to a place such as this? Joanne had walked in small steps when she came in through the front door as if fording a quick moving river, and she carried a creel wicker basket in her right hand that was full of different colored yarns and an assortment of glinting new crochet needles and aluminum afghan hooks. She could laugh now when she thought about it, how provincial and silly that had been of her.

At the time she had not been able to laugh. At the time she had been terrified.

Not one of the faces seemed to welcome her. She had thought to turn and run back but instead, she fingered the tiny golden crucifix that hung from her neck and she seated herself outside with her basket and her pattern book. She had kept her head bowed intently to her weaving, refusing to acknowledge the faces around her but never forgetting them, the whole time wanting to leave but held still by some kind of intense fear and shame. Every second that passed was slow and awful, and Joanne watched the quick, nervous movement of her own hands as they worked below her, felt her pulse beating through her neck, and wondered, "Is anyone else as terrified by such common things?" It seemed impossible.

But the night had moved forward and the faces after a short time forgot her, more interested at last in other people, more interested at last in other events. With this easing and the tonic of her drinks, Joanne's antennae had begun to move slowly, receiving now rather than blocking, and she slowed in her knitting and she allowed her ears to pick up on small pieces of the activity around her, attuned now to the phlegmy loud voices of smokers and to the quick laughter broadcast from coarse throats, attuned to the low obscene comments of men accepted like gifts by women in tight levis who smelled of pungent floral perfume and hair product. She had looked up finally from her small square of afghan and allowed herself a cautious laugh. The men and women had laughed back, acknowledging her graciously. Joanne allowed her eyes to open up fully like camera shutters. She was amid a small-sized crowd. How had she ignored them for so long? Their faces were not so threatening, their faces were easy and mutable with alcohol, and suddenly and magically the night seemed to hold possibilities.

So Joanne had swallowed shots of Petron out of glass tumblers with a busty woman named Michelle, who wore purple cowboy boots and sang out loud to "Sweet Home Alabama" when it came through on the blown speakers outdoors. She felt good, powerful even. And the men noticed her. The men looked in her direction without disgust. Joanne could tell by the way that their eyes moved over her in sections that they saw her as a prospect, as someone they might consider. She had the sense that something important would happen tonight, but she did not know what. Then she saw Abbot's rangy form leaned up against the trusses of the small overhang outside and she knew right away, that was it. She knew that was what she had coming.

What she noticed about him at first was his face. It was strangely beautiful but frightening. There were deep furrows like dugout canals, and his skin was razed scarlet purple with acne like the worst teenage affliction. He had sharp blue eyes that would catch on things and then deconstruct them silently. Joanne remembered thinking that he had a face that Hollywood might pick up for certain bizarre roles.

He had been part of the large group on the outside patio (her group, her people for that one strange night), but he was always just skirting the perimeter with a kind of impetuous, unnoticed superiority. He would laugh at strange moments and shout out cynical things that had a philosophic bent like, "That is what happens, Bobby, when you lay pearls before fucking swine." Then he would flick his cigarette butt over the fence like punctuation in a long and beautiful arc.

He had seemed to her so distinct and separate and lethal.

Joanne had not been able to take her eyes off of him. She would look away, but she was always drawn back, as to a crime scene.

When she asked, Michelle told her, "I don't trust him. There's just something snaky about him. His wife is home dying, and he's here tonight drinking like an Indian and shouting out fancy words. I'm not one to judge, but there's just something snaky about him." After a moment she added, "But I'm never wrong about people." Michelle looked over, and when Abbot was looking right at her, she turned away quickly and snorted.

He came back with, "Well, Michelle, when you have organized your famed intuition into some kind of actual coherent understanding, *then* we'll talk, sweetheart." His words were tactile and caustic with a self-important weight.

As the night went on, he became the only presence, taking up Joanne's whole awareness as he paced on the periphery, sucking down cigarette after cigarette. Finally he pointed at her with his Pall Mall as if elucidating a key point and said loudly, "Now that girl has got it. At least she is over there creating something while you fellows are over here humping each other's legs like a bunch of primates." Everyone looked towards her table, and Joanne blushed deep red.

After this, Abbot focused on her fiercely; she was the single object of his study, but he used his eyes only. He did not address her, and in his silence he seemed to become monolithic. She could not forget him. Every time she looked over, he was staring right at her. Joanne could only look away. Privately she was thrilled by the attention of such a force, but she had to go inside because she felt that out there with him she could not breathe.

He followed her when she went inside, and he stood next to her and set his drink down on the lacquered bar-top. When he told her his name, Joanne looked down at her own drink next to his and she stirred

70

it with her finger she and replied, slowly, "Abbot, like the Catholic monk."

"I hadn't thought about it," he said. Then, "No, not the monk. My mother-in-law might say Abbot, short for *abot-toir*." His laugh was sub-vocal, more of a quick movement in the general area of his mouth and a slow vibration in his gut.

"It's a place where they slaughter cattle," he told her.

"I don't think I've heard that before," she said. She took a long drink and then remembered to tell him, "My name is Joanne." She almost added "Joanne Farmer," but she thought better of it.

Abbot dropped his voice lower and he told her, "I don't want to bore you Joanne with family details, but I thought I would tell you up front that my wife has adenocarcinoma. That's stomach cancer. It's from eating too much fucking salted foods," he said. Then he held up his hand anticipating a rebuttal and he told her, "Well I'm guilty of it too," as if to clear his wife in fairness from full responsibility. He leaned in close when he spoke to her, and his breath was sticky and sweet and fermented.

Joanne touched his hand quickly and told him, "My grand-mother died last December from lung cancer. I know it's not a spouse, but her house always smelled like cinnamon and her yard smelled like compost and wood chips. When I was a kid, she read me *Peter Pan* out of a large, leather book with gold cursive on the cover."

"That sounds lovely, Joanne."

Abbot bought her drink after drink, and Joanne hummed along to the jukebox music and moved from the hips slowly, hoping that she would appear fluid in some way, hoping that she would appear casual, or maybe subtly provocative. Instead, she was aware of her silly wicker basket, aware of the little square of blue and gold afghan that was lying on top. She could feel the wooden way her body sliced through the bar's smoky atmosphere that had settled down like an inversion. She hoped that Abbot saw her somehow differently.

He had stayed with her all night right until the last call, and his attention had been complete and focused in a predatory way. It was as if they inhabited their own small space of reality that night, and what was outside did not matter to him at all. He was high on their dynamic, and he was sure of his power over her.

Joanne knew that Abbot wanted her in some way. She was not sure what she had done to deserve this interest, but she thanked God for it quietly.

She knew that she would have to do everything right.

\* \* \*

Early the next morning, Joanne had found Abbot's ring lying on her bathroom sink. When she held it up to the early gray light of the window, she could see the numbers 1-9-9-7. They were scripted into the underside of the band. There was also a message that was etched on the inside in thin cursive that you would need good eyes to make out, but Joanne had not allowed herself to read it. She would never allow herself to read it. The easiest way for her would be to not look in certain directions.

The ring made a sound like a fingernail tapping when she set it back down onto the cool porcelain. It was five a.m. and she had not slept. Joanne watched the sun rise, and she listened to the footsteps of someone waking up above her. She lay back down on her bed and watched Abbot as he slept. She liked to watch the irregular rise and fall of his chest with his breathing. She was already starting to glimpse certain hazy possibilities; she was already forgetting the ugly rhythm the night had taken on, how Abbot had not undressed, only slipped his pants down past his hips, his cold tongue and cold hands on her. She forgot the beer caps on the bed that had cut her back, and his final failure of arousal, and the moment he finally rolled off of her and mumbled, "I can't look at you. I need the right fantasy to make it."

Joanne had understood that his own shame caused him to say these things. He had slept close to her all night afterward, snored lightly with his arm draped across her, and did not move away. When he muttered in his sleep, she wondered what he was dreaming about.

\* \* \*

His knock was particular. It was two quick thuds with his open palm. When Abbot walked in, he set his unopened bottle on top of the small stack of cooking journals which sat on a wooden stand under her transom. He said, "Thanks, Joanne, for seeing me. Maybe you should have told me to go fuck myself."

He did not look at her directly, but she could see that his eyes were dried red from lack of sleep. They looked inset and buried in the tired skin around them. Joanne thought to herself, "I only want to calm him." Tonight, she would run her fingers through his thick hair. She would feed him and play soft music on her stereo that would help him to sleep.

She said, "I'm making hot tea and soup. It will be five minutes."

"Forget the tea," Abbot told her. He grabbed his bottle at the short neck and he walked with it into the bedroom.

Joanne hummed in the kitchen while she cooked. Her tune ebbed and flowed; it rose and fell with the spontaneity of a young child's song. She knew that tonight was so important for them. The new latitude would allow them the breadth to rest in each other, to become intertwined like the two tree lovers from the story; it would allow them to crystallize their connection in the way that she had thought of when they first met.

She would be able to tell her father and Mr. Paul at the clinic that she was in a relationship now. She could see Abbot smiling when she introduced him. Taking her father's hand firmly. Telling her over his paper in the morning, "you make me a better person." Joanne remembered the night that she had made Abbot laugh when she used the phrase, "death on crackers," pointing at the starved, painted model from the Revlon commercial. He had laughed about it a second time even, later that night.

That feeling of happiness passed through her veins now as she cooked, and she set that feeling into the close future, where she would make Abbot laugh over and over again. The future allowed her to soften all edges. Joanne could see things in a gentle clean light because they had not yet happened. Only in the present did things have claws and sharp edges and the sour stink of life like sweat.

Abbot could see that Joanne had prepared for him. She had arranged new pillows like couch cushions along the spine of her bed where it butted up against the wall, and she had moved the small television so that they could watch it easily from her bedroom. He looked around him. There were small wreaths the size of portholes on the walls that hung just above chair rail level. They were made out of walnut branches and different colored silk flowers. The walls themselves were a light blush red color with the trim of the windows painted white.

He thought that Joanne almost had a woman's sense of interior style, but then there were tall files of plastic Ikea storage units, piles of consumer magazines like leaning towers, wall sconces that would never be hung, and other weird pieces of unused décor. Just an overall clutter of shit, with a path to the bed blasted out like a tunnel. Joanne had a snow-white cat named Ghost which moved expertly in and out of the small spaces that wound through the mess. It was in Jo's nature to be slovenly, to start on projects that she would never complete. He saw an analogue between her habits and her physique. They finally lacked beauty and definition. He felt that this was reprehensible in a woman. But Abbot understood that Joanne loved him, and that she put him above herself. So he kept returning to her.

Abbot broke the seal on his bottle and dropped the little piece of curled plastic onto the bedspread. He lit a cigarette, drew on it deeply, then turned on the cable box. He could use her black mug as an ashtray.

Joanne walked in with two steaming bowls and a clay mug on an aluminum bed tray. Abbot looked up quickly and he told her, "I'm not hungry."

"You should eat. It's cream of chicken soup and red potatoes. Home-made."

"I'm not hungry," he repeated. He flipped through the channels with the controller. He knew that he needed her tonight in some way but he could not see how to soften. Abbot looked at Joanne's broad back reflected in the mirror above the armoire. She was only twenty-seven, but her size had relegated her to the double-plus racks and to the dress barn image of middle-class mothers.

Joanne set the tray down on top of her dresser. She knew it had been Abbot's idea to come over. She felt that this gave her some kind of opening. So she sat down beside him on the bed, and although she was scared she took his hand and she told him, "I know that you loved Jennifer deeply." There was a quick winded feeling that Abbot might confirm this, that he might discount her in one swift stroke.

He did not look at her, and he only said, "No one loves deeply." There was no sign of anything in his voice. He was becoming frustrated with the remote, pointing and clicking repeatedly now.

"I don't think you believe that," Joanne said softly.

Abbot kicked his shoes off and he loosened his belt. "Jennifer was pretty. Thin and as pretty as the next pretty girl. I was proud to be seen with her, to introduce her to my friends, to my mother." Abbot took a long drink from his bottle and Joanne watched as some splashed down onto his shirt, onto her lavender bedspread.

He snubbed his cigarette out in the black mug and then he lit another. "It might not sound like much, but she was more than anyone before or since."

Joanne flinched as if struck and Abbot felt a quick charge of shame like lightning. But it was replaced by the immediate, stronger impulse to strike again.

Joanne wanted to say something, but she only whispered, "Abbot. . . ."

"I don't want to talk about it right now," he told her.

"Okay," she said.

Abbot took a deep breath. He needed to calm down. Start over. Go easy tonight, he told himself. Abbot picked up a cup from off of her bed stand and then he tilted it slightly and sniffed.

"Water," Joanne told him.

He poured some of his Scotch into the cup with the water and then handed it over to her. He chinked his bottle against her cup.

"Thank you," she said. She knew that the drink was his way of apologizing.

Jo left the bed, and she grabbed the tray off of the top of her dresser where she had set it earlier. When she was up, she angled the television slightly. Then she resituated herself on the bed with the tray on her lap and the scotch and she kissed Abbot on his cheek. The soup had cooled and had thickened into a skin layer on top. She poked through it with her spoon.

Joanne shoveled the cold soup into her mouth; when she looked back up at the television screen she gasped involuntarily. The picture showed an old man who had been beaten to death with a large car battery. The bloody battery was setting on the tall grass, there was a small pond beside the dead man, and a large algae bloom had grown in the pond. The body was propped up under an orange tree with a white painted trunk but it had gone limp and the man was doubled over at his waist like a decommissioned puppet. There was a cap on his head, but the blood had soaked through, making it deep purple.

"Can we change it?" Joanne asked. "Please? It's too much." She knew her imagination. Images like this imprinted on her mind and they would not let her sleep at night.

Abbot did not respond, so after a few moments Joanne said, "Is there nothing pleasant on?  Wouldn't you like something pleasant tonight?"

Abbot said, "There is nothing pleasant on."  His bottle was already at less than half.

Then he pointed at the television with his cigarette and said, "What is funny to me is, there is really nothing special about death.  It is not fascinating.  It is not dramatic."

"Okay," she said.

"Don't say 'okay.' Don't placate me," he said, "That's condescending."

"I'm sorry," Joanne said.  "I didn't mean to."

Abbot nodded as if he accepted this.  His eyes were on the television screen, but he told her, "Her mother took care of her for those last few months.  I hated it there.  There was an adjustable hospital bed and the smell of Lysol that covered up worse scents.  There were used tissues everywhere and a clutter of cards and flowers and crosses on the bureau.  She would hold my hand and look out of the window and say, "I don't want to go to Purgatory.  That's where most people go.  It's like Hell, only God lets you leave once your sins are burned out."  Abbot talked in a slightly high-pitched voice when it was his wife speaking.

"She talked about Purgatory all the time.  She was like a doll with a pull chord.  It was a definite, geographic place that she was being sent to, like Siberia.  Apparently, she did not think Hell was an option," he told her, spitting a piece of tobacco from his bottom lip.  "All that I could think the whole time was that it was disappointing," he said.  "Unfantastic."

Jo could not speak at his flat venom, and in that space of silence what came into her mind was her long Greyhound ride last winter.  The mountains and then the frozen, plowed fields mottled with dark ice that had passed along outside of the coach window.  She remembered, they were revealed to be a part of a vast hallucination, a show of some kind disguised as substance and earth to the others on the train who did not know what she knew, who had not known the death of a loved one so recently.

"Why are you doing this?" she asked him.  Tonight of all nights she had expected some kind of gentleness from him, some kind of restraint.

"I am not doing anything," Abbot told her.

"Why would you talk about your own wife that way?" Joanne's voice was a fine tremor when she spoke. Her eyes were full green wells.

Abbot looked right at her for the first time that evening.

He could see that she was attempting to manipulate him through tears, through pleading, just as a child would. But he would not be suckered in such a simple way into her shame. Joanne had not known Jennifer—her simple morality that she carried with her to church, to her mother's house, to the grocery store like a shiny acquisition . . . then swept under the bed, and fucked whoever would have her. Never took time with him. She spat words at him through white, straight teeth from the kitchen as she cooked, or from the bathroom as she brushed her long brown hair that hung down past her waist. *Impotent. Loser. Punk.* As if he were a slug that she had found inside of her new tennis shoe. And he had stood there quiet and charged, on the edge of something. Her beauty had given her a leverage over him that he did not understand.

He might have killed her, finally. He might have killed her while she slept, but the cancer had gotten to her first.

"She was a whore," Abbot told her, flatly.

The noise coming from the television was strange now; it seemed much lighter than the rest of the room. They sat on the bed and they were each aware of the other in a quiet locking of horns. Joanne could feel Abbot's leg against hers, and she could feel his long calloused fingers that were still resting on her skin. She suddenly needed to remove herself so urgently from the close heat of his body. She knew it was best for her to move away slowly so as not to provoke him. But when Joe inched away Abbot only moved in closer to her. It was as though he sensed her distaste and he wished to amplify it, to provoke her in some way.

Her heart moved up into her throat anticipating him and Abbot laid his hand behind Joanne's back and with the other hand that was holding the bottle he pushed her down onto the bed. He said, "There," as if he were speaking to himself. As if he had just figured out how some piece of furniture assembled. He took one final drink from his bottle and then rested it on the bed stand without looking. Joanne knew by his rhythm that he did not think of her when he kissed her at the waist, or when he moved his hand down her large, inert legs. He did not think of her as he kicked impatiently out of his ripped blue jeans or as he hiked the thin cotton skirt which she had put on tonight just for him. And as part of this same series of motions Abbot moved up so that he was lying on top of Joanne, and he said lowly into her ear, "You don't get respect just for dying." Joanne could hear by the tight controlled pitch of his voice that he was angry. He was angry with her, but he was attempting to focus. He faced away from Joanne with his eyes closed, and there was sweat beaded up on his brow like small dewdrops. It was the same rhythm as the first night but it was claustrophobic this time. His leaden mass seemed to bury her. Joanne felt as if she were suffocating. She could feel the tenseness of Abbot's muscles like thick-braided wire, and it hinted to her of brimming restraint. Joanne understood that he was capable of great violence towards her. She knew that it was best for her keep still until it was over.

She also knew that there were certain thresholds that Abbot could not cross.

* * *

His breathing finally became regular and heavier until Joanne could hear that Abbot was asleep. She stood up from her bed, switched the lights off, and then sat back down again on the bed beside him in the dark.

After a short time Joe could hear a quiet noise that sounded like an infant gurgling in its sleep, dreaming of black and warmth. She looked over at Abbot, and when her eyes adjusted in the darkness she could see the wet bubbling up from his lips. He rolled over onto his back with a wet drowned cough; Joe shook him at his arm, but Abbot did not wake up. Then she rolled him over gently onto his side so that he would not choke while she was gone.

Joanne got up from her bed, walked into her bathroom, and pulled two of the hand towels from the rack on the bathroom wall. She dumped her toothbrush and her floss from their holder into her sink basin, filled that cup with warm water, and walked out. When she returned to the mattress she sat down beside Abbot and started to clean his mouth out silently, hooking her pointer finger covered with the first cloth, and sweeping the pungent bile into the second towel which rested on top of the other hand. Then she took the first cloth again and she dipped an unused portion of it into the cup of water, bobbed it until it was saturated, and began to rinse Abbot's mouth out slowly. When she was finished, she carefully cleaned his neck and his chin. Abbot still did not stir. Joanne pulled his stained shirt from off of him as he slept, threw it towards her hamper, and then cleaned his chest with the same detailed care. She would wash the sheets in the morning. She would not wake him up now.

Joanne touched Abbot's forehead with the back of her hand gently, and then she rose, walked over to the hamper, and threw the towels in. She did not go back to the bed to check on him. Instead she walked over to the large chair by her window and sat down quietly. Ghost jumped up onto her lap, and she sat stroking his thick white fur as he purred in the darkness. She did not know how long it was that she sat for. She had no thoughts to measure it by. She was locked in a static, numb unknowing in the dark.

It was still dark, but graying when a small sedan pulled into the parking lot outside of her window. Two bright spotlights came on suddenly, and Joanne watched, squinting as the outsized shadow of the sedan passed across the brick face of the building. One of the two spotlights was positioned high up in a tall Eucalyptus tree, where she could see that the branches had been limbed with a small buzz saw. It was strange that she had never noticed it before. The light was very bright and it pointed almost directly at her window. Joanne held her hand up to her face with the palm outward, shielding her eyes from the bright glare.

She thought, "There are so many things that you did not even look at that were right in front of you. . . ."

# In Bird Territory

The week of my eighteenth birthday Tommy told me about camping in the city. "Sign me up," I said. It didn't matter that I was sick as a dog. I stumbled out to my baby pink Cadillac and let Tommy drive. I was convinced my sickness was tied to my parents. They were the sun blacked out. They were cyanide added incrementally to my cereal each morning. My dad was a financier with electronic tickers for eyes and a shit ledger for a brain that added up everything wrong with me. My mother was depressed and wandered vacantly through our cavernous house like a concussion victim. She talked softly and politely when we crossed paths, like I was a stranger who lodged there. She spent most of her time in the backyard with her brood of chickens, clucking with them in some strange dialogue. Leaving home was an easy call—I stuffed a backpack with bras and panties, my hygiene products, a dog-eared copy of *Zen and The Art of Motorcycle Maintenance*, and we booked.

When my fever broke a few days later, I found myself staring up at the empty walls of an abandoned railway warehouse. My body screamed with hunger. There was no refrigerator to comb through. No cabinets to raid. Some squatter had left behind a half bag of barbecue Lays, though. And there was a warm Coke, too, still fizzy. I almost shrieked, I was so happy. I raised the dock door, stuffing my face with chips. When the sunlight flooded in I felt lucky, like I had just risen from the dead.

I had seen the inscrutable Bird-faces of the Analysts as I tossed and turned in my fever dreams: their polished gemstone eyes and hooked, blood-purple beaks. The Bird-Men stood behind thick red curtains, pulling long levers with their human-like hands, and cawing into the sky like crows.

If you were lucky enough to see an Analyst on the street, in the real world, he was almost always wearing an uninventive black suit, like an FBI agent, like a professional of some sort. (That is why the moniker, Analyst, stuck, after all.) But in my dreams the Birds were naked and spread their large wings like terrifying angels. Their plumes blazed so brightly it was like staring into an eclipse.

The Bird-Men were slippery—you might see an Analyst one day (in the supermarket, perhaps, picking through produce) and the next, you'd forget the encounter completely. Which is why the media called the Analysts, *"folie à plusieurs"* or "the madness of the many."

Certain people remembered more than others, though; they could just hold on to Birds better. Tommy and I were two of them. The armchair theory among Birders, as we called ourselves, was that the brain had to be wired a certain way to even register Analysts. It was a rare, perceptive ability, like synesthesia. The popular multi-player video game *In Bird Territory* had been written collectively by Birders like Tommy and me, someone who had talked with, or even lived among, the Birds for a time. We referenced the game and its wiki page like an encyclopedia of fact, the closest thing we had to a bible of bird culture.

Whatever their fugue presence really meant, the very existence of the Birds gave a star-gazer like me a reason to live, because it meant there was more to this world than shopping malls, melting glaciers, dead-eyed parents, and dead-end jobs. The Birds' elusiveness endowed them with holy-grail-like-status to those who knew.

But the occasional glimpse wouldn't cut it any longer. I needed more. I had to find a way to snag one, to force my entry into the Birds' strange world. They could fix me, I was certain . . . maybe add some kind of measurable *meaning* to my life.

That's what I decided as I stood on the loading dock that morning, soaking in the desert rays like a sun-greedy Lazarus. I saw my Cadillac before I heard it. The faded pink beast was unmistakable from a block away. Tommy piloted the pink dragon, his white shock of hair also unmistakable. The car threw out a cloud of black exhaust as it pulled to a stop. Four bodies spilled out, and Tommy ran up to me.

"Kat!" he said; "You ready to get out of this hell-hole?"

"Fuck yes," I told him.

He opened the passenger door for me and took the driver's seat. It was a warm October desert afternoon.

We drove around the valley with the top down, blasting Misfits, stopping at Circle K for EmergenC, tall-boys, and tuna sandwiches. Tommy had money; I didn't ask where it came from. I was starting to feel better with each bite, though. Alive again.

"Where do you wanna' go drink?" he asked me. "Your call."

"Golf course," I decided.

I loved it there because it was so green and smelled like mown grass. It didn't feel like desert at all, but like rolling, green countryside. More importantly, it was a hot-spot for Analysts, and right then I felt even one glimpse of a Bird could recharge me, calm an unexpected nervousness I was feeling at having left my parents. Being homeless was this uncomfortable buzz of being unanchored, of floating through the desert like a stray black balloon.

We walked around the golf course drinking our Schlitz. Two humming birds buzzed us like large bumble bees. My red hair drew them. Fire-truck red. Dyed one week ago. Tommy threw the empties into his backpack and pulled out two more. He laughed and ducked from the birds.

"This is a great day," he said. "You with me on that?" He grabbed my hand and swung my arm, like we were two five-year-olds traipsing at a carnival.

I knew Tommy was in love with me, but wasn't sure I could ever fuck him. There was something angelic and underdeveloped about his body. He once told me it was some kind of hormone imbalance—congenital—but didn't like to talk about it.

He stopped walking suddenly, pointing down the chip-seal.

"I see this Bird everywhere," he said. "He runs all over the city. Always in those same shorts." He paused. "It's like he never stops running."

Tommy's memory for the birds was remarkable, the best I had ever known. The shorts he spoke of were orange Adidas running shorts. They were shiny and super short, and they shimmered in the sun like orange insect wings. Yes, I remembered this Bird as well. Always running. Always orange shorts.

I made a quick calculation: I'd stand aside, and at the last moment hurl myself into the Analyst's path. I imagined the collision in my mind's eye, an entanglement of limbs and feathers, stray down on the wind like a raided hen house. Perhaps we would fuse like some mythical chimera. Maybe the bird would pass through me like smoke. Whatever. It would be an interaction. It could be the start of something.

"I'm doing it," I decided.

But the Analyst stopped short of us. He planted his lanky arms on his sides, leaning forward at his hips, then walked back in the opposite direction. He took a seat by the pump house, stretching his wiry legs onto the green as his plumed chest heaved.

He truly was a stunning Bird. His chest was red like fire. Short explosions of cobalt tipped each long and wondrous plume.

"This is *too* cool," Tommy said.

A Bird stopping in such close proximity—at least according to *Bird Territory*—could be taken as an invitation. Nothing was accidental when it came to the Analysts. They saw many distinctions we missed due to a developed sensitivity often regarded by Birders as "psychic ability." My heart hammered a blast-beat as we walked on over.

"I saw you running yesterday," Tommy said to the Bird, playing it cool, "by the Golden Saguaro. And the day before that," he said, "at the canal park." He took a long pull on his Schlitz, his cheeks filling like water balloons before gulping down.

"That's possible," the Bird said, "Quite possible. Although I hardly bother to think of where I ran yesterday."

His large eyes were startling blue, and inscrutable as reflecting pools. He motioned for us to take a seat beside him. We did. I reached into the small pocket of Tommy's backpack and pulled out a notebook he always carried for me and a red sharpie pen. The last thing I had written was, "What is the I-Ching, and why do the Birds 'toss' it????? Look into this. . . ."

Impulsively, I began to draw the Analyst with my sharpie. It was shaky and unskilled—a child's drawing, with stick arms and legs, stick fingers and toes, and a triangle beak. A bubble coming out of the Bird's mouth read, "Quite possible."

I tore the page off and handed it to him. I'm not sure what possessed me. I was no artist, obviously. I just felt the overwhelming need to give him something. I fished through the same pocket searching for my Marlboro lights and lit one, shaky with excitement.

"I've quit like a thousand times," I said, suddenly self-conscious the Analyst might pass judgment on the habit. Tommy just looked at me strangely.

"I usually smoke cloves," the Bird said, "but I don't carry them when I run." I offered him a Marlboro light and he accepted.

"This is just right," he went on, studying the picture as he smoked. "May I give it to my daughter? She collects such things."

"Sure," I said, scratching my head, "but I don't think it's very good."

Then the Bird began to whistle, "Jesus' Chariot." His whistle was clean and resonant as a well-tuned instrument.

We sat and talked as the sun lowered in the sky, Tommy and I getting drunk, and the Bird whistling on with such beauty and precision it put the warblers in the lemon trees to shame. We learned his name was Arpeggio, that he was training for the Pike's Peak marathon. He had recently run an Ultra in Death Valley. Many Analysts, apparently, were also ultra-runners.

"We may not fly like our fleet-winged cousins," Arpeggio said, nodding up to the lemon tree beside us, "but that doesn't mean we can't run like the fucking wind." We laughed to hear an Analyst cuss. It sounded like such a surgical attempt at hipness.

We told Arpeggio we camped in the city. He told us he camped above town with his daughter, near the old tire stockpile. Did we know the spot? We assured him we did.

Strangely, all the questions I thought I'd ask once I had an Analyst to myself dropped off. I never asked, for instance, if the Analysts sat in the shade of young beech trees, pouring wine down the bark of their greenish trunks, or if they whispered and courted them with poetry like lovers. I didn't ask if Bird society was truly anarchistic, as we Birders believed, with no concept of status or power based on such bullshit markers as wealth and profession. We simply kicked it for an hour or so, like old friends catching up. We actually talked music. I learned Arpeggio was into Arcade Fire and The Flaming Lips. I told him that lately I had been getting into '90s era east coast hardcore—bands like Agnostic Front, Sick of It All, and Life of Agony. I promised him a comp.

Arpeggio glanced at my drawing once more and said, "Kat, I'd like to start working with you. Weekly. Find me Friday, at my house, and we'll start." With no further explanation he stood, and after a few quick hamstring stretches, sprinted off nimbly towards the piss-colored horizon.

"Shit, Kat," Tommy said. "Holy shit! You just scored a session with an Analyst."

We Birders knew that those who went into session with an Analyst were headed for great things. For unimaginable realms. That was the expectation, at least—an expectation of transformation, and of many mind-blowing miles through Bird Territory.

Shit was about to change.

Everything had a wide-open feeling that night. My blood rushed under my skin like a hot river. I felt I was standing on the rim of some

84

inviolate canyon. I wasn't sure why I deserved this good fortune. It was better than the grand prize. Better than fame, I thought.

I wasn't in any kind of mood for sleep. Tommy and I talked all night by the railroad tracks, drinking and smoking like champs through to dawn. When he was drunk enough, Tommy kissed me. I let him. Life had given me something, so I needed to say *yes* in return. It seemed simple—a kind of quid pro quo. The soft scream of locusts wrapped us in a globe of sound, and when we were done fucking we lay naked in the dirt and listened to the drawn whistle of the train and watched the slow pull of shipping cars as they chugged past us under the creamy stars.

\* \* \*

I found Arpeggio's place that Friday afternoon, close to the tire stockpile, as promised. He was sitting in the sun when I arrived, popping cherry tomatoes into his mouth from a wooden dish beside him. He had ditched his orange shorts for the day and was wearing the more traditional Analyst suit. His jacket was thrown casually over a tree stump, revealing dark suspenders and rolled shirt sleeves. A wreathe of fire-red plumage exploded from his collar.

"Kat," he said, "You found me. Good. Let's head inside, to my office." The Bird's house, if you could call it that, sprawled unevenly over the baked ground without much of a plan I could sense, save perhaps the steep roof which I learned channeled drinking water into the large catchment below.

Before going in, he whistled up at an impressive treehouse anchored solidly in the fork of a large black oak tree.

A small chick appeared at the opening, who I guessed was Arpeggio's daughter. She held a large remote control in her hand and toyed with the levers, summoning a robotic dog to her side. The riveted creature let out a brassy bark.

"Don't play all day," Arpeggio said, glancing at his wristwatch. "This afternoon, you need to work on *Biography*, Cali. It's very important. Don't procrastinate. Do good work and I'll have a Nikola Tesla card for you, or possibly a Joan of Arc."

The chick's wings fluttered in a blur of excitement at the prospect of new cards—collectibles called *Biocards*, according to Bird Wiki. They were a type of holographic trading card highly valued in Bird society.

Arpeggio and I entered the rickety structure and walked down a tortuous hallway to an office-type deal. It was separated from the rest of the house by a thick dividing curtain. The curtain was red, like in my dream, the office threadbare but cozy.

"Now, first meetings are a type of introduction," Arpeggio said. "Or, perhaps it's better to think of it as an acclimation. Your body needs to adjust to Bird Territory. You're moving from the land back to the sea, so to speak."

"Okay, sure," I told him, but wasn't.

Arpeggio directed me to a high-backed chair. A few ribs of armature had ripped through the greenish upholstery. There was also a tattered second chair, a large bookshelf, and a table thrown together from splintering palettes. A window looked out on the dull land, a potted bonsai resting on its sill.

It was too calm and quiet. I felt out of my element, suddenly, and wasn't sure what the expectation was.

"Don't be anxious, Kat," Arpeggio said, tapping a clove from his pack and lighting it. The room filled up with spicy incense. He considered me silently. "I want to tell you that I love the sound of your voice. Your voice is what clued me in to what Analysts call your Self-Actualization-Potential.

"Your voice—the amplitude and pressure of its sound waves, combined with more personal details such as style, word choice, elongation or compression of syllables, and other factors—paints your portrait much more accurately than any gene sequence might. There are so many fine distinctions in the human voice. It is as complex as the cellular structure of that juniper"—he pointed at the bonsai with his smoke—"and we Analysts have the proper microscope to read it with, so to speak."

"Cool," I said, "I can see that." Like how Arpeggio's voice was sharp and clear and seemed to burn away fog. My father's voice: an army recruitment ad. My mother's voice always sounded as if it came from a shy ventriloquist in some adjoining room.

He went on, "You might not realize it, but you are already changing, acclimating to Bird Territory. It began on the golf course the other day. As you spend more time with us, you will be reborn. I'm not talking spiritually, although that is certainly a factor, but physiologically. This is more than the normal regeneration of blood and skin cells which is taking place all the time in all living creatures.

Your heart will restructure—its electrical system will rewire. You will also re-set neurologically. Signals normally filtered out by your nervous system as unnecessary to survival will begin to take on visibility, importance, and dimension. The world, in other words, will blossom into a vital, teeming sea full of the most fantastic and abundant and mysterious life. Does that suit you?"

I imagined bio-luminescent life forms, swimming in a swift, wine-colored ocean. Hell yes, I wanted to live in a world like that.

"And perhaps most importantly," he continued, "you will come to know yourself." He paused. "What we Birds will receive in return, is in-depth knowledge of you, as a completely unique and powerful human being. And we will add our knowledge of you, in the form of Emotional Biography"—he indicated the musty bookshelf with his clove cigarette—"to our cherished library of humanity."

"Deal," I said. Really, who would say no to that kind of an offer? It seemed like a win-win to me. I stood and walked to the bookshelf. I brushed my finger across a long row of hardbacks, stopping on a thick volume with a brocaded spine. The decidedly un-fantastic name, "Cindy Mack," was spelled out in gold-woven letters.

"May I?" I asked.

"Certainly," Arpeggio said.

I pulled the book out and gently leafed through the pages.

"It felt like someone was clamping her heart in his fist," I read. That was the entire first page. The next page was a sewing needle glued with polymer to a sheet of thin tree bark, followed by many sheets of fulminating color: fuchsia, gun-metal, sea-foam, cobalt—all shuffled and molded into pyramids and decagons and beating hearts and blazing synapses. The book was insane, alive, unstructured. I felt Cindy Mack's story like an infusion. She sat alone on the stone bench of a busy plaza, an anxious young woman who was much too frightened to look at the milling faces around her, but still needing their heat, their voices, their bodies, even as she ducked her head to sewing and drowned them out with headphones. Then, years later, Cindy Mack with eyes sharp as cut diamonds, as she stood below her epic tapestry which churned and swam like a Van Gogh painting. The awkward girl had flowered unbelievably in one swift moving cancerous explosion. I had the feeling of being possessed by her. The hairs on my arms stood up as if lightning was about to strike.

"Holy shit," I said.

"Yes," Arpeggio concurred. "That's what we call empathetic possession. It is the breaking down of the self and the inhabiting of another's emotional core."

I went through a whole row of Emotional Biographies before sitting back down in stunned silence.

Something in the room had changed over the course of our hour together. The potted bonsai on the sill had grown. It had moved, I realized, deliberately. The plant's movement was different, of course—it wasn't our pedestrian movement of one foot in front of the other. The plant's movement was growth, an explosion of cells towards the light, towards nutrients, towards sun. I felt myself moving in the same way towards the awesome Bird creature beside me. I felt myself growing through the thick slabs of silence between us.

Arpeggio's final words that afternoon were, "Next Tuesday, Kat. And please bring running shoes."

* * *

When I pulled up to the warehouse, two squatters were out front working on a demolished Chevy truck. It belched dark exhaust and stalled each time they turned it over. The kids just laughed and sucked down their Old English. Then when finally, the truck didn't die, they shut themselves in with their forty ounces, and squealed away, cackling like devils towards downtown. The sunset cast the tall office buildings in pink light. The world seemed like a fantastic place to me. Even the weeds that grew in our dirt patch bloomed bright yellow. The dock door when it rolled up was industrial, powerful, strong. Everything had lost its dish-water aura and gone high-definition.

But I realized this wasn't my vision. I was piggy-backing on Arpeggio's consciousness—borrowing the Bird's wavelength, so to speak, and looking at things through the rose-colored reality tunnel of Bird Territory. No way could I maintain such sight. I was no Cindy Mack, after all. I was certainly no Joan of Arc, or Nikola Tesla. As quickly as I thought that, everything turned brown again. It was fucking depressing. Then I became intrigued by how that happened—how clarity and beauty had evaporated the instant I thought it would, and how subtle the mechanism of that change had been.

I thought about it as I walked around the warehouse district that night with Tommy. We stopped at the Green Motel, which was what we had named the Desert Motel Inn because of its unnatural mint color like cheap cake icing. It looked like some tenement building in candy-land. We liked it there, though, because no one bothered us. We hung out by the pool with the prostitutes, who lounged on the deck chairs like jaded lizards, waiting for some john to sidle over with a twenty or two.

Tommy and I talked Birds, of course.

I remembered something from my session. "Arpeggio said the Analysts are not a mystery to solve," I told him, "but a mystery to accept." Tommy chewed on that for a while, then said, "Like life in general, I guess."

"In France," he told me, "the Birds are worshiped by artists and Bohemians. There is, like, this movement, this whole school of art, which only paints Analysts. Really bright paintings of tropical, psychedelic Birdmen, but wearing suits, of course." He paused, lit a smoke. "The French see them more easily, for some reason. Per capita, they have far more Birders than we do. Genetics, I guess." I nodded, as if this was all very natural—as if I could now consider myself of the same ilk as Parisian artists.

We found an open room later that night, and I showered with the brittle soap bar and the pungent shampoo-conditioner combo. I looked at my face in the mirror afterwards, rubbing a circle from the fog. I was hoping for someone different. I guess I was hoping for someone greater.

I went out to the bed after my shower and sat there, letting Tommy stare. When he came over I kissed his small face, pulled his soft body close to me. I licked the delicate ossicles of his inner ear and thought, "this is how men must feel towards *us*—hungry, rapacious, dominant." I remembered Cindy Mack's blazing eyes as she stood beneath the tapestry. I wanted to be like that. I wanted my soul to be a sharp, shining diamond.

\* \* \*

"Kat," my father said flatly. He just looked at me dead-eyed, and went back to his paper, radiating stern disgust.

"I'm just here for running shoes," I told him.

My mother stood up from the couch. "I just saw them some-where. The pinks?" she asked, pulling at her hands, and staring at a spot just above my right shoulder. My mother was scared of eyes.

"I saw your note," she added. "Thank you, dear, for letting me know you were leaving." Like I said, she was always so polite to me. It freaked me out.

"It's been good," I announced," just living at this place, this really nice place, and trying to, you know, make sense of the chaotic pantheon of gods and demons battling inside my chest."

My father started to cough violently—"God's and demons Shit, Kat. How about resumes and cover letters?" He shook his head in a gesture of disbelief and snapped his paper taut.

My mother, sensing a battle, walked away and began to prattle under her breath about chickens—something about the Andalusians and Delawares, the Andalusians being a less hearty breed for winter. Then she started moving from room to room, opening closets erratically, and searching, I guessed, for my shoes.

"It's okay," I called. "I know where they are, mom. They're upstairs."

I felt sorry for her sometimes—the way the slightest conflict sent her spinning off into some strange orbit, where nothing could reach her except her pet chickens and the fat orange fish swimming in the pond out back. My mother had never been an anchor. Not even close. She was always right on the verge of collapse.

I was fourteen years old, or in the neighborhood of fourteen, when I realized that my parents were actually just as confused and full of shit as everyone else. It was a moment of great insight for me. Their parental authority was nothing more than a massive con. They knew as little, maybe *less*, than I did about life, but insisted on pretending to the throne. I had never *rebelled*, when it came down to it—I had disregarded. There had never been any decisive battle or split in the Parson household. We all just disliked each other thoroughly.

I walked upstairs and found my cross-trainers, then sat for a time staring at the teal walls of my old bedroom. There was a box of Sweethearts on my dresser and I tilted my head back and poured the chalky candy into my mouth. When I went back down, the living room was empty. I looked out through the transom into our back yard. My mother was sitting by the pond, tossing crumbs in to the pearlscales and roughies that swam in the clear water. The coop door was open, and the hens strutted in the dirt, doing a little dance around her. She was wearing this rice farmer's hat Aunt Paula had brought back from Shanghai a few years ago. With her conical hat and crooked back and the burnished, nuclear sun above, she looked like a sad Japanese painting.

* * *

There were vast tracts of BLM land to the north and west of the city where Arpeggio and I went on our runs. The land was scarred dependably by a network of two-track roads we used as trails. Our first time out, Arpeggio dusted me mile one. His light, avian musculature, and his two-toed ostrich-like feet, carried him easily over the baked ground. He seemed to glide like an air-hockey puck through the desert, that fuck. I, on the other hand, was ill-coordinated as a drunken toddler. My legs moved in a different rhythm than my hips, my hips went against the tempo of my center, my center was out of sync with my spindly, pumping arms. Each graceless heel strike was painful.

When I found Arpeggio waiting at the first junction, I was sucking air hard. He sat on a crate of bottled water he had cached in the shade days earlier. He tossed me a bottle along with an orange, gel-cap pill that looked a lot like a Dayquil.

"What's this?" I asked.

"Think of it as a crutch," he said, "until you find your balance."

"You're not dosing me are you?" But he was already off again. I shrugged and swallowed it down.

Whatever kind of Bird magic that little orange pill contained, it changed my run completely. I felt its warmth spreading from my stomach outward, until I could feel each millimeter of my body wrapped in it. Each contraction of muscle, each smooth expansion of viscera, each electrical stroke of heart muscle, worked in a profound and rhythmic unison. I felt all the blood and water in my body dropping down, aligning with the pull of desert gravity. Each footfall was easy. My body buzzed and hummed as I sped through ravines and washes with a new gentle strength, past the towering saguaros with their pleated trunks, past the iron-skillet faces of red rocks. The recent rains had spread green carpets through the arroyos, and the desert was smiling.

I found Arpeggio waiting for me at each junction. He'd toss me a water then sprint off on the next leg, showing me the way. By the time I was finished drinking, he was already a blip on the radar screen.

As the sun started to set, I found myself running alone through a narrow slot canyon. There was something off about the shadows in this particular canyon. They looked out of place and cockeyed, not quite lining up with the sun. I saw movement like a heat shimmer on a scree slope hugging our trail, and a shape blew around me. It had slippery texture, and dimension. Then, just as quickly, everything snapped back to a harmless contour. I was not sure what had just happened but chalked it up to confusion and exhaustion. I did pick up my pace, however. The ridgelines turned pink as the sun sank behind them, and everything looked friendly again.

When I found Arpeggio back at the vehicle, we were both ghostly white with alkaline dirt. "Not bad for your first run," he told me. "Even with the pill." He thought for a moment, then explained: "The pill drops your consciousness into the center of your body, here"—he rubbed his stomach in circles—"and allows you to direct your movements from that area, rather than with your thoughts, *here*." He tapped his forehead; "This is the worst place to direct movement from. Soon, you'll understand the feeling of that, of moving from your center, and you won't need the pill at all. You'll run like the wind."

Arpeggio cooked up a meal that night of sautéed chard, bright steamed vegetables, and braised pork so tender it fell apart in my mouth. I was mellow from our run and the wine Arpeggio kept pouring. Cali had her cards out as we ate. The Birdling activated one card by placing her finger on a metallic sensor imprinted in the corner. Nikola Tesla's handsome, Slavic profile emerged carved in light. His photonic eyes burned with intelligence.

"Now, what is Tesla's essence?" Arpeggio asked the chick. "Feel into him."

Cali started anxiously pacing, gearing up for something, until she finally blurted: "Death Ray Abandonment. Cortisol Shaman Fantasy structured into lonely, castellated Dynamo." She was breathing heavily and seemed spent from her effort.

"Perfect!" Arpeggio clapped. "Now, Joan of Arc."

Cali activated the proper card. Joan's young, haloed profile emerged. "Somatic Belief Armor," she said. "Crystallized innocent bravery of strong, soft heart."

Arpeggio smacked down on the table, and Cali beamed at her father's encouragement.

He turned to me with lustrous eyes like geodes. "Your turn, Kat. Let's start with . . . hmmm. Your mother."

"My mother," I repeated. I was at a loss.

"Parents are hard," he said. "Your ingrained ideas about them make them very hard to see. Think poetry," he said, "not narrative. It sometimes helps to close your eyes."

I closed them.

"Chickens," I finally said.

"Chickens," he confirmed.

"That's all I've got," I said, opening my eyes.

"We'll work on it," Arpeggio said, and passed the wine.

\* \* \*

I noticed my body becoming looser and more sensitive with each long desert run. Before long I was staying on Arpeggio's heels, following his orange shorts like a gleaming beacon through slot canyons, past petroglyphs, into hidden valleys which opened up into grassy range. We gunned past cattle tanks, flew by rusted car frames and shot-up saguaro cacti surrounded by red shell-casings. Arpeggio would sometimes leap into the sandstone bluffs and hop nimbly around with a flock of mountain rams, before spreading his wings and coasting back onto the trail like a hang glider.

Running was becoming very important to me, something I enjoyed and felt proud of. It stripped me down to my elements, allowing me to live physically, from the inside out. My body was this amazing thing—somehow, I hadn't taken much notice of it up until now. Arpeggio liked to say running, "cleared the fog of programmed thought," allowing us to receive all the brilliant, physical transmissions of life. I loved it. Until one run when it became too much.

It was a ten miler. Our trail carried us through a massive patch of dead Gambrel Oak and thick chaparral. The oak trunks were skeletal. Their foliage had been stripped by a plague of insects that had long since moved on. Yet I could see the phantom swarm. I saw it a mile wide, mowing down trees like a brazen, gluttonous beast. The swarm's trilling collided with the sounds of crickets and warblers around me, of hidden life burrowing in cool dirt, of chitinous insects rattling in cheatgrass, of lowing cows in the surrounding range. The sound kept building and building, until the desert became a bleating orchestra. I stopped running and fell onto the trail, clapping my hands to my ears. The sky above me was sharp and loud, the sun raw and nuclear. My whole body was drummed by paralyzing pressure.

"Fuck this," I screamed at the desert. I was both terrified and amazed. I was a drowning sailor who for the first time knew the murderous ocean.

The shadows were gathering again. They moved into the open from behind creosote bushes and ironwood trees. They moved in and circled me like spectators with vaguely human shapes. They started to fill in, black cloud turning to larval faces without eyes. I felt something reach through to my spine, clamping down nerve clusters like a spectral vice. I was a beetle, pinned to a board.

Then Arpeggio's hand was on my shoulder. The noise stopped like a record. The shadowy faces snapped back to tree shade.

"Get up," Arpeggio said firmly. "We need to leave this spot. Now." He pulled me to my feet and I lumbered along behind him down the dusty jeep trail, my head pounding like the worst hangover.

"What the fuck was that?" I asked, back at the car.

"What do you think?"

"I started to hear things. See things. I couldn't move. I'm not sure." I shook my head.

"You're starting to see is what happened," Arpeggio said. "*See* with a capital S. You're becoming sensitive to new signals –signals your old nervous system filtered out or discarded."

"Well, I'm not a fan of seeing, then," I told him.

"The first few times are always chaotic and frightening," he assured me. "Soon, you'll learn to structure those experiences into digestible form. Your mind and body won't react so violently."

"And the shadows?" I asked. I knew he had seen them too.

Arpeggio lit a clove and thought for a moment. "An embodiment of the desert," he said, finally, "although that's simplifying. Let's just say they were entities who saw your vulnerability. They would have taken you over, without a doubt, if I hadn't returned. They are attracted to strong emotion, especially the emotion of fear. They wanted to eat your awareness, Kat. They are predators who hunt energy, as mammals hunt meat, and they are as hungry as devouring vultures. Your enhanced awareness, coupled with your fear, made them gluttonous. You are becoming susceptible those types of forces, now that you're starting to See." He paused, then added, "Heightened awareness isn't all roses, you know."

I lit an unsteady cigarette.

"Next weekend is Southern Cross. I trust you've heard of it, through your video game. Tommy can come," Arpeggio decided. "I think we deserve a party." He patted my knee, then threw the pink beast into drive and shot off down the jeep trail.

When I was alone again, I kept my eyes on shadows. I became absorbed by the dark silhouette of an ocotillo painted in spidery charcoal on one wall of the warehouse. The agave beside it was a stark, rigid bloom, opening to the sky like a dark-armored flower. The combination of shadows had such minimalist precision, I considered some artist might have landscaped the plants solely for the beautiful effect of their shadows on this particular wall. Intrigued, I watched until the sun was gone.

I thought about the beings who had wanted to "eat my awareness," as Arpeggio put it. Now, instead of fear, a strange pride surged within me. Life was humming, expanding into delicious and dangerous territory. I was a warrior, my energy coveted by malevolent predators from different realms. If they engulfed me, well, at least it was a fucking worthy way to go.

* * *

That Saturday we made our way into the deep desert. Arpeggio drove and Cali had shotgun. Tommy and I were in the back. Des Cadenza screamed from our blown door speakers to the thrashing assault of Greg Ginn's guitar.

"Listening to Black Flag with an Analyst," Tommy remarked, shaking his head in disbelief at his outrageous good fortune.

We finally drove up to a condemned-looking building absurdly isolated in the desert hinterland. Its mirrored windows flashed at us. Arpeggio screeched the caddy to a halt in front. The whole structure looked unstable and bent. It was the Leaning Tower from *Bird Territory*—ground zero for Southern Cross, a kind of transportation ritual which conducted the Birds into arcane realms we Birders only guessed at.

"Does he always drive so recklessly?" Tommy asked.

"Yep," I said.

95

"Looks like a death-trap," Tommy noted.

"Yep," I said again.

The front door yawned open and we walked inside and climbed a winding metal stairwell to the rooftop. In contrast to the cement stories, the roof was earthen, and as dark and rich as planting soil. I took off my shoes, digging my toes into the cool, moist dirt.

A brood of Analysts milled up top, each dressed in a trademark black suit. Wreathes of dense neck feathers strayed from each avian collar. I had never seen so many Birds in one spot! One Analyst had the blinding red plumage of a tanager, another the bright yellow feathers of a goldfinch, yet another the blazing blue coat of a stellar jay. I saw the dull gray smock of a sparrow, and the blue-black down of ravens and crows. The Birds were in constant motion, gathering then dispersing, winding in ribbons, never settling into groups for long. *Dancing*, almost, as their conversation buzzed steadily like the wind. A series of clay ovens were set up along the perimeter, sending small columns of smoke into the hot sky. There was a large pool at the center of the roof, which gave off a briny smell like the ocean. Arpeggio and Cali disappeared almost immediately into the strange marine layer.

Tommy and I walked on over to the basin. Despite its gigantic size, it was as primitive and rough as a hand-dug well. The cloudy water teemed with marine life: water bugs, fish, sinuous ocean flora. Glowing trilobites sailed just beneath the surface of the water like armored ships. We stared slack-jawed at the elliptical bodies of the ancient sea-kings. I felt the trilobites' ancient power, recalling vague memories of ocean bloodlines. My whole body hummed electrically. My skin absorbed the wind and mist like super food. My blood churned a raging river, bright red as anemone. I was strong. I was in my element here. The trilobites responded to me with a blush of gorgeous light.

A new Bird stood beside us.

"The human paleontologists got a lot right," the Analyst said, gazing at the impressive creatures, "but they got a lot wrong, as well. They never guessed *bioluminescent*, for instance. Trilobites use light in a very advanced system of communication. They are highly intelligent creatures." The lobed bodies of the Cambrian rulers breathed and burned below us like embers.

"Callahan," the Bird said, extending his hand to me. He had steel-colored eyes and smoked a filterless cigarette. His feathers were the dull green color of tarnished copper.

"I'm going to tell you something no Bird's ever told you before," he said. "Not all Analysts are heroes, no matter how you've built us up in your games. Birds can be ambitious, spiritually ambitious. Always trying to attain higher and higher levels of awareness, to move up into the stratosphere, so to speak. It can get us into trouble." Then Callahan nodded in the direction of three gaunt looking Analysts who wore the blue-black feathers of corvids.

There was certainly something bent about them. Their eyes were mechanical and greedy, and their bodies were twisted as wind-battered pines.

"The corvids should have died centuries ago," Callahan said, "but they have found ways to prolong their life."

"Like how?" Tommy asked.

"By burying themselves in the earth for months at a time, in order to steal its power, for one." Callahan said. "They're also Therianthropes, or shapeshifters, and can take the form of wolves or coyotes and other types of mammals."

"No shit?" Tommy asked.

"Swear to God," Callahan said, making the sign of the cross. "Joking, by the way, with the cross thing. I'd never buy into such a ridiculous cosmology as Christianity." He spat a piece of tobacco.

Arpeggio and Cali had rejoined us. Arpeggio gripped a bottle of wine by the neck. "True power is as gentle as a breeze," he said; "it doesn't look like that, obviously."

The corvids sidled like crabs to the edge of the basin. Their eyes were empty, crustaceous. They chilled me to the bone.

I shifted my gaze back to the teeming water. It drew me like flame.

"If you sounded this, you'd find its several fathoms deep," Arpeggio said.

I dipped my foot in. "Warm," I noted.

"Most of the fish are deeper," he told me. They like cold." He paused. "You're diving, by the way." He handed me a plastic bag containing three translucent crystals blue in color. He drew a pair of goggles from around his neck and tossed them to me.

"Blue Magic," he explained, nodding at the bag. "It's cobalt, bound in an organic molecule. The crystals absorb oxygen from the atmosphere. Your body heat will release it once you're under. It's better than an oxygen tank, and much less cumbersome.

"It also has the side effect of increased metabolism," Callahan added, "which will keep you warm down there."

"Good luck," Arpeggio said. He said it in a way that made me think we would be parting ways forever. Then he stripped off his suit and tie in a series of fluid motions and disappeared beneath the seafoam with a flourish.

Callahan followed his lead. Within moments the other Analysts were breaking the surface with the hypnotic swishing of their dives. The rooftop became quiet and deserted.

"He could have warned me so I could have prepared psychologically maybe. Fuck," I said, my earlier sense of power and presence quickly replaced by a sinking dread. I popped the Blue Magic into my mouth, feeling it dissolve on my tongue. As soon as it did, I was saturated, literally dripping with oxygen.

"You lucky bitch," Tommy said, smiling, and pulling me in for a hug. "I can't wait to hear about this."

"I can't wait for this to be over," I said, not knowing at all what I was getting myself into, just certain it wouldn't be simple or easy. I stripped down, threw on my goggles, took a deep, resolved breath, then dived past the glowing trilobites into the abyss.

Some tidal force drew me down and down that finally let up in the inky depths. Terrified and blind in the murk, I immediately started back up to the rooftop. In the direction I thought was up, at least. I had no real bearing. No lodestar to guide me. My shocked brain was telling my body to breathe, breathe, breathe, despite the Blue Magic. It took everything to resist the spasms in my gut.

Then a glowing white sea-star floated idly past me, followed by an electric-blue fish that was impossibly thin, as thin as cardboard. It looked more like a cross-section of a fish, and before I knew it, the waters around me were pulsing with bioluminescent life. My eyes began to adjust, making sense of lines, shapes, and direction.

"You need to head down not up, Kat," I scolded, swallowing my fear. I kicked my feet out behind me and dove.

As I swam, three large sea-creatures sailed past me in a gang. They were the size of whales and slapped their electric tails in unison. The creatures disappeared into the darkness, but returned shortly, circling me and appraising me with mechanical eyes which spun like the gears of ticking clocks. Their blue-black scales shined like oil slicks. They smacked their fat purple lips at me as I hung in the water. Then a large flock of Birds approached, their feathers billowing out in flowing clouds of vibrant color. The Analysts encased their shape-shifting brethren in an awesome school and spirited them away into the dark like water faeries.

Something switched on inside me as the cells of my body became sensitized. My nerves modulated to each shifting degree of pressure and current in the ocean. I felt the icy waters on my skin, yet my core was warm under the spell of Arpeggio's Blue Magic. Every square inch of my body was charged, the least minutia of sensation vividly experienced. I felt cells regenerating and nerves communicating. I felt capillaries eating oxygen, and genes expressing on and off like molecular strings of Christmas tree lights. I was changing. The Bird Ocean was inside of me, mutating and building, my veins channeling its waters in tiny blue rivers.

When I reached the ocean floor, I kicked my legs up and rested on a large landform that emitted a green ink of light. The reef grew, expanding up and out right before my eyes, like those Magic Rock gardens from childhood, only gigantically green. A school of fat orange fish swam through the shifting tunnels. The small fish looked so ordinary in the waters of Bird Territory—they were the kind of fish you'd expect to see in a stream, or a backyard pond. Their slick hides tickled my body as they carried me along in their soft, orange cloud.

And just as the fish called to my mind a memory of home, an image of my mother was projected holographically from the strange reef in technicolor. I watched her as if on a movie screen: She was standing in our back yard in a purple bath robe, her skin white as frostbite against the deep purple, a smell of burning leaves in the air. She reached into the cold water of our pond, patting the head of a large orange roughy as it swam past along the edge. "I just patted the fish's head." It was such an unexpected gesture. The gesture expressed—I don't know— lonely, unaffected caring.

"Chickens," was all I had come up with at Arpeggio's dinner table.

I watched her invisibly. She cut such a sad figure, alone in our back yard with her fish and chickens and coolie hat.

And as simply as mom patted that fish's head, I got her. It's what you'd call an insight, I guess. Arpeggio said insight was "the grasping of a chemical reaction without the formula." And, he insisted, insight was the only real learning, because it was an experience of truth. You couldn't forget its lesson even if you wanted to, not like you might forget the quadratic equation or dates from a history test. Your whole body was imprinted by insight. Your whole being understood it, not just your intellect, which, Arpeggio argued, was only one aspect of intelligence, and a shoddy, one-dimensional aspect at that.

I got my mother suddenly. Every cell of me got her.

My realization was deceptively simple: she was fighting a quiet battle . . . and losing.

The hostility sloughed off me like heavy dead skin. I felt lighter, and now the movie screen showed her on a bulleting subway train, reading her James Patterson, not at all absorbed in it. (She resisted things, even the books that she read.) Her resistance was a whirring white noise living behind her eyes, made up of a cocktail of half-thoughts and confused emotion. The other passengers on the train were just as cut-off in their own tunnels with their papers and iPhones and relentless internal dialogues, their bodies lonely meteorites jostling each other in cold, crammed, commuter orbit.

A large bony eye shuttered open on the reef, followed by another and another, along the entire length of the now-giant range bulleting up from the ocean floor. A strange fish swam over to me. It was striped black and yellow and was about the size of a football. Its human-like eyes were brilliant-blue and bloodshot.

"Any outer revolution must be preceded by an inner revolution," it gargled cryptically. "Real change," the fish emphasized, "must be preceded by a real change of heart." It shat tiny fish turds in the water as it expounded.

"Your heart," the fish went on, "is a seat of deep and sensitive intelligence." It flickered holographically, and, without warning, bulleted straight through the center of my chest, and out again the other side.

My charged heart began pumping a strong rhythm. It beat a forest rhythm of drum circles and ground-pounding. I could feel the chambers pumping and releasing, followed by a sharp sensation as the muscle expanded its vascular roots throughout the dark concourses of my body, growing and mutating, weaving over and around a jigsaw of organs, intertwining an already complex network of veins and arteries, of motor and sensory nerves, of interconnecting neural pathways. My whole body luminesced in a soft, golden glow as I hung there in the water, some brand-new kind of animal.

I couldn't end my mother's suffering, or anyone's suffering for that matter, but I could certainly *ease* it. Because—as a wise man had once written—"the effect of a vital soul is to vitalize." And that's what I was. I was simply, powerfully a vital-ass soul. Easing suffering was so obvious to me, suddenly. It was a talent of mine, of all of ours, that I had buried along the way, but which now emerged from my blood in a shocking flash of crystal fury.

The fish stared fixedly with its bright, bloodshot eyes. It seemed to smile. "True Compassion," it concluded, "is the highest and rarest form of intelligence. Congratulations, *human*; you're not a dipshit." Then, as quickly as it came, the weird fucker darted away through the murky waters, disappeared into the reef. When I lost sight of it I swam back up towards the surface and the golden light of the desert sun.

Tommy was waiting for me. He wrapped me in a towel. "What the hell?" he asked, grabbing my shoulders, and looking closely at my eyes. "You need to look in a mirror, Kat," he said. "Seriously, your eyes are blue, with these little flecks of gold, like, I don't know, *goldschlagger*, or something." He rubbed my cheek with the back of his hand. "And what's up with your skin?"

I looked down at my body. My skin was radiant—a luminous, golden-brown, with a slight hint of transparency suggesting the enhanced vascular networks below.

"How long was I gone?" I asked.

"Five minutes," he said.

I called bullshit.

"Maybe six," he reconsidered, looking at his watch. He squinted at me. "What happened to you down there?

I couldn't answer Tommy. I didn't have the words yet.

Then the Analysts began to emerge from the rooftop sea. One by one they rocketed into the darkening sky, a large fish trapped in each purple beak. They spread their magnanimous wings, and shook water from their plumage, which came down on us in a pelting rain.

Southern Cross, as the Birds called it, turned into one gigantic fish-fry. The Analysts went to work gutting and preparing their catch, dipping strips of fish meat into flour, Old Bay and panko. They heated oil in gigantic skillets which they shoved into those clay ovens. The mesquite smoke rose into the sky and the rooftop sizzled. The wine circulated freely, of course. Sometimes I thought the Birds could dry out a little. It was hard to keep up. I picked delicate pieces of fish bone from my teeth.

"Whatever happens," Arpeggio told me, pausing to suck meat off a rib, "to this planet. To the Analysts, to your human race, whether the water tables fall and the fisheries collapse, whether it all ends tomorrow in a flaming catastrophe, or whether it crawls along for another billion years, what matters the most," he seemed to be searching for the words, "is to keep a real flame burning. It hardly matters what inspires you, so long as you burn dimensionally. That's most important, I think."

Arpeggio shuffled away, and he came back with a book which he tossed into my lap. My name, *Kat Parsons*, was brocaded on the spine in gold-woven letters. The volume pulsed in my lap like a small sun, powerful as all hell. The floodgates were open, the world spread out in front of me like an awesome jungle. I didn't know what was ahead. Shit, I barely grasped what was behind—what, for example, I had learned here in Bird Territory. I couldn't explain it if someone asked, anyway. The chemical reaction of insight was important, I decided, but you needed the words in order to share it. Words were the formula, the expression.

I put the living biography aside and watched the thick moon rising in the sky, as a flock of sparrows flew in strict formation above me. I reached into Tommy's backpack and pulled out my journal, then began to write: "It was the week of my eighteenth birthday that Tommy told me about camping in the city. . . ."

102

# Creature:
# A Children's Story

Summer vacation started tomorrow. It should have been the triumph of Lindsay Black's eleventh year, but the girl sat stone-like in front of the old Zenith television set while *Blade Runner* played on mute. Rutger Hauer rode up to meet his maker. Lindsay watched, listening for the sound of footsteps, or a movement of the bedroom door on its hinges. Her mother had not left the room for three days.

A freight train bulleted by on the rails outside. It vibrated the walls and furniture of the small house, and Lindsay could hear her mother's vapid moan bleed through the locked door.

Sometime during the past year Maddie Black had singled the trains out as her primary burden in a neurotic way. The hammering scream of the flat cars, the violent way the train rocked the tracks, the mini-earthquakes that inspired the girl, sent her mother spiraling into a private hell. Tonight she groaned like a patient too drugged to express her pain. It crushed Lindsay to hear it. She did not have the stomach for anguish. There was nothing she could do. She turned the volume back up to drown it out.

\* \* \*

When the movie ended, the girl made turkey and lettuce sandwiches for herself and Maddie, and she cut them into squares carefully. She felt it was important that she take care of things while her mother could not. She grabbed the ice-trays from the freezer, filled two glasses with cubes, and poured the orange Fanta. She wanted to be disciplined about it. It always started out that way.

From the kitchen window, the girl could see the ruined steel mill. It towered, a dominant shadow in the ash-grey mature evening, the central ruin of Sykesville. The sprawling building was visible from any house, or any window, anywhere in their high desert town. The stacks of the old blast furnaces shot up towards the sky like the spires of an ancient stony church.

The mill had shut down one year ago, after the mines had gone dry. The residents who remained in Sykesville were stragglers and hangers-on, a strange mix of small-engine mechanics, hawkers, traveling merchants, and social pariahs. The few who were left standing with resources irrigated swaths of valley soil and planted desert crops of watermelon and cotton. But the town no longer had a center, or an economy of its own to speak of.

Lindsay's father was one of the many who had left for greener pastures when the company split town. He had taken off in the early morning with an old footlocker and their Impala, leaving behind everything else.

The girl set up in the living room with the food. She heard the door finally, and saw her mother move towards the bathroom, shielding her eyes from the hallway light.

"I made you something to eat," Lindsay said when she came out. Her small arms trembled slightly under the weight of the dishes.

Maddie stopped at the girl's blockade, resting against the wall.

"I'm not hungry right now," she said. "I need more sleep, Lindsay. That's all." She had dark crescents under her ruined eyes. She ran her fingers quickly through her daughter's red hair. "I'll be better soon. I promise."

Maddie reached into the deep pocket of her dirty robe and pulled out a fist of money. The bills were mixed with lint and mostly smoked cigarettes.

"Go get me a carton of Marlboro Reds from Mr. Mackey's store," she told her. "Use the change to buy whatever you want."

Maddie dropped the bills onto the dinner plate. Her skin was as white as frostbite against the deep purple of her robe—bloodless, as if she had not seen the sun in weeks. She drifted back spectrally.

The girl was thrown by the phantom figure of her mother in the quiet hallway. She felt she inhabited a ghost town, that she did not really belong here, that she was seeing everything through thick glass.

* * *

The moon was nearly full outside and the stars blinked clean white light as she started the mile to Mr. Mackey's store, which Lindsay knew might or might not be open, depending on Mr. Mackey's mood. The loud song of summer cicadas surrounded her like a globe, like a vital structure of sound, and the girl smiled, because she knew there was a carton in the freezer, that all of the money was in fact hers. "Little victories," she thought. But she could not help it. She looked back at her mother's bedroom window.

Instead of the lighted square she saw a pink glow coming from the back yard of her house. It was new. The girl backtracked, and as she came closer, she saw that the glow was coming from the pool, that the light pulsed from some source inside of the basin. A craggy object took shape as her eyes adjusted to the dark. It was a gigantic meteor, with wild ribbons of glowing pink.

The girl raced forward and hockey-stopped at the edge of the pool. But it was moving, it was breathing, and Lindsay fell back with a startled scream. "Holy shit," she yelled.

She stood and picked up a small rock from the ground and tossed it underhand at the living thing in her pool. There was no reaction, so she tried to provoke it again, this time by making noises in a loud string of inane monkey sounds.

A quiver ran through the creature's naked mass, heightening the coral luminescence in a shimmery wave. The girl could make out the general diamond shape of the body. Its armor was craggy and rough, like lava rock.

Lindsay walked around and stood in front of it. She looked into its round, smooth eyes. It had wild, living eyes, and the girl realized she was staring into the face of a gigantic toad.

The size of the creature was impossible. But it was there, right in front of her. It was as definite as the house she lived in. It was as definite as the large black oak tree planted beside it.

The toad filled the dry pool completely, busting into the tiled sides. Its triangular head rose above the rim regally. The creature was trapped in the tight space, unable to propel its mountainous body up and out of the confinement.

Lindsay raced in for her electric lantern, sweeping books and clothes and DVDs from under her bed, and she ran back out with the light to study the rough, living skin of the creature. She swept her light along the complex banded pattern of its armor, illuminating the ribbons of electric indigo, and deep, saturated red. There were streamers the yellow-green color of budding spring plants, and serpent bands of dark ochre and cobalt. Its whole body was iridescent under her light, like insect wings.

She could not let go of the feeling that it had come from the bedrock—that this creature had been born in lava.

She did not know how to gauge the toad's intelligence. She had no knowledge of any wild language to communicate with. But the girl was certain that the creature was not dangerous, as she knew some dogs were friendly. There was a powerful stillness in its deep eyes, inaccessible and potent.

And the creature was hers.

Lindsay was certain that it would somehow prove to be the answer to everything.

The girl went in for her sleeping bag, taking the stairs in one stride, electrically. Arcturus and Vega burned on the horizon, and the sky was a blaze of white-hot constellations.

It was summertime, after all. Everything felt new and good.

\* \* \*

The sun rose.

The girl woke up to the sound of the toad's loud snacking. She stretched and yawned. The creature's pink tongue shot by her, the tacky muscle grabbing two mating locusts from a bunch of pampas grass in the yard beside her. It sounded off a chorus of thin insect rattles when it chewed.

After breakfast, Lindsay wanted to find Tree.

He knew a lot, more than other adults, and the girl wanted someone to share this with. A discovery like her toad could not be hoarded. But she would never knock on her mother's door. The girl understood that the mystery surrounding the creature couldn't survive Maddie's ruined atmosphere. She would dethrone it. Somehow.

\* \* \*

When the girl arrived at Tree's house, Diesel was chasing a black squirrel out front. She scratched him behind his scarred ears, then slapped his abdomen, raising a cloud of brick-colored dust. The mutt trot-hopped to the back, and she followed him.

Diesel was missing a front leg. It made him Tree's dog more than anything. Her friend collected misfits the way that other men in Sykesville collected guns, or beer steins.

He sat there at a rough table in his yard, a door raised up on cinderblocks. The table was set up beneath a copse of pinion pine. Tree was a giant., but his eyes were gentle and heavy-lidded, richly brown like loam. His skin was a much lighter shade like raw silk. From where the girl stood, he was a ponderous shadow in the morning shade.

"I have something you need to see," she blurted out. "At my house." She stood there in her polka dot pajamas, rattled.

Lindsay had not meant to sound so urgent. But suddenly she felt afraid that Tree would not come without a clear explanation, which she could not give him.

"Lindsay," Tree told her. "Sit down and tell me." He patted the bench beside him. He looked at his watch to remind the girl that it was still very early. He always interacted with her deliberately, a way that he had of training her patience.

"Well, it's a surprise," Lindsay said, restructuring her approach. "Anyway, you need to *see* it." She sat down coolly.

There was an oak-slab chessboard on the table in front of her. A gouge and a carving knife rested on top of the board. Tree's fingertips were black with dye, and curlycues of wood were settled lightly at his enormous logger's boots.

"I'll come," he said, "as soon as I'm done here."

"You're building a set?"

"Not building. Carving is the opposite of building. It's subtractive. You remove the parts that you don't need."

Tree held up a wedge of pine, which was the size of a young child's building block, and, in his other hand, a finished rook.

"Subtractive," the girl said. She enjoyed the exactness of the word. She liked how it remained after she spoke it like something solid, like the chess piece that Tree held.

He lifted a darker basswood piece from a small bowl beside him. His primitive black dye smelled acrid, like rust and vinegar. "Well, maybe they're ready," he said. "I'll just finish the white Queen. You can tire Diesel out for me. His rope is behind that creosote." He pointed with the rook to indicate which shrub exactly.

"I'll tire him out. Don't worry," the girl said.

They thrashed towards the rockery.

Diesel worked himself into the crevasse between two sangria boulders, and chomped hackberries from a low branch there.

Lindsay shouted, "He wouldn't fit if he still had his front leg, Tree." She saw some poignancy in this.

107

The girl felt at home here, in this yard, with Tree and Diesel. But now there was the creature, and its pull was much greater than comfort. She saw the creature clearly every time that she closed her eyes.

* * *

As they approached the girl's house, they heard an extended low vibration like a foghorn. It was followed by a long braided ringing sound—a trilling, like a gigantic insect calling. The sound was full and alive.

"It's in the pool," Lindsay said.

Tree stopped at the edge of the basin. "H. Christ," he exclaimed.

"It's friendly. I think it is. . . ." Lindsay would not say *magical*. Tree would expose the word as childish. "From another place," she concluded.

To demonstrate the creature's gentleness, she lay down on her stomach and extended her arm to stroke the thick skin. It felt dry, like cornhusks. At the girl's touch, a vibration moved through the creature's naked mass, charging the serpent bands electrically. The flush was a blood response, hematic and spontaneous.

Tree lay down on the cement deck beside her. The toad's tongue shot out, threading the space between them to snack on a dark beetle.

"I think *it* is a *she*," Tree said.

"Why?"

"My gut is telling me."

"You mean, it has a female vibe?" She looked into the creature's large eyes. They were reflective turquoise pools. They gave the girl no sense of gender.

Tree laughed. "Yes. A female vibe."

"I've never seen anything like it," Lindsay said. "Like *her*."

"She is a mystery, isn't she?"

The creature's presence suggested the patience, the endurance of landforms. The toad waited as though a river would one day carve her from her confinement. Her rough armor suggested brutal landscapes cut by wind. Tree thought he saw something slow and intelligent in her calm eyes.

"I petted her this morning. She still felt moist," the girl said. "Now she feels so dry." She walked over to the spigot and opened the valve; then she unwound the hose and dragged it with her. The water spilled out weakly. Lindsay fogged the stream with her thumb, and walked around the pool, misting the creature.

Immediately the baked skin softened, and the color radiated cleanly from the serpent bands of the creature's slaked armor.

"You are beautiful," Lindsay whispered.

Tree told her, "I have a nozzle for that at home. I'll bring it with me tomorrow."

There was some sort of majesty here, he decided, caged and unfamiliar. And it had been placed right in the girl's lap. Tree knew that he was committed to this, although he did not know what that commitment would mean, because he could not see ahead. They had started down some new, indeterminate course together.

But he would be here with her. He cared for Lindsay deeply: Tree recognized a certain potential in the girl for extreme independence. It was rare.

He pointed and said, "Your mother is up. I'm sure it was all the racket."

Lindsay looked in. The curtains were mostly drawn, but she caught some dark movement.

"Does she know?" Tree asked.

"She's been sleeping," Lindsay told him.

Tree knew about Maddie's long sleep cures from the girl. In town, she was known to be subject to great depressions, and also strange, violent abreactions.

The girl hung her head and walked.

Inside, the refrigerator door was open, and Maddie stood in the space. She lifted a carton of milk and smelled the contents before selecting a glass from the cupboard.

She turned and saw her daughter there.

"Lindsay. You gave me a scare." She did not look frightened, though. She looked tired to the center of her bones.

But she was up, and drinking. The girl knew it was a good sign.

Maddie filled two glasses. She set the cups down on the small kitchen table. "Give me a hug," she said, and beckoned Lindsay with her arm. "Don't worry about me. I'm recovering. I'll be as fit as a fiddle soon."

The woman rested her chin on her daughter's head and began a slow dance with her beneath the yellow cabinets. Lindsay could feel her through the dank gown. She was as slat-ribbed as a refugee.

Maddie pulled back and their lilt stopped.

"You have been using my hairspray, Lindsay. I smell it on you." She looked at the girl's face. "My makeup, too." She wiped a trace of smoky red lipstick with her finger, which the girl had pilfered the night before. She studied Lindsay's hands, flipping them.

Maddie's slight body had become tense and shivery. Her eyes were awake now and half-wild.

The girl leaned in and hugged her mother fiercely. The hug was her pleading. She knew her mother's anger could spike violently from these calm moments.

Maddie breathed long and deep below Lindsay's powerful hug. Then, with great intention, she picked up the earlier rhythm, dancing slowly with her daughter in the kitchen.

"I'm sorry Lindsay," she whispered. "I'm not well yet." A quick sob rattled from her throat.

\* \* \*

The following week was full. The girl felt happy. She spent every moment she had with the creature, whom she named Oya. Oya fit perfectly because the name was beautiful and unfamiliar, like her creature. She liked the way that it rolled off of her tongue.

Tree had erected a ramada for Oya to shade her from the brutal sun: four large mesquite posts and a gigantic blue tarp fastened down. Lindsay imagined that the trill of the creature once the shade was erected was—thankful. She was starting to hear the messages in the creature's sound.

From her new post in the yard, she could look back and see the dark square of her mother's window dripping condensation. Maddie did not know yet of the creature's existence. There might have been an ocean separating her from her back yard.

Tree had taken over most of the inside responsibilities. He helped the girl cook and clean, and he made sure that Maddie ate at least one meal a day in her bedroom. He would remind Lindsay to brush her teeth, because the girl was so rapt in the spell of the creature, she could forget simple hygiene. Tree would ask about her reading, and they talked books. Lately, it was Ray Bradbury. Lindsay consumed his whole catalogue as she sat under the ramada with Oya during the long summer days.

In the evenings they sat in old lawn chairs, the girl so deeply interested in the shifting colors, the pulsing luminescence of the creature's armor, and reliably Tree beside her, toying with a bishop and drinking strong coffee from his blue camp mug.

One evening when the weather was cool, the bluish emanations of the creature matched the deep blue-black of the approaching night. Tree had cooked up a light fish stew with sea bass and cilantro. He brought it outside in a steaming decanter and poured the meal into three bowls. The girl brought one dish to Oya, and the creature's powerful tongue over-shot the target. She placed the bowl again, this time at a distance, and Oya hit her mark, capturing some of the meal but projecting the dish side-wise like a bowling pin. The meal splashed Tree as he sat in his chair, and the girl fell over with laughter. She found a method of pouring the soup into Oya's trusting jaws. Everything was good.

When Tree left at night, the girl stayed outside with the creature. She hardly went inside at all. It was too vacant. It felt barren, like an empty schoolroom. But the beauty of the creature absorbed and excited her. Nothing else had ever brought Lindsay to such a level of attention. She began to draw Oya on her Strathmore sketchpad, although she felt that the picture emerging was much too clumsy. She did not have the ability to capture the alien beauty. Some dimension to the creature could not be recreated with lines and curves and her average skill.

The creature watched her, as well. Oya's hooded eyes followed the girl as she worked setting up her tent at night, or gathering the hose for her watering, or slapping her knees like bongo drums, or whistling some tune she had heard on Tree's crank radio that day.

Every morning when Lindsay crawled out of her sleeping bag, she found that new transformations had taken place in her yard.

Dewy ferns had shot up from small breaks in the weathered cement deck. With each sunrise, there was an accumulation of slick moss, and putrid wetland mud. A population of emerald caterpillars crawled beneath the stems of the new vegetation. The bracken ended abruptly where the cement deck hit her dirt yard. It was a square oasis of green, with Oya at the center.

Then one day as Lindsay sat with Tree, the message in the creature's sound was suffering. Oya's wail emerged sharp from the general quiet. There was no mistaking the grief in it.

The girl was distressed by the revelation of pain.

111

Tree told her, "Oya is alone and trapped. Maybe more alone than we know. Perhaps there is no other creature like her."

But Lindsay did not think that made sense. "Then who does she cry for?"

Tree did not have a good answer.

He said, "But she does not look well, Lindsay."

The creature seemed diminished in her confinement. She no longer had the stature of a mountain. The skin around her eyes had gone loose and sick gray, like spoiled meat.

After that, the girl became occupied with freeing Oya. Her ideas were mostly improbable: military jets hoisting the creature from the basin, flying her to a remote expanse where she could thrive with others like her. When she looked at the towers of the old mill, Lindsay considered mining equipment and huge mechanical claws resurrected from machine graveyards. They would tear up the ground and release Oya from her prison. She saw Oya loaded onto a freight car and bulleted away to some magical land at the bottom of the ocean, where the train tracks ended in the silt. The girl's images were always this clash of machine and creature, of industry and wild. Her imagination veered towards the technological, a habit she had acquired from science fiction.

Oya had remained their secret. It was never a discussion that the girl and Tree had, but it worked out that way. The girl's mother was in such a dark place that she could not see outside, and they did not generally receive visitors. Their closest neighbors, the Randalls, were a quarter mile down Tuckerman.

Both Lindsay and tree understood on some level that they could not blurt Oya out like a tabloid headline. They knew the character of their town. If Oya were discovered, there would be conflict.

But there was no practical way to hide the massive toad. So it was a relief when Don Forrestal broke into their world that Sunday afternoon. The waiting was over. Now certain cards would be dealt.

\* \* \*

Don stood on the edge of the basin, running his fingers through his thin hair and wiping beads of sweat from his brow with a dark bandanna. An inarticulate noise rose and died in his throat. He crossed himself, and gripped his King James Bible closer to his chest.

The girl watched as he walked around the pool. He checked the spectral armor of the creature. Don slipped on a matt of slick moss in his polished church shoes.

"It is crawling with electric serpents," he muttered. "Strange, charged, snake-things."

He shook the mesquite posts of the ramada as he walked under the structure, as if it might be rigged to collapse on him. Don studied the girl and Tree. Their faces were impassive.

"What, in the name of God, is it?"

"Her name is Oya," the girl said. "She appeared in my pool one week ago. We are trying to get her . . . home."

"Appeared," Don said, nodding. The explanation satisfied him. "From the depths," he added, sub-vocally. He wore a pair of khaki pants and a white tee shirt. The plain dress matched his pale skin. His spine curved gently like a sodden stalk.

Don had been courting Lindsay's mother, or something like courting, for the past year, ever since her father had split Sykesville, but he worked without apparent passion. He had been pursuing Maddie with the metabolism of a snail.

Don held a carnation, which he dropped down to his side. He asked, "Why hasn't she told me about this?" Then he added, "She still does not trust me." But he spoke in a rote and automatic way. He knew that it did not matter. He was used to casual rejection. The real issue here was the beast.

He did not know yet what God wished for him to do. He did not know what the *real* meaning of the creature was. But a dull horror churned inside of him as he stared at the beast. The proportions of the creature were incorrect. It smelled of ozone and wet dirt and algae bloom. There was a deep underground smell surrounding it like decaying wood.

Don stared at Oya, but he spoke to the girl, "You and your mother were not at church, so I thought I would come by. I need to talk to her. Now." He felt fear rising inside of him like ice. His knees wanted to buckle beneath him.

Don stumbled towards the back door of the small house.

He muttered, "Serpent of the earth. Yes. Serpent of the earth. Certainly."

He thought of the old iron mine where he had worked all those years ago. He saw the gaping wound of the pit, like an open mouth to the center of the earth. And in his vision, there was a strange substance growing on the buried ore that burned with the cold light of the beast, attracting and collecting like small pools of mercury to build the unnatural creature. The image was strong. It was true. Inspired. Don looked up at the hot sky.

The girl watched as he pulled the door to her house open recklessly, and stumbled over the threshold toward her mother's bedroom.

Things had changed. The town would be there tomorrow.

"I think we will need our sleep tonight," Tree said. He hugged the girl to his side before he left. "We will figure this out, Lindsay. Your Oya will be all right." But he could not bring himself to promise.

The girl looked at the creature. She resembled an anemic god in the swimming pool. Lindsay pulled the hose and fogged Oya with water.

Maddie's bedroom light was on, and Lindsay heard Don's raised voice through the glass, although she could not make out what it was that he said.

Tonight, Lindsay would sleep beside the creature in the wetland growth. She wanted to lie right on top of Oya, feeling the warmth and movement of her live body, but she would settle for closeness, and the warm cloud of the creature's breath.

\* \* \*

The next morning, Maddie Black sat eating her grapefruit with the flattened eyes of an insomniac. It seemed as though she was viewing everything through a small keyhole. Her daughter sat across from her at the breakfast table drinking orange juice, the girl's red hair matted with sphagnum. A streak of green mud had dried across her cheek. Maddie had the vague thought that, as she slept, her daughter had turned wild.

Don had seen to it that she would be up today. He had told her that she would have visitors. That she would have to stand. He needed her to go through the motions. It was crucial. He would help her figure things out, but not today. Whatever demon it was that possessed her soul, he would learn of it, he promised her. He would ask the Lord for insight, and when he prayed, God listened. When he prayed, things happened.

But tomorrow, he was sorry, she would have to stand. Everyone else went to work, he told her. They showered, they watered their plants and took the garbage out, even as they suffered deeply. This was life, he said. A trial. It helped if you knew there was a God, but she did not know, did she? She would not be so hopeless if she had *faith*. He would help her. It was important that she understood this.

The crucial thing at the moment was, he was calling a meeting that very night about the creature. As he pontificated, he became convinced that the very soul of Sykesville was at stake. He stood up and paced the room when he spoke. He seemed to be on fire. When he sat back down on the bed, he slid his hand underneath her gown and between her slight legs. Maddie had never seen such passion from Don. He was a new man, heated, and his blood boiled with purpose.

* * *

The first visitors came peacefully. They rapped on the door lightly and carried small gifts with them. Sarah Engels came, holding her family rug pattern on a piece of yellowed paper. Maddie had asked her about it years ago. She had found the intricate, Rotarian patterns striking.

Sarah handed the paper to Maddie and said, "A get-well gift. We heard you were feeling ill." She walked towards the window as she said it, and the brittle gift fluttered to the ground.

Sarah pulled the drapes. "My sisters and I can weave that pattern," she continued, "with our eyes closed. We know it when we are born." She spoke hypnotically.

The bracken almost hid the creature from her view, but Sarah saw its rock-ribbed armor above the vegetation, rising and settling with the creature's slow breathing. She stumbled towards the door.

Lindsay threw her favorite pink cap on backwards, and followed Sarah Engels outside. She took up her post by Oya in the wetland growth. She sat on a soccer ball and rolled a pine baseball bat thoughtlessly under her foot.

She said to the creature, "They can look, but they cannot touch you without going through me."

The girl knew that Oya was in some kind of danger, although she did not think the inhabitants of her town would risk open violence. She

115

thought of King Kong, then of Oya, displayed on a platform under harsh stage lights.

A low-ranged sound erupted from the creature. The notes were deep and muscular. The girl looked up at the dark sky. The sun was hidden behind thick clouds. It was a canvas of purple, threatening rain and wildfire.

But the weather held off as the morning passed. The trickling in of the first curious visitors had turned into a crush of bodies by noon. Hundreds of feet turned the space into a dust cloud.

Lindsay was aware of the rally in her yard like the loud drone of an air tanker behind her. But she was not a part of it. She did not know if Tree was there, or if her mother and Don stood together. The girl could not stand back and look at Oya through their telescope. That was what adults liked to do, view things from a distance, condemning or approving them. Separate. They planned. They made pronouncements about the nature of things.

But the girl was in contact with the creature. She wondered at Oya almost every moment now. She was sensitive to every small sound that rattled from her body; her world was Oya's warm eyes. Each impulse that ran through the creature's armor was a new and shocking spread of color. Emerald caterpillars from the oasis crawled over the girl's shoes. Some clung to the delicate stems of the vegetation, or hung upside down from the light fronds.

Lindsay heard a sharp voice say, "Where else? Of course it came from the mine. That land is . . . black. Of course it did."

A yellow sarong and a pair of platform shoes crowded in beside the girl. Lindsay did not know who it was that spoke, because she did not look up. The girl did not speak one word to the visitor. Or the next. There was a broken line of bodies throughout the day—the brave souls who wanted to look right into the eyes of the beast.

But they did not dare to break the silent solidarity of girl and creature. On some level they understood: their intrusion here was shameful, they did not belong, they were disrupting something vital. In this way, the girl protected the creature . . . to an extent.

Oya's health had worsened noticeably since the night before. Even as she radiated her beautiful light, the creature's bearing was wilted. A filmy serum covered large areas of Oya's armor, and a spongy growth like mold carpeted the sack of her throat.

116

The girl opened a ziplock bag that rested on the ground beside her. It was full of raw, salted fish. She fed the trout to Oya, then laid her hand on the creature's giant head. When she pulled her fingers away, they were covered in slick membrane.

"Oya," she said. "What can we do about you?"

Lindsay looked up at the dark sky. It was a harsh steel curtain now. One small break in the clouds not far from the horizon blazed with the swift orange of the setting sun.

She heard a man say, "The roads are gonna flood. You know they are. Well, we haven't had rain since February."

Someone added, "We aren't getting across Fat Man once the rain starts."

The storm was setting up nicely over the valley. From the Blacks' back yard, strikes could be seen lashing the far ridges violently, or side-striking from cloud to cloud. Gray colonnades of rain hung solidly over the far peaks.

An updraft whipped the girl's cap from her head. It touched down lightly on the creature, before skipping across the yard like pink tumbleweed.

As the hot air rose, the creature gave off her light in a new way— it was a solid, primary glow. The shifting bands of color were gone, and Oya's body breathed and burned with the steady radiance of a burning charcoal.

The gathering outside of the oasis was moving now. Some of the crowd gathered their small children and moved towards the vehicles out front. They wanted to beat the hammering of weather that was certainly coming. But the majority of the crowd stood stock still, arrested by the sight of the creature's dynamo, hypnotized by Oya's cool fire.

The girl stepped back to better watch the spectacle. Then Tree was beside her. He pulled the girl back further, and unclipped his bowie knife and released the long blade.

"Your reflection," he explained. He held the knife for her, catching the porch light and using it as a mirror. Strands of the girl's hair stood out statically.

"Is this dangerous?" she asked, smiling.

She enjoyed the silly image, but moved back as Tree had suggested. The girl felt the excitement of the building storm in her blood.

Her mother stood near the porch with the group from Calvary Baptist. She was side by side with Don, their arms hooked loosely unaware of each other's bodies. There seemed to be a mutual disinterest between them.

The girl thought for a moment that her mother was looking at her, but Maddie's eyes were half closed, her skin blanched, her mood unfocused. Neither the girl nor the creature held any interest for her. The rising winds did not key a warning. She stood because Don required her there. She did not have the energy yet for self-direction.

The heavy drops of rain started down slowly. With the downdrafts came hard ground currents—missiles of wind that channeled over the Blacks' back yard from all directions, attracted to the creature centrally. Oya opened her jaws and drank the strong currents of air.

Don Forrestal watched with fierce gray eyes as the creature burned and pulsed in the basin. He watched as the beast ate weather with the appetite of a primitive god. He was incensed by the magnitude of the biblical display.

He studied the rapt faces of the Calvary group, keen with the wonder and fear owed only to the one, true God. He knew then that he would slaughter the Scarlet Beast, with or without the consent of the town. It was all that mattered. He would bring his rifle tonight while the girl slept.

The rain fell harder, and the yard swirled with stinging grains of sand and microtrash. Don swept Maddie inside, and the remaining crowd clamored towards their vehicles, most of them forgetting to lock their hubs as they bulleted off with the realization that they had likely waited too long.

The rain came down in sheets now. Tree was a monolith, and Lindsay anchored onto him. The glow of the creature was abstracted drunkenly through the heavy water. Oya pulsed like a beacon, her light fractured by water fall.

And then it was dark; the girl could not see the creature, until her light appeared again, burning brightly beneath the black oak tree. "Oya!" Lindsay cried. "Oya!" She jumped up and slammed down in the slick desert mud. "Hah!"

The creature tore off into the wild, berserk with her new freedom. She bounded into the country with earth-shaking strides. She did not pause to say goodbye. She did not know about such courtesies. She only knew life and movement and deep primal power.

Lindsay chased Oya's glow, maneuvering through the dark desert, infected by ferocious joy. She hopped over creosotes and jumped cacti. She threaded between agave plants, never loosing her footing. The girl was possessed unaware by an expert grace.

The creature bobbed and winked in and out of the ravines. Her light lilted and pulsed against the easy slope of the valley floor, wavering like heat. They ran.

Lindsay could not keep up, but it was enough to have Oya in her sight. They moved farther from the buttoned houses of Sykesville, and from the strange, buttoned lives. They passed old car frames and beaten cattle tanks—industrial trash owned by no one and half swallowed by the desert sand. In the open valley Oya was a lit tank moving heavily over the terrain. When the creature leapt, she left craters the size of mountain lakes behind her, filling with rainwater.

The girl came to the south fork of Fat Man Creek and stopped at the swift channel. She had never seen it so swift or heard it so roaring. It was the end of her trail. She sat down on the muddy bank and watched Oya's light recede towards the rocky peaks. Without the light of the creature close by, the desert became inky.

"You changed everything, Oya," she said to the creature as Oya's light disappeared behind a knife ridge.

The girl's clothes were saturated with rainwater. The desert air was warm, and she felt strong, as though Oya had left behind a piece of her animal heart, which beat inside of *her* now.

And later that night, when Lindsay lay down to go to sleep, she found that she was not able to. She lay there instead, studying the crude drawing she had made of the creature underneath her book light. She closed her eyes to see Oya more clearly. An excitement like a low bass line traveled through the girl's body, her mind alive with thoughts of the future, and all of the awesome possibilities life held.

# War Story

I have my first war story. Three of us from Zion National Park were called up to Oak City, Utah, to help fight a ninety-acre wildfire that was burning primarily in Pinyon Pine and Juniper in the nearby mountains. The locals managing the fire were desperate for bodies because at the time most Utah fire resources were up north in Montana, Idaho, Oregon, Wyoming, etc., fighting wildfires in those areas. (The north was an inferno in mid-August, and our local activity had calmed down quite a bit.)

I was woken up from a deep sleep at 6 a.m. on Thursday August 17, by my front doorbell ringing. I stumbled out of bed, wrapping a sheet around me toga-style. It was a crew member, Sean Powell, all geared up in nomex and fire boots, trying not to burst out laughing at this oddly private moment and at how disoriented I looked. "Hey, we gotta go to a fire. We tried to call you last night. We'll meet you at the EOC in ten minutes." I muttered "fuck" and shut the door in his face. (I really hate being woken up, and I usually blame the messenger.)

We were going to the (ominously named) "Devil's Den" fire. I learned that the incident had two hand crews on order, who would be coming from New Mexico, but that these resources would not be arriving on the fire for another twenty-four hours at least. So the local BLM office from Fillmore had called Color Country for assistance. Color Country in turn threw together a hodge-podge handcrew of twelve, including the three of us from Zion, deemed us Color Country Squad Seven, and we were on our way. We figured we would spend one full shift on the fire, and then leave as soon as the other resources had arrived from New Mexico, as we needed to get back to our home units to be available for local IA. (IA = initial attack, the first twenty-four hours of suppression effort on a fire, and the most crucial.)

Let me start by saying that working on the Devil's Den fire was a shit sandwich from second one. We drove to the established staging area, met briefly with the Incident Commander (IC) and the IC trainee, who told us that they did not expect much activity out of the fire, because the day before aircraft had "painted" it with fire retardant. We

120

were not briefed on weather, safety concerns or strategy before they began shuttling us into the fire via helicopter. Someone should have spoken up about that, but no one did. This was the first time in four years of working fire that I was *not* briefed at an incident. But we simply did what we were told, like good soldiers, and hoped that these things would be clarified once we were in the black.

Another thing that was sketchy from the get-go: the helispot they were shuttling us to was located in a saddle, between two ridge lines. This saddle was at the head of a steep draw—Devil's Den—the canyon in which our fire was mostly established.

One of the first things they teach you as a first-year firefighter (and pound into your skull every following year) is that canyons and draws act to intensify fire behavior exponentially. They act as a funnel for wind, and as fire moves through a canyon, the heat it generates cures out the fuel on either slope, which in turn ignites quickly and rapidly, spotting easily to either side, and creating even more fire intensity and even quicker rates of spread. Finally, with enough intensity, a fire creates its own convection winds, feeding the cycle even further. Basically, fire + steep canyon = shit storm. Unfortunately one of our tactical points on this fire was at the head of this canyon. If the fire did blow up, it was coming right for our helispot. But in the minds of the IC, the fire was "out," and did not pose a real threat.

All of these were red flags in the minds of our crew. We were aware of them, and based our actions accordingly, but no one spoke up. No one said to the IC, "This is a fucked up way to manage a fire. Step back and re-evaluate."

When our full squad had been shuttled in, our crew boss (also my station manager at Zion and a bad-ass, solid firefighter) made contact with a local crew, who was to line us out on our specific assignment. Apparently we were to hike down into the draw from the north (right toward the fire's head) and begin securing the east flank of the fire. At the time there was not much activity from the fire's interior, but our crew boss did the right thing and refused the assignment. Attempting a frontal assault on a fire is one of the eighteen watch-out situations that we are taught and continually reminded of. Also, "Steep terrain makes escape to safety zones difficult." In our situation, both of these statements were apparently true. An uphill escape route is to be avoided at all costs because fire moves faster uphill and we bi-peds move slower.

Let me give a little background and say that our crew boss for this assignment is an ex-hotshot. Shot culture does not take the refusal of an assignment lightly. Shots have a "let's fucking kill this fire; we can get it done; we are bad-ass superhumans" type of mentality. You refuse an assignment only in what you believe to be a life-or-death situation.

I think he took one look at that canyon, and knew on a gut level that we would be sorry if we went down into it. He has the hair trigger instincts of a salty fire fighter who has seen shit. He suggested the alternative of approaching the fire from the south (towards the fire's heel) where we would put in a good anchor-point and begin our sawline. But soon he would decide that even that was too dangerous.

Not a minute after we had turned down our assignment, groups of trees started to torch out in the fire's interior, putting up thick, white smoke. The afternoon sun was drying out the fuels in the canyon, and our "dead" fire was quickly becoming active. Our crew boss told us to find a safety zone in good back, where we would observe our fire's behavior before we committed ourselves to any assignment. ("Good back" is a burned area through which a fire has already passed, which is devoid of all fuels and has no re-burn potential.)

Our safety zone was on a burnt-out mesa top that extended to the west rim of Devil's Den. This was also a great vantage point to observe our fire's behavior. Our squad kicked back for a while, ate our lunch, joked around, walked to the canyon rim, and checked out the fire and the topography. We guessed at what route we would take into the canyon, and made comments that unfortunately we had not managed to escape the sea of cheatgrass and juniper typical of southern Utah. We fantasized about a more sub-alpine environment, about ponderosa pine and fires in Montana. We traded bags of chips and different flavors of juices like school kids. We were killing time, enjoying the scenery and each other's company.

At about 13:00, we heard the first round of radio transmissions from Spencer Koyle. One thing that sticks out in my mind is Spenser's observation of the continuous cheatgrass throughout Devil's Den. He told the IC that given enough time, the cheatgrass would carry the fire through the canyon and up to the saddle where helispot one (H-1) was located. In Utah, cheatgrass is one of the primary and most volatile carriers of wildfire. It is dry, cured grass that provides a very sensitive fuel bed, which fire moves through with lightning speed. Spencer talked with the IC about implementing Plan B. From what I gathered, Plan B was a burnout operation starting from the closest ridge line to the north of Devil's Den. This method of "indirect attack" would keep crews out of Devil's Den and therefore out of harm's way.

This seemed like a very smart plan, and I am not sure why it was not carried out immediately, but it wasn't. Immediately after Spencer and the IC discussed putting Plan B into motion, we were told that "a spot fire" had been found while scouting the main fire, and that we would "work" this spot fire using Zero Romeo Lima (the type three helicopter assigned to the fire) for bucket drops.

Most of us listening to radio traffic did not have a very good concept of exactly where Spencer was. We knew that the observer was scouting the main fire, working spot fires in an attempt to make it safe for crews to work in the gulch.

At the time, most of us believed that he was working those spots somewhere near the fire's heel. After the fact, we realized that he was near the head of the fire. Even to a rookie, that seems an act of extreme stupidity or insanity (no disrespect to the dead intended), especially given the terrain and weather conditions. The winds and topography were aligned perfectly that day. The upper level winds were pushing the fire from south to north, which was the direction of the canyon. The cheatgrass was continuous, making for extremely volatile fire behavior. How could a sharp observer miss these things that are so obvious? Why did he ignore them? Maybe he was just too comfortable. Maybe, for whatever reason, his years of training were occluded by that narcissistic impulse that allows us to think, "It can't happen to me."

But the IC knew exactly where the big boss was. He should have had enough situational awareness to realize that he needed to get out of that canyon. This was his responsibility as the IC.

It's not my place to judge the IC, and I sympathize with him. As a close friend of big boss, and as the top official responsible for management of the Devil's Den fire, the death of our big boss is a fuck-up that the IC will have to live with for the rest of his life. I imagine that being responsible for the death of a close friend is an extremely personal and claustrophobic type of hell. I imagine it follows you around like a demon that is assigned to you, bringing years of tensed muscles and grinding teeth. A kind of ever-present tension and uneasiness that takes away something vital from every good thing you experience. Not to mention the inevitable and explosive episodes of (Mormon?) guilt. You would have to ask yourself if you deserve happiness anymore.

The IC probably has legal battles to look forward to as well. But I imagine that the introspective nightmare will be much, much worse.

Of course, in my mind, the responsibility for our big boss's death ultimately falls on his own self. He was an experienced and seasoned firefighter who should have known better.

The next episode of radio traffic told us that more spot fires had been identified both above and below the big boss, who was using Zero Romeo Lima for bucket drops, directing them from his position on the ground.

About this time our color country squad was given a simple and safe assignment that we felt comfortable with. We were told to secure the west flank of the fire, which included the cold edge of our safety zone. It was inactive except for a few duffers and burning stump-holes. I think this was more or less busy work to keep us occupied until conditions allowed us to work on a more productive assignment.

As we began to leave our position along the rim of Devil's Den, our fire exploded with an intensity that I have never witnessed before, and that I will never forget. It was, to say the least, awe inspiring. The smoke column quickly grew in size like a Hiroshima explosion, and ice-capped, shearing off sharply at the top, where it must have hit those upper level, south moving winds. We heard the roar of a rapidly growing fire, which sounded to me like launch pad thrusters during a space shuttle launch. It was so incredibly loud that we stopped in our tracks and stared, unable to speak.

The last radio transmission we heard from our boss was, "I think I'm in trouble." Then, it was chaos. The IC was screaming into the radio, "Drop your pack, and get the hell out of there." Other voices asked who was where. The IC was pointing with his combi tool to where the fire was exploding. "You fucking have someone down there?!" The IC calling over and over for Spencer on his BK but getting no response. Then the IC was throwing his radio, dropping to his knees and punching the ground with closed fists.

James walked over to us and gathered us into a circle. "Pray," he said, "if that's what you believe in. Because that guy is probably toast." The original IC was too distraught to continue command. James told us he was taking over as IC of the fire for the remainder of the day, leading the search effort once the fire died down enough. "You are going to hike back to the vehicles," he told us, "And tonight we are getting the hell off of this fire."

We stood there for a while, absorbing all of this. At that point, I was too shocked to feel anything at all. I felt blank.

I imagined the big boss appearing over the rim of the Canyon. I did not know what the man looked like, so it was just the staggering silhouette of a firefighter that I saw, faceless. First and second degree burns, but alive. I imagined him collapsing into our safety zone, and everyone huddled around him in a large circle, one of the EMTs checking his vital signs, and telling everyone to move back, to give him room to breathe.

But I knew that in actuality the chances of survival were zero.

Then I imagined that it was Sean Powell, a crew member from Zion, who had once been entrapped, and this thought provoked a few tears. Here was some emotion, a way to bring this experience closer. I felt like an alien, observing all of this in a petri dish. I needed this to be more personal. (Now I understand it was shock, and not spiritual callousness, that made everything seem so distant and unreal.) Next, I imagined it was me who had died because, after all, it might have been. We had been ordered into the canyon, but we had refused. Another few tears. The thought of myself not existing was too hard to process, I think, because I still felt numb. Then I imagined it was my brother, and that here I was up on the rim, completely useless and impotent, just having to accept that my brother was most likely dead, unable to do anything but wait, the whole search for him governed by a bureaucratic process that had nothing to do with me.

This was the thought that got me. I was completely shaken by this thought, and my whole body reacted to it. All of a sudden I felt violent, frustrated, torn-up. I thought that I might throw up. I wanted to punch the ground just like I had seen the IC doing. (I remember reading somewhere that the same neural pathways are activated by the memory of an event, as by the event itself. Your mind does not distinguish between the imagined or real event. The violent reaction I had to the thought of my brother dying is a perfect example of this.)

We all milled around on the mesa top for a while. It did not seem right to start hiking back to the vehicles right away. We were each in our own world, all reacting to this in our own, private ways. A few people on our squad were apparently upset and crying. One member of our squad had just returned home from Hamadi a few months earlier. He looked sick and pale, like he had just seen a ghost. (For the next several days, as we were being interviewed by federal investigators, as

125

we were going through "stress debriefings" and quasi-group therapy sessions, this guy kept that same kind of eerie and unreadable remoteness.)

We finally hiked back to our vehicles and the helibase, where we staged for the rest of the day, along with the life-flight folks and a few representatives from the sheriff's office. The seconds ticked by. We were stuck there, waiting for our crew boss who was now the IC. That place was very bad medicine, as the natives would say. I wanted to get the hell away from Oak City and its environs. However, a part of me was extremely disappointed that our squad was not included in the search effort. I wanted to see the body. I have never seen a dead body before, and my curiosity in matters like this always takes precedent over my sensitivity.

Maybe it is better that I did not see him. I know that some who did see the body wished that they had not. When James finally came down that night, our whole squad moved towards him, expecting that he would have something to say to us, or at the very least he would let us know what our hotel arrangements were. Maybe he would just say, "Load up, we are leaving this god-awful place." Instead, he looked at us and said "I really don't have anything to say right now. I just got done peeling that guy's femurs off of the ground." Then he walked away.

The search party had gridded past the body several times in Devil's Den before they actually found it. I heard someone say that they had mistaken his body for a charred log.

There were about thirty of us back at the helibase as the sun was setting. All resources were finally off of the incident. The waiting was absolutely painful at this point. I wanted to get the hell away from Devil's Den, drink a few beers, and go to sleep. We seemed to be just prolonging a day that had already been entirely too long. Everyone was standing around the helibase, apparently doing nothing, not even talking. Finally, it became obvious that we were waiting for the transport of the body.

I remember it was dark enough that the headlights of the morgue van, still hundreds of yards down the road from us, drew everyone's attention as it moved very slowly towards our location. But it wasn't so dark that we couldn't easily make out the white, vinyl lettering on the side of the van as it passed: Southern Utah Mortuary. Everyone became incredibly quiet, and all you could hear was the light hum of the van's

126

engine. The vehicle pulled off of the gravel road, wobbling in little waves as it drove over the uneven field towards Zero Romeo Lima. The body bag was transferred without ceremony. It became extremely dark very quickly. It was a new moon, or close to it. The van drove away slowly, its headlights boring through the blackness. The guy on our squad who had been to Hamadi and a few others held their baseball caps over their hearts. It was a strange and potent memorial. That whole sequence is imprinted on my mind visually like some of my most vivid childhood memories.

Our day was finally over. The next morning we found out that they would keep us in the Fillmore area for another two days. We had to talk to the investigators, and we had to attend a stress debriefing.

I think it is good that they have these stress debriefings, and I definitely understand why they do it. I think having this outlet helped some people on our squad. Still, I found myself feeling defiant in the face of our so-called therapist. He was really nothing more than your standard government employee, who had been given some kind of course in "sensitivity training." I found myself wanting to throw a wrench into his trite analysis and his grab-bag of clichés. I wanted to ask him to help me understand why death is so hard for us to deal with. To help me dig. Is it because it reminds us that we are also going to die? Why is death so tragic to us? And why does it hurt so bad? Life is so painful for many people, and this pain is only interrupted by these brief moments of real happiness; if we are lucky we become numb to the pain, so why is the thought of an end to that so terrifying and so unacceptable to us? Is it because death cannot be understood in the way that this computer I am typing with can be understood? Because we cannot dissect it with scientific instruments, and we cannot probe it with satellites? Death is one thing that is so real, so undeniable, so present in this life, and yet so completely inaccessible. It is a complete mystery in the truest sense of the word. Thinking about death tests faith—your religious faith or even just faith that there is any type of meaning in the scheme of things. There are infinite possibilities of what happens next, the most terrifying possibility being that maybe nothing happens next. But I am no philosopher.

Still, this punk kid inside of me wanted to ask these questions, just to hear the System's apologist stutter. He was soft and pudgy in his cheap suit, with a vacant look on his face, the type of guy who might show up on your doorstep trying to sell you a set of steak knives. I know

I am being harsh. I am sure he meant well. Still, it seemed almost like an insult to me to have him there. He brought nothing to the table.

Finally, after stress debriefings and the like, most of us were allowed to return to Zion, and to our respective fire districts. However, the team kept our IC in Filmore for an extra day because of his close association with events on the Devil's Den fire.

I did not know the dead man personally. I did not even know what he looked like. This experience was not nearly as close or as upsetting to me as it was to a lot of other people who were involved. But now that he is dead, he has somehow become important in my life.

The main question I had for myself after I had returned to Zion, to my bed, to the engine bay, to my crew, to familiar surroundings, was how I could integrate this experience into a deeper part of me. It was important that I did not just have some vague sentimental notions attached to it, or for my thoughts about it to become some indecipherable haze to me, or to fade. It did not seem like that would be a good way to honor the seriousness of what happened on the Devil's Den fire that day.

The only way I can think of to say "thank you" and "goodbye" is to write this, and to keep alive the memory of what has affected me.

# Letter to Jenna Miller

My name is Phillip Baxter. I know that your name is Jenna Miller. I am writing you this letter because I want to tell you how amazing you are. You are so amazing that I can't even talk to you, just looking at you hurts me. I know it sounds like a line and I wish I could be more poetic for you, so that maybe you could understand that I am sincere, but I have never been able to get my words exactly right, although I get by.

When I first saw you (at Tully's Coffee Shop, maybe now you can guess who I am), it looked like someone had just painted you standing there in line. Your face was so unusually perfect, so completely smooth and flawless and unblemished. I remember how everyone who stood next to you looked blurry, they were not as defined as you were, they all looked pixilated somehow.

Look, what I am trying to say is that you are a prototype of something perfect. You stand out like an archangel among pissing and whimpering malcontent.

It is not just because you are physically beautiful, even though you are that, Jenna; it's more like, you just radiate goodness. It is so calming for me just to look at you. I know that green is your favorite color, especially clover-green, because you wear it almost every day, like a child who wears green, who is so loyal to it, because they love turtles and praying mantises. I think that you are very pure and good.

Look, all I am saying is that you are better than they are. I just want you to know that I can see that.

I want to tell you a little bit about myself, so maybe you can decide if I am someone you might be interested in meeting. You already know that my name is Phillip Baxter. I am 6 feet, 1 inches tall, which women seem to like. My weight tends to fluctuate and I will admit that it can fluctuate a lot sometimes, due to my medications: Clazaril, Haldol, Navane, and all the others. Most people do not realize how chaotic the metabolism of the medicated can be. It is the final affront to those of us who have already been thoroughly fucked over in life. But I am not bitter.

When I am skinny, people say I look like Gary Sinise, and I think that you will agree that he is not a bad-looking guy. But I have blue eyes, the opposite of Gary's brown, which have been described differently to me by different people; as icy or intense, calm or chaotic, caring or abusive, depending on what mood I am in. I think that you will find that my eyes are always kind when they look at you.

I have to admit that I am balding slightly, but I still have enough hair so that as long as I part it on the side and comb it over, it is hard to tell that I am balding at all. I am not horrible looking, I can promise you that. I am not someone you would have to be embarrassed about, Jenna, but I am not Adonis, either. I just want to be clear on that.

Right now I am working as a clerk, but this is just until I start my own business. I'm already networking and making connections in that direction. I have a million ideas that could turn into something, Jenna. But until that happens, I work at Same Day Payday Loans in Southeast Portland, and I drive a Ford Focus, although that car is only for now. I plan to upgrade to a higher-end vehicle sometime in the near future.

Look, I am not an idiot. I am the smartest person I know, really, and I am definitely smart enough to figure out how to procure a little bit of wealth. The thing is, I have had a few problems in the past, and I am just getting back up on my feet now. But I will become a force to be reckoned with, I can promise you that. Someone with my talent and personal power is destined to go places. You will be happy, then, that you know me.

However, when it comes down to it, I don't really think that details such as cars and jobs are that important to you. And this is one of the things I like about you, Jenna. I just admire the way you don't get caught up in the externals, like everyone else does. You might wonder how I know this about you, but you only wonder this because you don't understand how perceptive I am yet, how my insights into people can border on psychic, how sensitive to patterns and processes I can be.

Look, if you need me to label it for you, to dangle verbal tags so that you can understand, I can just tell by the way you give special attention to certain people. Like how you always smile so sweetly at that young bike courier who comes in to Tully's, the one who has the acne-covered face that looks like it has been dipped into a vat of acid, the kid who always tries so hard to smile, but who can never quite pull it off.

Or the obese woman, you know the one I am talking about, Jenna. The lady who plays solitaire and who throws a fit if her coffee drink is too strong or too weak, or too hot, or not hot enough. The one who is so repulsively ugly and full of self-loathing. I notice how you always go out of your way to talk to her, and when you address her, you do so closely, in physical proximity, how you might touch her shoulder lightly with your finger-tips as you speak, as if there is an intimate fraternity between the two of you. She is influenced by your beauty and perfection, Jenna, and for those two minutes in your presence, she almost becomes beautiful, too. But as soon as you leave, she is average again. Just as average as everyone else is.

I have never been married before Jenna, which means that I have never been divorced, either, and I hope you will agree that this is a good thing. It should tell you that I am less jaded and bruised than your average adult male, and that I am more available for a union that is entirely healthy, rather than reactionary and spiteful, as so many marriages turn out to be.

Look, I will admit that in the past loneliness or physical need may have encouraged me to settle for someone who did not meet the full criteria of my value system. Someone who was not my equal, as you are. Fuck, I am not perfect, Jenna, and I don't pretend to be.

The woman who came before you was named Margarate. I first met Margarate when she came into Same Day to get a loan for a special pair of shoes that she needed. My first impression of Margarate was that she looked like a twisted and gnarled tree, one that was dying. She was not very attractive at all Jenna, but I have to tell you, her looks were not really all her fault. Margarate suffers from multiple sclerosis, and because of this, her left leg is several inches shorter than her right, which is the reason that she needed that special pair of shoes in the first place. To get to the point, I signed Margarate up for a loan, and then I took her home that same evening.

Look, Jenna, it's just that I was intrigued by Margarate, by how rock-bottom she was, by this certain aspect of abandon she had in her personality, how she had these eyes that saw but did not see, black animal eyes. If you met her, I think you would understand what I mean by abandon. She was as natural as a fly or a mosquito in the ecosystem that is Portland, and with the same insect dumbness, too. I admit that I might have had more patience with Margarate if it were not for her twisted limbs, or the dark hairline above her lip, or if, in bed, she was

131

something more than a warm body just lying there. Or, perhaps more importantly, if you had not come into the picture, Jenna. I am so glad that you did.

I broke it off with Margarate after the very first time that you and I spoke at Tully's. Maybe saying that we spoke is being a little bit too generous. I should say, I broke it off with Margarate after the first time that you said something to me at Tully's. The funny thing is, I cannot even remember exactly what it is that you told me.

Look, it is not that what you said was insignificant, because everything that you say or do is significant to me, Jenna, it's just that your presence, and the impression that it made on me, have completely wiped out any other memory of dialogue or detail.

Your completely fearless and unforced eye contact . . . I do remember that, Jenna. And how your presence was like a mild electric current that passed through me. This was a very dear and physical sensation. I can remember your particular scent, it was like rose water and vanilla, and how it seemed chemically engineered for the comfort of others, how it made me feel like I was inside of a pleasant dream, or within a childhood memory of safety and happiness. When you walked away a few seconds later, I was in a state of light shock. I could not remember how to order coffee. I just stumbled towards the bathroom like a man with a concussion.

I don't think that you understand the enormous talent that you possess, the way that you can benefit people just by being present. It is amazing to me that you can be so unaware of yourself in this way.

Look, I am sorry to go off on these tangents, but I wear my heart on my sleeve, Jenna, and I am very proud of that. There is no shame in that.

I do not have too many hobbies right now that might interest you, Jenna, but I am confident that we can find some common ground in our leisure lives that we can build upon. I know that simple things like this are important to a lot of couples. I have not been into recreation so much lately, although I do enjoy reading, which is essential. What interests me the most are the psychiatric trade journals. I think that it is important to keep up with all the new forms of psychosis that are surfacing, primarily because it is fascinating to me, and it reassures me that I am right about other people when there is science to back me up in this way. What you start to realize is that everyone, from Gandhi to the Queen of England, falls somewhere on the continuum of mental illness. But that

132

thought is not my original, I think it was Dr. Becker who first told me that, although the more that I learn, the more I start to see the basic truth in it.

Other than reading, I spend most of my time outside of work with my parents, who live in northeast Portland. My parents are very important to me, Jenna, despite the fact that they have never nurtured me properly; they have never once given me the credit that I deserve. The thing is, they are even worse to each other. You will see it when you meet them, how there is this other, ugly thing that is always going on just below their dialogue.

If you need more than that, last night when I visited, they were arguing about a sink that they are having installed in the kitchen, and how it was not finished on time. It was nothing all too exotic, Jenna. If I had it tape-recorded for you, you would not find the exchange memorable at all, you would think that it was like a thousand other arguments that people might have when they are married. But if you had been there, if you had actually seen it with your own eyes, I think you would understand what I am talking about when I say, ugly thing beneath the conversation.

My mother complained that the workers were not worth their wages, she said that they were slowly destroying her kitchen, but the look that she delivered was one of clear hatred, of pure disgust, for my father. You could tell that it was not the sink that she was upset about, Jenna, not really. It was something that went much deeper than that.

My father told her that maybe she should mention that to the workers, instead of to him, but you would have thought by the look that he gave her, that he was not talking to his wife, but to some kind of a slug he had just found inside of his new tennis shoe. It was utter disregard mixed with nausea. This look must have lasted for over twenty seconds. A punch in the face would have been more subtle, Jenna.

Look, I am telling you. You were not there. I know it does not sound so dramatic to you. But it is the combination of their constant Dick and Jane dialogue, which is so simple, and this undercurrent, this thing that they are really expressing, which is something much more vicious. Somehow they mix it just right so that it is perfectly painful for me.

It is almost too much to take, because it points out their major lie. The thing is, it is impossible to actually fall out of love and into this type

133

of contempt, Jenna. What my parents and everyone else like them cannot admit is that they were never really in love in the first place. I am starting to think that they are all incapable of it.

It is funny to me how ninety percent of the songs on the radio are these love songs. Let me put it on the table and say that I have no problem with love songs, Jenna, not on principle. I am not so cynical as that. If the Buddha or the Dalai Lama or maybe Jesus Christ were to sing a love song, and someone were to play it on the radio, I would listen to it. I certainly would not change the station to search for a better song. But these pop stars have not explored the idea of love at all; they have not meditated on it in the least. It is some fuzzy, romantic notion to them at best; at worst, it is just a word. And it is the most sold out word in history. But people still cling to it like flies on shit. They throw it around like an old rag doll. They have turned it into a syllable from the mouth of a parrot.

Look, I am not saying that I am an expert, Jenna. But love is something I have thought about. It is a concept that I have spent some time on. I feel like I can almost grasp it.

What I've come up with is, you love someone when their pain hurts you as if it were your own, and when their happiness lifts you up as if it were your own. This seems right to me. But their pain must truly hurt you, like your insides have been put through a wringer and twisted without pattern and rubbed against the grain with sandpaper. Alternately, their joy must make you cry.

The only problem is, we are not wired for this kind of empathy, Jenna, not really. If there is one thing I am sure of it is that selfishness is in our blood, it goes right down into our bone marrow, no matter what any optimist will try to tell you. There are only a few key people who have almost got it, who could say the word love, and have it not be a complete joke. There is maybe one or two who have actually made it there.

I watch you with everyone at Tully's, and it is obvious that you are one of those few people. Look, I know this about you, even if you do not know it yourself. There is this poetry to each small thing that you do, Jenna, and to every word that you speak. I don't know how to explain it, you could just move your finger and it would be cinematic. The reason is, love is somehow instinctive for you, with you it is biologic somehow, it underwrites everything you do, and makes it beautiful, because you are composed of it.

You don't realize how lucky you are, how far ahead of everyone else. You must have figured something out, Jenna, something that is inaccessible to me. I know you can help me get to where you are. Look, I am not saying that you are above me, our strengths are just in different areas.

I am not sure exactly where to go from here. I know that this letter changes things, that it has erased the space between strangers, the space that allowed us to keep distant, and safe. To get to the point, I do not have a phone number that I can leave for you right now, Jenna, but I will be at Tully's at seven o'clock on Thursday evening, and I need to see you there. Please realize the gravity of this situation. I will be wearing a red polo shirt, just in case you still can't picture me. Either way, I will spot you. Trust me when I say that this is the beginning of something really amazing.

Yours,
Phillip Baxter.

# Selling San Clemento

I sell. Or as San Clemento would say, I help those in the market for spiritual renewal.

I can always tell when a prospect is going to buy. There are several signs and they are not, on the average, very subtle. It could be the way that a client smokes his cigarette in our lobby—one long breath down to the filter with short breaks for air. Perhaps it's the compulsive way he continually smooths his beaten-up blue jeans as he waits, or the mumbled curse with which she shoves her hair back from her eyes to reveal an acne-scarred forehead, only to have it slide back down on a slick of facial oil.

Body language is completely individual, a true snowflake of misery. Almost every person you meet, San tells us, is in some way handicapped by sorrow or anxiety. The whole world, he assures us, is potentially a client.

Now, I am undeniably excellent at what I do, but I am not the only element in our office that makes this operation a successful one. To give credit where credit is due, everything that the customer experiences from the time he walks in the door is an essential part of the eventual pitch.

To get an idea of the brilliance of our whole operation you must experience it—not as a potential customer but as a seasoned professional with respect for a completely original and undeniably effective sales presentation.

Our receptionist, an Ohio girl named Lilly Pinkwater, approaches each client waiting in the lobby and offers him coffee. Lilly is very attentive to details, such as how much cream and sugar the client would like, the temperature and strength of the coffee, even the preferred thickness of the brew. We have a choice of seven different beans—three Columbian, two Turkish, and two Arabic—which Lilly can name with the skill of a barista.

Lilly is perfect for our office. She is San's niece, so her job was a family handout, but she has become an undeniable asset. This is because Lilly has a Midwestern look and is extremely average in a way that clients automatically trust. She is slim as an iris, with pasty, buttermilk skin that is generously freckled, and thin brown hair that looks as if it has been washed too many times. Her bangs, in fact, look as if they might dissolve upon touch.

After a client sips on his coffee for a minute or two, Lilly comes back and escorts him to the listening lounge so he can get a taste of our product. Lilly asks the prospects to make themselves comfortable on leather recliners the length of deck chairs, and then situates them with a headset through which they can hear San Clemento's soothing, butterscotch voice.

But I should qualify that last statement. The prospects only believe that they are hearing San's voice. San has been a smoker for almost his whole life, and his voice, in actuality, sounds like gravel being sloshed around in a puddle of phlegm. It is not San on those tapes but a hired actor whose voice is all cream and honey—more soothing than a caring pastor who hears your laments with deep, personal concern.

The proxy San calms his clients; he talks with them one on one, about the only important thing in life: happiness.

During San's talk of joy, GHod, and the importance of self-understanding, soft music plays under the vocal track, like something you might hear at midnight mass on Christmas morning. This audio portion is a string quartet overlaid with a type of choral chanting. It rolls just like waves in the middle of an ocean. The music is almost inaudible, but it is engineered to certain frequencies that cause relaxation.

San puts the insomniac to sleep. He temporarily cures the headaches of the anxious. Visitors in the listening lounge lose the ropey tension in their shoulders for the first time in months, or in some cases, years. The voice of the recorded San is like the light of the Holy Ghost. The client, if all goes well, starts to see the possibility of a life where he can relax and once again be as carefree as he was as an eight-year-old.

It is my job to make the client believe that this happiness can and will be permanent if he buys our deluxe twelve-tape course.

I once saw Lilly open a box of marketing pamphlets, which was reinforced several times over with packing tape, by beating her fists against the box with a force that was amazing considering her small hands and arms. She simply couldn't find the box cutters. The display approached shocking.

When I try to think of a way to sum up my sales style, I always think of this awkward image of Lilly, beating all hell out of an Airborne Express box.

If the listening lounge relaxes the client, I equivalently pummel him once I have him in my office. I find that the client is in a sense confused into buying my pitch, like a nascent tourist who takes the advice of the first shady taxi driver he happens to meet at the airport.

I let the prospect know, first of all, that San has a relationship with God. A very special relationship. San's god is not simply a Christian god or a Muslim god or even an inner god, I assure them, but an all-inclusive, democratic god. I give them examples of those San has helped and ask them how they can argue with *results*. Results, after all, are not opinions. Anyone can claim to be gifted in the art of self-help, I say, but how many are as affluent as San? The charlatans don't have food to put on the table at the end of the day because people don't pay for crap, for God's sake. I show them a cover of the *Phoenix New Times*, which refers to San as the up-and-coming "Self Help King." (The article inside is skeptical at best, but most clients don't know this.) When the client's mood shifts just a little bit at this display and the distrust starts to leave his face like a slow leak of air, I know that I have him. At least at this point it is a ninety percent certainty.

I start with the personal questions next. I probe the prospects about their family life, their love life, and their professional life. I ask penetrating questions about their relationship with their father or their lack of one. Do they inadvertently feel that they don't have the right to success in life because their father was a drunk? Are they burdened with the idea of genetic limits? These questions are designed to convince the clients that they are not working with the average salesman but with the sophisticated consultant. I don't stop until the prospect walks away in mid-sentence or decides to buy. That is how you have to work as a salesman. It is hit or miss. You just have to swing the bat more than the next guy—this is the law of averages.

One thing that I can assure you is that I will always swing the bat more. That's how I will always keep my advantage. I have what you would call drive.

Today has been good to me, so I smile graciously at Lilly, looking at her with just the slightest hint of sexual need, which is enough to make her blush. I like the effect I have on her, even if she wouldn't be my first choice for a woman. There is the element of sexual hierarchy between us. I am a dominating man, and she is a little doe of a woman, ready to be submissive. There is really nothing romantic about it.

I visit Lilly on average about once a week. I know she would like to see me more often, but I seldom have the energy to interact, with her, or with anyone, after a day of work.

See, I operate on a schedule and must complete what I set out for myself to do on any particular day before I allow myself to socialize. I am what you would call disciplined.

Lilly sometimes makes fun of my schedule because I will get up in the middle of eating or maybe watching a television program, and make an important change in my day-planner. She says it makes her think of an artist who is so inspired by some creative idea that he must stop everything in order to write it down. But it is only a schedule, she reminds me, and giggles at this for a long time, as if it is very funny.

Lilly laughs a lot. It makes me feel relieved that she is happy without me having to try hard to please her. It is lucky for me, I suppose, that she is so simple.

I arrive at Lilly's apartment later in the evening and find she has had it wallpapered. "Professionally," she informs me with pride. It was a gift, from her uncle, for her birthday. I find the idea of a wallpapered apartment ridiculous, but I tell her it looks beautiful and I kiss her on the cheek. The flowers that I sent to her are still sitting on the coffee table in a thick glass vase.

We sit outside on Lilly's balcony at one of those cheap, plastic outdoor sets. Lily asks me questions about my family. She wants to know about my aunt, who lives here in Arizona. She wants to know about my mother and my father. She always asks about my family, and my answers never seem to satisfy her because the next week I find her asking me the same questions, as if she was unclear on what I said the last time.

I know that Lilly wants to hear stories, something picturesque that she can smile about, but I find that I cannot garnish my family history with interesting details like I can with San Clemento.

I answer Lilly's questions because I have no choice, really. But she believes that I am confiding in her, a sign of trust and affection, and she takes my hand gently in hers to show me how much it means, and caresses my palm with her thumb.

I ask Lilly questions about her family also, in particular about her uncle San.

I know for instance, that business is expanding. We are expanding regionally and, if the past year has been as kind financially as I believe it to have been, we will be going national, and maybe even public somewhere down the line. The self-help industry, I predict, has as much growth potential as silicon, if not more. Humans suffer by nature after all, and that equals job security. I know it sounds like a marketing slogan, but it is not a theory. It is law.

Does San have any prospects in mind for regional manager? Does he plan to promote from within? These are things that I need to know. Being that San is a Texan, I can be sure that he promotes based on personal favorites rather than on sales history. My record is impeccable, but does San like me? I have to ask Lilly.

It finally comes out.

Lou Dobbs.

Lilly doesn't say the name but drops it, wishing after she sees my expression that she could pick it back up again.

Lou Dobbs was named an up-and-coming business visionary by the *Utne Reader* for the year 2003. Lou Dobbs has an MBA from Princeton. Lou Dobbs has a beautiful wife and a prodigy son. I have a rock in my gut.

Lou Dobbs is flying in from Tennessee. His father is an old friend of the family—an oil baron, like San's own father. Lou will eventually run the new branch of San Clemento's down in Tucson.

Lou Dobbs has Plans, I find out—big plans. He is the young, innovative type. He has *ideas*. He will take San's business far, and will be compensated nicely in the process. Corporate training programs. Focus groups to improve our product. Lou will streamline the outfit for the new millennium. Make ours a company worthy of respect in the business community.

San knows I am his best salesman, Lilly assures me, and wants to keep me at the flagship office in Phoenix.

This expansion, of course, will be good for everyone. The more business we do, the more employees will be compensated. And those who are worthy and work hard enough will find themselves upwardly mobile.

Yes, everyone will benefit, I agree, but especially Lou Dobbs. He will benefit the most.

In fact, Lilly tells me, acting as if she has just remembered, Lou will be flying in for the work barbecue on Sunday.

On this note Lilly moves inside. She does not walk exactly, but gallops lightly to her closet and fingers through her summer dresses, anticipating, I assume, what she will wear on Sunday. Her fingers come to rest lightly on an ankle-length, honeydew colored summer dress. A private smile engages her lips as she thinks to herself, perhaps imagining what she will look like on Sunday in her dress, hugging her uncle San.

Lilly removes the dress from her closet and lays it gently on her bedspread as if it is something of great value.

I have seen Lilly wear the dress once before. It seems that it is her favorite. She does not look stunning in it, by any means, but rather she looks comfortable. It is a landscape that she blends quietly into.

Lilly is unassuming, although not in a fairy-tale sense. She is not a quiet maiden who sits in the corner, combing her fingers through long hair or the like. She is not the *intriguing* type of unassuming. Not even close. Lilly is unassuming to the point of not being noticed at all. I would have never taken a second look at Lilly myself if I did not work in the same office with her day in and day out.

Watching her now, I realize that Lilly is out of place. She should be living with her family, on a cattle ranch in rural New Mexico, or in some equally idyllic scenario. Her innocence, somehow, calls for this. But she is answering phones in Phoenix instead of milking cows, and living alone in a small, ratty apartment with her new floral wallpaper to keep her company.

Lilly does not seem to worry ahead to spinsterhood, as any reasonable girl with her particular qualities and appearance might find herself doing. She does not, in fact, exude loneliness or insecurity in the least. If she were a potential client, I would decide after observing her that she was a no-sell. There would be, in my mind, no question about it. It is amazing, I realize, how impenetrable she is.

But right now, I have to remind myself, there are much more pressing things to think about. I have to prepare for Sunday's barbecue and it is already Thursday night. I have 59 hours between now and Sunday, which is plenty of time, if I use it properly, to prepare myself for the challenge of San Clemento and Lou Dobbs.

I must do what I am good at. That much is obvious. I must sell. I must sell San the idea that he made the wrong choice in picking Lou Dobbs as his right-hand man. This may not, of course, change the situation at hand in any concrete, material way. I realize this. I am not the type to live in some kind of fairy tale.

But if I know that San recognizes, inwardly, that he has made a bad decision, or if I even produce a shred of doubt in his mind, I will be able to rest much easier on Sunday night. I am definitely not the type who is okay with coming in second.

I will have to be composed, first off, and appear completely natural and competent throughout the evening, not slipping once. I will present myself as a paragon of marketing competence when business is brought up. But I must appear humble at the same time, as if I cannot help but relay this vast store of knowledge that rolls off the tip of my tongue so naturally. (I make a mental note to stop by the bookstore, pick up a few business bestsellers, and glean a handful of relevant phrases and concepts from the text.) I will read Sunday's *Wall Street Journal*, because there is no doubt in my mind that Lou Dobbs has. When and if he brings up the articles, I will be in the know.

I must be charming also, and with a biting sense of humor. I will make underhanded jokes about business ethics, and say clever things such as that morality, like the law, is only a set of arbitrary rules.

Everyone, ideally, will laugh at my Machiavellian wit.

San Clemento will understand that I am not trying to impress anyone but am just being myself—grossly capable—because I know of no other way to be.

I become excited just thinking about Lou Dobbs trying, vainly, to keep up with me. There is no way that he will have put in all the preparation that I plan to.

The only problem, I realize, is Lilly.

This is the first month that Lilly and I are driving up to San's barbecue together. We have arrived together on previous Sundays, but always as part of a car pool. Driving up just the two of us, in my mind, is equal to posting announcements that we are together. In an official sort of way.

I would prefer a much more inconspicuous arrival, but I found myself one night, in the sedate after-glow of sex, suggesting that we attend one Sunday together, as a couple. Lilly has not forgotten my comment and gives me excited reminders, as if I had promised her a spectacular evening at the opera or something equally extravagant.

The problem here is that if San Clemento believes Lilly and I are a couple, it is over for me. San is sure to look at me as a predator, or at the least not worthy of his pure little Lilly. This is actually what he calls her sometimes—his Lilly of the Field. It is interesting how relatives can see you as so much better than you actually are.

I can't have this disfavor, not with so much on the line.

I am angry at myself for allowing Lilly to manipulate me in this way. I feel like one of my own clients, pressured to put up a title loan or to refinance their home in order to buy a bad product.

Lilly comes out of the bathroom where she was, no doubt, freshening up for my benefit. She is still drying off her face, freshly washed, with a hand towel. She smells like eucalyptus soap and baby powder. It is a pleasant smell and somehow comforting, but when she puts her hand on my leg I find that the heat of her fingers is unwelcome and I want to squirm under her touch. The Sunday barbecue, after all, has become a problem because of her.

But I have 59 hours to get ready for Lou Dobbs and to figure out what to do with Lilly.

I give Lilly a hug and tell her in a deliberately weak voice that I don't feel well. Her small arms draped around my neck and her pleasing scent almost convince me to stay. I have to remind myself about priorities.

Lilly walks up to me from behind her desk, and her small feet barely impress the carpet. Her figure is framed and put into relief by the looming picture of San Clemento in the background, looking like a vivisection of rodeo barker, infomercial czar and oil baron. There is an interesting contrast between uncle and niece.

Lilly feels my forehead with the back of her hand, and tells me that I might still be a little warm. I roll my eyes, but in just a way to let her know that I like her fawning and am really just pretending to be annoyed.

"Tea or coffee this morning?" she asks me. Her voice is mild and soft. Lilly has a tendency to alter her voice depending on the time of day. In the early morning she speaks as if she is trying not to wake someone in the next room.

"Tea," I answer; "sugar and cinnamon, Lilly. Please." I pause. "Any calls, qualified leads?"

"There is someone in the listening lounge now."

"I think that would qualify as qualified," I say and wink.

Lilly smiles. I can tell I will be right on the mark today. Witty. Confident. Thank you, Lou. I think I will sell my ass off out of spite.

Lilly hands me the prospect's completed questionnaire and I take a look at it.

Billy Summers, I think to myself, is mine. And when I have him standing in front of me, looking pock-faced, lonely and skinny beyond being excusable, I know that I am right.

Billy, let me tell you, is a salesman's dream. He is the type who agrees with you just so he doesn't have to let on that he has no clue whatsoever what you are talking about.

He is beautiful. Perfect. I want to tell Billy how beautiful he is to me. He is a glass slipper that somehow fits perfectly onto my big, awkward foot.

"The charlatans," I tell Billy halfway through my pitch, "don't have food to put on the table at the end of the day because people won't bet the farm on a pile of horseshit. Would you bet the family estate on a heap of fertilizer, Billy? Certainly not." I come back before he has the opportunity to answer. "You are too smart for that." The adrenaline starts to kick in like a high-powered stimulant.

And then Lou Dobbs appears at the back of my office. I know it is Lou Dobbs without even having to ask. He holds up a clipboard with the San Clemento logo on the back to show that he is family, so to speak, and nods at me to continue my pitch. As if everything is just fine. As if this intrusion is somehow excusable.

I can see Lou from where I am sitting, but Billy cannot. Lou has raven hair that is short-cropped, well-combed and gelled. Sure enough, there is a *Wall Street Journal*, rolled up like a dog swatter and positioned under his right armpit. Power suit. Burgundy tie that stands out sharp against his black dress shirt. The works.

I find that I am nervous, goddamnit. I am not ready for Lou Dobbs. This meeting was supposed to take place Sunday after all, and it is only Friday morning.

Now, Billy is mine, and has been since he walked in the door. Finishing my pitch is only, in essence, a technicality. A pitch must be completed. A sale must be closed. So I continue. And I don't, for an instant, look towards the back of the office.

I barrel into Billy, a linebacker sacking the quarterback. I ask him if he is a man of action or a man of procrastination. I pound my fist down onto my desk to accentuate my points. I put it to Billy that if he is a real man, which I know that he is, he will leave this office with our twelve-tape course. If he looks deep inside and decides he doesn't, after

144

all, have the necessary testicles to make an investment that will change his life, he can go out and buy a Wayne Dyer book instead. He can go do this along with the millions of others who have also bought the book and have likewise failed completely at improving their lives in any type of measurable way.

After a good pummeling, I take it down a notch. I give Billy what I call the "living example" close.

I sit back down in my chair so that we are eye-level. I tell him that I was, only three years ago, sitting where he is right now. In this very office. And look at me, I advise him. I wear nice suits and I drive a nice car. I became a success, I assure him, because San Clemento helped to calm my inner turmoil and helped me to understand the limitless power inherent in the human spirit. I became, in fact, so aware of my inner strength—at this point I clutch my heart—that I knew I could go anywhere and do anything. And does he know where I went? Does he know what I did? I came here to help put San's tapes into the hands of the masses. And I'm doing nicely with it, I add, picking a small piece of lint off of my pressed Armani suit. You can do the same, I assure Billy.

Three minutes later, I am holding a check signed by Billy Summers. When Billy leaves, I remain in my chair. I look over at who I know to be Lou Dobbs and say, as disinterestedly as possible, "Now how can I help you, sir?"

"Lou Dobbs," he announces as he walks over to me "I'll be running San's new operation down in Tucson." Lou runs his fingers through freshly cut hair, then holds out his hand. I take it, and lift myself out of my chair just enough to suggest getting up, but I make sure to stay in my seat.

Lou clears his throat, a little embarrassed that I don't reply to his introduction. "I am only in town for a few days, but San thought it might be a good idea for me to, ah, observe the operation, and get an idea, first-hand, of what needs to be, ah, improved upon."

Lou is younger than I expected. His accent is very eastern and proper, but I know from Lilly that he is from Tennessee. He is the type of young, streamlined southerner, I imagine, who finds his home state backwards in some fashion and wishes that he was from Washington D. C. or New York City instead. I find that when I am face to face with Lou Dobbs I feel reassuringly superior. Despite his vaunted education and supposed ingenuity, he is what you would call a new fish. This won't be as hard, I realize, as I had imagined.

"Well, yes," I advance. "A little first-hand observation might be a good idea. So the company isn't just an abstract idea to you from one of your textbooks."

Lou smiles, an embarrassed little half-cocked smile. His lips are not what you would call big but what you would call full. He is one of those undeniably attractive Adonis types. "The little bastard," I think to myself. "Good looks on top of everything else."

"Do you mind if I comment on your pitch?" he asks, extremely polite-like.

"Go right ahead," I offer. After all, I closed the sale. There is nothing Lou here can say that will change that.

Lou takes a seat on the opposite side of my desk.

"You have the potential to be an excellent salesman," Lou starts; "You have the energy, and you definitely have the charisma. . . ." Lou takes the tone with me of a motivational speaker. It turns my blood molten.

"You have the energy," he continues, "but you come off as phony as a three-dollar bill, if you'll excuse the expression."

I start to put up an argument to defend myself, but Lou shakes his head and cuts me off in my own office.

He says, "You have to stop pushing for sales so desperately. We are not carpetbaggers. We are not Bible salesman. We are not selling cutlery. We are selling confidence. Happiness. Success. Only ten percent of your presentation should deal with confirmation and closing. You were closing during your whole pitch."

Lou says this very kindly. He is a mentor advising his student. He is, after all, only trying to help.

Lou walks over to the coffee maker and pours himself a cup. He slurps on it in that annoying way young executive types do. The slurping, I imagine, somehow makes him feel superior.

My first inclination is to strangle Lou Dobbs with his necktie.

I suggest that it is San's name that motivates the customer to buy. It is similar to brand recognition at the supermarket. I am just here, in a manner, to give the client's ass a proverbial push over the line.

Lou shakes his head "no" for about three seconds.

Finally he says, "No, No, No. You have it all wrong. I'm sure you were trained to believe that is true. Now, you are not in danger of losing your job. But things are changing around here and you are going to have to adapt. I don't want you to lose your job. In fact, I will make it my personal mission to make sure that you do not. Properly trained, I would like to have you on my team in Tucson. In fact, I would love to have you on board."

Does Lou notice the blood boiling over out of my eye sockets and running down my cheeks in tiny red streams?

"Now, I don't have the time to give you my whole sales seminar here in your office, but I will give you a few pointers that I think are obvious." He holds up his hand to show that he did not mean for the comment to be taken offensively.

"First, you should never stand when a client is sitting, which I noticed you did with the young gentleman who just left. That's number one."

Lou goes on to tell me numbers two three and four, respectively. Lou would really love for me to read Sylvia Brown, Phil McGraw and several other self-help types. He wants me to see what I am going up against.

I want Lou to die a painful death, something involving hyenas, red ants, and skillfully applied black magic.

Lou goes on to tell me about the nature of sales in the information age. How the average buyer can learn their market with minimal effort because of the wealth of information at their fingertips. How you have to approach your clients as equals these days. How even the least literate among them are potentially educated consumers.

Lou Dobbs, I realize, loves expounding his sales philosophy. He takes a tactile pleasure in his own articulations, as if they are containable and measurable—something he can carry home with him. Lou is an infomercial sales seminar.

I ask Lou if he would like a lectern. I think that there might be one in the storage closet.

Lou doesn't suspect my sarcasm. He doesn't suspect my hatred. He suspects good-natured humor. I imagine this is because Lou Dobbs is the type of guy that everyone likes. He is god-awful.

Lou asks if I would mind if he pours himself another cup of coffee. I tell him that I would love to have a cup with him, but that I really have to prepare for my next client. In light of everything he just said, I have to readjust my whole presentation, after all.

Lou smiles at me and tells me that you don't become a salesman overnight. Achieving full competence is a slow and arduous process.

147

But with my talent, he assures me, I will eventually become what they call top-notch. It is only a matter of time and discipline.

Lou shakes my hand and tells me that he very much looks forward to working with me.

I agree that it will be a rewarding experience.

"Swine bastard" is all I can think as I watch him walk out.

It feels as if there are deposits of ore building at my temples. I have aspirin in my office bathroom. I take four.

I must re-calculate. Concentration makes my head pound even more, but I certainly cannot sit here shiftless and invalid, not at a time like this.

Lou is good. He is even better than I thought. He must have his talons planted more firmly into the flanks of San Clemento than I originally gave him credit for. I do not blame San. San does not have a cast-iron cattleshit detector like I do. Texans, I realize, are too easily seduced by personality. The value of something as important as competence has completely fallen to the wayside.

It makes me sick thinking about it, having to defer to Lou Dobbs as my boss. I refuse to do it. San Clemento can only have one of us. I suppose that Sunday will decide if this is going to be Lou or myself. I was caught off of my guard today. The barbecue will be different.

San will see. He will have to. I will make it plain.

Lilly walks into my office holding a client questionnaire. She hands it to me, and congratulates me on my sale, as she always does. She kisses my forehead and then starts to brew a fresh pot of coffee. Her kiss relaxes me, and I let up my grip on the arms of my desk chair.

Lilly and the humid gurgling of the Mr. Coffee occupy my perception completely for a moment, like a memory or a dream. For a moment the scene feels very natural, as if Lilly and I live in a small apartment together and are participating in a slow morning ritual of sorts.

Lilly asks me what I think of Lou as she wipes stray cigarette ashes off of my desk and into the palm of her hand.

I tell her, "not much, really." I did get the impression that he was arrogant and quite full of himself. But not for long, I think to myself.

Lilly looks at me, with a little smile like she's in the know, and says that arrogance is really only a way to cover up your weaknesses early, before other people see them. I tell her that I agree with her, at least in the case of Lou Dobbs. His large ego, no doubt, is a pre-emptive strike against his many defects.

Lilly is solicitous. She asks me if I would like Tylenol. My face is red, she tells me, like it always is when I have a headache.

I tell her that I am fine and that she can send in the next client— Josh Hayward, I say, when I look at the questionnaire—whenever he is ready. She leaves to go check on his status, and as I watch her go, I wonder if we will stay together.

If I stay with San Clemento's outfit, Lilly will only be a detriment to my career. If Lou stays and I go, well, maybe Lilly and I can work something out. She is, after all, a decent girl.

I start to cheer up. I won't let a chimpanzee like Lou Dobbs destroy my mood, no matter what he thinks he might have on me.

What Lou doesn't understand is that I will always swing the bat more, and my swing will always have more force. In another forty-eight hours, San Clemento will know who is the greater asset.

# School Busses

From a distance they appear to be dark ghosts moving smoothly along the open road. As they approach, you realize they are not specters at all but tired travelers, limping along the asphalt pale and unfed. Alert despite their fatigue, they clasp hands forcefully like two lovers on the edge of an abyss. They hang onto every sound they hear, analyzing and interpreting the noises until they're certain the sounds are innocuous: the exoskeleton of a beetle raking the dry grass, a burrowing rodent, or the wind tossing an old saturated paper bag. The pair never stop for these noises, but they do walk backwards, watching, until it is quiet again.

The asphalt of the highway they travel is violently split, like two collided tectonic plates, and they pass exit ramps littered with the dead plastic of barricades and lights that no longer flash. They hope the highway will take them to a better place with some trace of the old practiced decency of civilization, even though they don't really believe such a place exists.

The woman's face bears two deep cuts along the length of her cheekbones, self-inflicted in defiance of a beauty she found finally useless. She is unable to attach meaning to anything now, even beauty. Vanity and aesthetic have become ridiculous. Despite her efforts, the woman is still wild and beautiful, with a tawny face, a sharp Mediterranean profile and a trim body. Her swollen lips are chapped and her dull brown hair is dreadlocked with dirt. Tomorrow she will cut it off with her knife.

The woman is insane. Sometimes she carries on a third-person narration, saying things like, "She is walking in the mud now" or, "She is looking for something blue that she dropped." The man knows she is insane, but she is beautiful and she allows him to fuck her whenever he has the need.

As she walks down the highway with the new man, the beautiful woman remembers a man named Alex. Alex was tall with light-colored hair and round glasses that made him look bookish. In her earlier life he had asked her to marry him. The memory of Alex is a word and a face now, like the title of a portrait memorized for some long ago history test. But, deep in the blood, a part of her still knows that she had once been in love with Alex, when things like love had been possible for her. Under layers of trauma  lies the memory of how she had wanted with Alex: to comfort, influence, love him, to know and learn from him, to encourage and listen to him, to terrify and to be terrified by him, to inspire, surprise, mystify and excite him, to seduce, explore, make love to and reveal herself to him; to masturbate, ride and fuck him; to  anger him, to be unable to sleep at night because of him, to nurture, accept, confuse and placate him; to enlighten, arouse him; to  touch, lick, cut, and feel him; to bring him joy, bring him comfort, bring him clarity  and cause him pain.

Somewhere in her blood, the woman understands she had once been very alive and capable of that passion; that those emotions had been possible in a life, in her life. If she is lucky, she might one day truly recall them.

After walking for several hours, the man notices a small stand of trees where they will take shelter for the night. He tells the woman, "It is almost time to sleep."

As they arrive at the trees, the woman collapses onto the ground, and immediately the cold begins to work its way through the soil into her bones. Moisture on the blades of grass inspires memories of rain and ponds and moist fruit. The man reaches into his satchel, pulling out several pieces of dried meat, tough calluses on which he  begins to chew. He offers meat to the woman, but she is staring at the sky, unaware of his gift. After eating he loosens his belt and enters her, pounding out a steady monotonous rhythm. The only sounds now are gentle grunts from the top of the man's throat and the couple's slow colliding. He momentarily seeks a connection, kissing the woman softly on her chin and then her eyelids, but she, absorbed in a dream of the past, does not notice his intimacy. Turning her face away, she whispers, "Remember school busses?"

# Tolstoy and G-Man

Kelly blamed Leo Tolstoy for her domestic unhappiness. She had kept *Anna Karenina* since her college days, glancing at the large volume on occasion as the years passed and its pages yellowed. When Snowmageddon shut them in, she opened the novel and began to read of unhappy families—casually at first—but soon found herself immersed in Anna's sensual and vigorous world. The prose was so rich it infected her with visions of icy cities, gulags and lead-colored mountains. Her cells screamed for new fuel to burn. It was then that she had started to drink Cabernet and listen to Tchaikovsky.

She watched her husband scour through his work files as they finished their meal. A docudrama on drug cartels played at low volume on the television set, and his focus shifted from work, to film, to dinner very neatly, without loosing track. He would clean his gun before bed. "I'm happy to see you reading the classics," he said. "Try *The Odyssey* next, or *The Illiad*." His dark eyes were sharp and intelligent, but this didn't comfort her. She imagined his heart fortified with technology, diodes connecting chambers, arteries pumping enriched blood that blazed red like anemone. She did not want perfection, but wanted her soul broken open. For now there were leftovers to attend to.

# Negative Space

He unrolled his bed on a rug that smelled of cat-piss, and listened to her fucking in the next room. She sounded feral, rapacious. He thought of the meteor shower, and how her eyes had flashed in the dark like a raccoon's. He suddenly pictured her on a mountainside. Perhaps it was because she had once spoken of Colorado, and how the dark space between stars looked like faces carved from light.

# Important Information about Alien Tumors

## published and distributed by

## Abby Holtz, Alien Tumor Foundation

Not all brain tumors are alike. Some are self-aware alien entities you bring back unwittingly from your research dive in the Falkland Islands. They begin as tiny organisms which slime their way through your ear canal and settle into your brain like fat royals at a luxurious five-star resort. They gorge on electricity, blood protein and brain fat, growing rapidly in the fractal folds of your cerebrum like those wacky toys from China that expand in water, only more insidious, as these tumors are self-aware and what you are experiencing is in fact an alien takeover.

Of course, you won't know this at first. You'll just continue your domestic and professional routine, none the wiser. On occasion, your newly anarchistic brain will release explosions of sex hormone, which puts the smackdown on your once-dominant neocortex, and causes mildly insane behavior such as drag racing and having sex with Danny Collins in the broom closet during lunch break. Then, one hour later, you return to said broom closet with the Croatian lesbian Leona. Her soft, Sapphic lips and muscular calves the size of tree trunks are suddenly and inexplicably too much for you to resist.

The next round of symptoms aren't as cool: the malaise, the headaches, the ataxia. Most of your friends think you've taken to the bottle again, prompting them to call your mother, who shows up on your front porch wielding the twelve-step manual like a Bible-shield and reciting the serenity prayer like a primal incantation that can detoxify you on the spot. To calm her, you agree to a family dinner. As your father is slicing the pot roast you do this weird thing where your arms windmill wildly, knocking over cups and salad bowls, and where your teeth clack away in overdrive like cracked-out castanets. (You have no memory of this, but your sister describes it to you later.)

If you are an intuitive person you have likely figured out that something is definitely wrong. *Perhaps something involving the alien colonization of your brain.*

Honestly, it may be too late. The tumor's intelligence has increased exponentially. It has already attained the cognitive abilities of a highly developed cephalopod deity. It can stretch its tendrils octopus-like along the hilly-gray pastures of your once-idyllic brain, placing perfectly calibrated pressure on your decision-making centers and, in the process, convincing you that such bizarre thoughts and behavior as you have experienced in the past month are, in fact, quite normal. In other words, you are its bitch, and you don't even know it.

Despite this, you have a few isolated moments of lucidity, where you recognize the truth about alien tumors. But the dissembling cancer stays your hand each time you decide to stab an icepick through your face as your final, brave act of sacred suicide, undertaken to save the human race from devastating, inner-skullar invasion.

Begrudgingly recognizing a warrior spirit within you that it wasn't prepared for, the alien tumor may try a new approach, kicking neurotransmitters into overdrive, and flooding your body with tidal waves of, say, serotonin and dopamine. For several days you just float by on a happy cloud, where you smile at old women and small children and watch morning news shows, never guessing there is anything unusual about your newly acquired, sugar-assed worldview. The tumor wants you comfortable and unsuspecting.

**DO NOT BECOME COMFORTABLE AND UNSUSPECTING.**

The evil nature of the unearthly cancer that has colonized your skull will show its true colors in time.

You might be walking in the park, or brewing a nice pot of chamomile tea one evening, when everything around you drops into an abysmal void and you are confronted by a cosmic blackness eons old, a blackness of empty space and archetypal hatred that throws you into a cyclone of existential despair almost impossible to comprehend. Beast-like screams batter your auditory cortex until you finally consider clawing your eyes out to divert the pain from the psychic to the physical. Then, the screams and blackness abruptly end.

*Fuck you very much, alien asshole. I guess I should be grateful?*

About month three, the Cthulhu tumor will have learned to speak with your mouth and vocal chords in a strange, croaking vibration that sounds a lot like the voice of William S. Burroughs. It has mastered this through artful synchronization of your motor neurons, synapses and energy pathways.

*Noog*, it will say.

*What?* you ask.

*Noog*, it will say again.

*I don't know what "noog" means*, you respond, impatiently.

*Clamp on Noog in the Wibbly Wabbly grackly-womb*, it croaks.

(The malignancy hasn't mastered English. Perhaps it's not as smart as you first believed.)

At this point, you start calling the tumor *Noog*.

Noog will insist on canned herring and buttermilk every morning, afternoon, and evening. It is more moody than a breast-feeding baby. This is because Noog craves fat, has a metabolic jonesing for it. *You* have a metabolic jonesing for it, too, as your two nervous systems have now integrated completely.

If you are lucky, driving home from the supermarket one evening after a mackerel run, you may finally notice the gaudy, dayGlo sign which reads *Madame Astrolight: Fortune Teller/Magician/Apothecary.*

A shadowy plan will begin to form in your traumatized and hijacked consciousness, prompting you to pull over and exit your vehicle as quiet as humanly possible. Noog, of course, must be sleeping for you to get away with such rebellious intent, as Noog can read the complex chemical patterns of your blood like a sanguine diary that spells your hopes and fears out plainly.

Madame Astrolight practically falls out of her seat due to the intense vibes of alien possession you throw off. She'll help you into a chair and treat you with exaggerated concern, as if you have just stumbled out of the evil woods all beat up and lobotomized at the end of a horror flick. She'll pull out her leather-bound grimoire and flip through it quickly, running her long, curved fingernail along columns of ancient typeface as she mutters otherworldly incantations which make you feel as though you are being sucked through the narrow end of a telescope.

Noog will wake up just as Madame Astrolight gets going with her mojo, making a series of quick, clicking noises with her tongue as she cries into a silver mirror that allows her to gaze through stubborn, inter-dimensional walls and metaphysical time-blocks.

*Waggly trapper Gack! Nogglang!* Noog will scream.

You will hear the tumor's panic and feel an immense surge of adrenaline and cortisol course through your body. For a moment, you may feel some sympathy for Noog as it faces its inevitable end. This is because you named it. You shouldn't have done that.

Just imagine a gruesome nest of extraterrestrial eggs about to hatch, like in the movie *Aliens*, but smaller, and inside of your brain. This will steel you. You will want to annihilate those motherfuckers.

Astrolight's holy-magic-mojo flushes the once god-like invertebrate called Noog out the base of your skull and into your body proper. You may faint, but will awaken to Madam Astrolight smacking you vigorously in your face. She'll start up an obscure app on her iPhone. She explains that it aligns tribal folk magic, pseudo-entropy, and occult purification technique into a type of handheld transporter which removes the alien body non-invasively. *Don't worry*, she assures you. *It is actually quite a pleasant surgery.*

Perhaps you will preserve your tumor in formaldehyde and seal it up in a mason jar to keep on your bookshelf, so as to never forget the crucible of your recent alien invasion.

**Someone you know, possibly your mother, could be a victim of alien colonization. Let's band together, and spread awareness of this rare, but cosmically relevant, problem.**

Abby Holtz
Founder, President, Member
Alien Tumor Foundation

# Drowning Danger is High
# When the River is Deep and Swift

Mary Tower stood outside of the Rivers Motel in a wide-brimmed gardening hat and a sensible pair of white tennis shoes, waiting for her ride to show up. She clutched her favorite pink purse close to her body, as if she expected someone to come along at any moment and snatch it away from her. Every noise from behind made her suspicious. She had never trusted California. She was only here because of family. Mary would be joining her sister and nephew this morning for a walk along the Kaweah River. Caitlin had made these plans for all of them, and she knew that she could have backed out if she had spoken up sooner, but she felt it was too late for that now.

There was heavy smoke set in the valley from a prescribed fire burning at the nearby park, and Mary brought her hand up to her mouth.as she waited for her sister. She coughed affectedly at the atmosphere, like you might for a smoker at the table next to you. The October sun ate through the cloudiness like hot forged iron. There was something violent about its light through all of the smoke. Mary Tower looked up at the star with a deep sense of foreboding. She was not at all happy about this River Walk. In fact, she had never enjoyed nature. "Despise" was not even too strong a word for how she felt about it. Almost as long as she could remember, certain images from nature had haunter her . . . and they were not pleasant images.

It had started out with one bird. When she was a young girl living in Douglas, Mary had freed her mother's plum-headed parakeet from his cage in the sun-room. She had acted as her friend Courtney had told her she needed to, on principle, because animals should not be kept in cages or even in zoos. That was what her dad had told her, Courtney assured her, and she of course believed him. Mary had liked the sound of that "on principle," because she wanted to think of herself as brazen, like the little orphan Annie, as taking no muck from anyone—and she had opened the doors wide to ease the bird's escape. Only moments after Jimson had alighted on a nearby mesquite tree, a large hawk came down at him from the sky like a piece of malicious and guided technology—as if the hawk had been told ahead of time what the girl would be doing—and the raptor had finished off the poor bird ruthlessly, right in front of Mary Tower's eyes. She remembered Jimson inexplicably calling out "peanut butter," just before his throat was torn by the predator. Mary had screamed and cried, and she beat her fists into the dirt until her pink knuckles bled, scaring the hell out of everyone. Courtney did not come to visit her so often after that.

That night her mother had explained to Mary that tropical colors cannot hide in the desert. She told her about something called a food chain. It had been her mother's way of saying, "that's just nature," which did not seem right to the young girl. She felt something much more diabolical lurked in nature—from hawks in the sky to sharks in the water.

That incident seemed to set off a chain reaction, and Mary Tower's scabs were still healing when she had been compelled to watch a nature show for her fifth-grade science class. She remembered that program perfectly. It was some special where you followed a mountain lion while it stalked a white-tailed doe. The final attack was vicious, but what had haunted the girl even more than the kill itself was the cold-blooded placidity with which, once its prey had stopped struggling, the large feline had calmly licked and cleaned that small dead Bambi, just like a mother cat cleaning her kittens. Such gentle indifference after that violent killing! Mary could not help but imagine a human corpse caught in that death kiss, and she saw her father's ashen face through Savannah grass under the resting paw of a beast so sure of its meal, its soft pink tongue licking the spectacles from off of his head. She suffered such anxiety from this fantasy that she had to visit the school nurse, with snot and tears on her once-proud face, and the children taunting her cruelly as she left the room. Mary had been excused by a concerned Mrs. Birch from writing the required 300-word summary.

And this time her mother had told her firmly, "calm down." She was letting her imagination get the best of her. She was much too old for this. And Mary understood somehow, it *was* an unacceptable way to behave. Or at least, that other children would not like her as much if she acted in this manner. The hard lessons taught by an indifferent, even malicious nature became ingrained, but she had learned to keep these fears perfectly to herself, like rare toxins in her bloodstream that she would not share.

Mary was fifty-two now, but these images were still with her. There were just too many for her to catalogue fully. Floods, Fires, Earthquakes, Meteor Storms—she feared these acts of nature the way that some fundamentalists feared a final, vengeful conflagration. Walking right beside the deadly river was not on her list of favorite vacation activities.

Now Mary Tower saw her sister's blue sedan sputtering down General's Highway. The car came to a stop, and Caitlin turned the hazard lights on. The back door opened, and Izaak, her eldest nephew, stuck his head out.

"Hey, Aunt Mary. You're in the back with us."

She got in. The car was small, and Mary Tower was not a small woman by anyone's standard. Her knees pressed hard into the front passenger seat as she arranged herself in the back. She took off her sun hat and she set it down on her lap. Then she wrestled the seatbelt across her hips.

"Well," she said, more for punctuation, now that everything was in place. She was breathing heavily from the exertion.

Caitlin began to drive away slowly. "It's so great to have you with us. Won't it be a perfect day for a walk along the river?"

"Yes," Mary Tower answered shortly. She did not wish to argue with her sister so early on.

"We never get to the park, and we live so close to a national treasure. I know it's hard to see, but . . . Rick, Mary. Mary, Rick." Her sister spoke to her through the rear view mirror. A pair of dark sunglasses dominated her petite face.

At the introduction, the man up front craned his neck and nodded shyly. He had dark eyes that were magnified by his thick spectacles, and a wiry salt-and-pepper mustache the consistency of brillo that overhung his upper lip. He gave Mary Tower the vague impression of an old cartoon character. She thought that he was an unusual choice for her sister. Caitlin's romantic history was mostly with blue-collar, arrogant types, men who got into bar fights and rode around on choppers and had skull-and-serpent tattoos drawn onto their masculine shoulders.

Once she was settled, Mary was able to turn her head to get a better look at Izaak. "When we get to the river I can get a *proper* look at you. Hmm, very handsome," she muttered, touching his soft auburn curls as if examining some expensive length of fabric for new window curtains. Mary Tower had always appreciated beauty. In Izaak's case she thought it was a genetic gift like intelligence that reflected well on her own gene pool. Her nephew had grown out of adolescence into a very handsome young man. She was happy to see it.

The young girl beside him, she supposed, was Izaak's girlfriend. He introduced her as Emma. The girl appeared to be uncertain of how to conduct herself in the situation, the same awkwardness that one has around new in-laws. She sat very quietly during the whole ride, with her hands on her lap and a faux-serene grin on her pretty face.

Caitlin finally brought the vehicle to a stop in the middle of a large chip-sealed lot approximately the size of a football field. When they left the tiny blue Corolla, it lifted from the lost weight of their five bodies like a buoy. Caitlin came around to her sister and said, "Now I can hug you." Her hair was stylishly messy and she wore a tight top and jeans that flattered her trim figure. She looked like the type of hip older woman who might give her children their first beer at sixteen.

"You are looking so thin, Mary," she said. "Aren't you seeing anyone in Tucson?"

Her sister believed that these two were somehow inexorably connected. And Mary happened to know that she was not looking thin.

"No," she told Caitlin. "And I am doing just fine on my own. I have my business, and the Book Club." She cleared her throat.

Mary Tower had never had children of her own, and her family did not understand this lack of biological expression on her part. It was a sign of illness to her mother that a woman might not wish to breed. It was too late for that now, but they still held onto the hope that they might marry her off, that spinsterhood could still be dodged like the fatal bullet.

The visitor center was throbbing with suburban weekenders clad in two-hundred-dollar hiking boots, their forty-dollar Sigg bottles reflecting the orange disc of late October sun. They were dollar-throwing tourists with a casual appreciation for nature epitomized in postcards, and as she walked through the middle of the bustle, Mary Tower thought they all seemed to merge into one massive entity, each individual an appendage, their eager camera lenses glinting like one thousand glassy eyes.

Izaak and his girlfriend were up ahead of them. The two youngsters had closed the distance to the information kiosk, excited for the river. But the adults made their way much more slowly, talking

161

about the weather, and repeating the latest Fox News sound bites on health-care rationing and swine flu.

At the kiosk, Caitlin said, "Mary, listen to this: The Kaweah River flows into Lake Kaweah, where most of its water is diverted for irrigation." She pointed to the system of flues carved into the foothills, carrying water to all the various powerhouses and fruit groves. But Caitlin's words blended into a general undifferentiated noise in Mary Tower's ears. What occupied her perception fully now was the grim, black-and-white announcement stapled crookedly to the particle board of the kiosk. There were two copies of the same announcement planted on the wooden post to the trailhead marker.

"Oh no," Mary whispered, bringing her hand up to her lips as they mouthed the print in front of her.

The only color on the advertisement—if you could even call that aberrant post by a label that was so benign—was the word CAUTION printed in alarming, blood-red capital letters. Underneath was the Spanish translation, *Cuidado*, followed by the warning, "Drowning danger is high when the river is deep and swift."

The photograph on the poster was the floating corpse of a woman, her overturned body very strong and muscular even in that grainy black and white, her arms and legs spread in a prostrate submission to some final judgment of the elements, as gone and empty now in the river as a piece of driftwood washed up after monsoon.

Who in the name of Jesus Christ would post such a thing? The words alone would surely have sufficed to get the point across, but now she had this photograph to contend with, just one more image that was to be imprinted on her brain finally and indelibly, as if through some gruesome initiation ceremony, just one more impression to keep her from sleep on the nights when her mind was moving too fast, those nights by herself when there were only horrible visions of crumbling brownstones and skyscrapers spinning in her brain, and when she saw the asphalt floors of cities undone, reclaimed at the end by camelthorn and knapweed and stalked by wild creatures.

Mary Tower stared at the announcement, her fat fingers frozen close to her lips, very still in her tracks. You would not guess that there was a warm current beneath, that there was a wild and unsteady heartbeat like broken syncopation.

Caitlin was shaking her gently, "Mary. Where are you?"

162

What broke her trance was not her sister's gentle voice but the drawn-out wail of a police cruiser from the nearby highway. The cruiser was pulling over a mini-van, and the family was hanging out of that moving vehicle with their camcorders, trying to capture video footage of a small buck. A Chihuahua in the parking lot next to Mary Tower was howling at those sirens with its scratchy vocals, reaching back to some long-dead wild instincts, and the owners of the dog were laughing and taking footage of their own, delighted. It was a carnival.

Mary shot a sideways glance at the couple with the dog. "Listen to that ridiculous animal," she said to Caitlin. Then she straightened up, checked the hat on top of her head, and said, "Well, let's do this, after all."

Mary Tower started down the river walk ahead of them. She marched steadily like a woman on a mission. Her shoulders were thrown back, her head was held very high, and her hips were switching a stout rhythm inside of her white gabardine beach pants. She was only trying to walk at a sane and steady pace. She knew that Caitlin's eyes were on her back, and that her sister would soon begin to worry. It had been like this since they were very young. Caitlin's sensitivity to her mood was extreme, and it never ceased to annoy Mary Tower that she had to watch herself so closely in her sister's company, so as not to upset her.

They matched her steps quickly, and Caitlin hooked her arm through Mary's. "It's *so* good to see you," she told her again. "And we get you for a whole week. Next time I promise to make it to Tucson." Caitlin rested her head quickly on her sister's shoulder, just as she had done when they were younger

Mary Tower knew how to recognize it. Whenever Caitlin worried for her, she tried to strike just the right chord of cheerfulness. Her sister understood that she would never talk about the things that disturbed her, but she always hoped that she might acquiesce finally, out of an inbred sense of social decency, and attempt cheerfulness herself. Well, she did not wish to be difficult. She just needed this day to be over, and to be back again in her hotel room, away from the river and the noise, and safely reading under the covers of her bed.

As they continued down the walk, everyone that they passed was talking casually and snapping photographs, and occasionally bumping into other tourists. This brought good-natured apologies all around, and then offers from each side to play cameraman for any group

163

pictures. Mary Tower thought the walk was as congested on Saturday as a clogged drain. The chaparral and oak common to the foothills were replaced by willow trees and large wind-cracked cottonwoods along the river's edge. It was not the right season for wildflowers, which must have disappointed Caitlin. The only flowers to be seen had been recently undone by the colder weather and looked like deflated faunal trumpets, their large white petals falling toward the ground like week-old lettuce.

"Rick and I are going to visit Mama in two weeks. Then we'll stay until Thanksgiving," Caitlin said. Rick smiled gently, took Caitlin's hand as they walked, corroborated quietly. Mary saw exactly what his role was. He was the gentle accommodator.

"Company will do her some good," Rick said softly. He leaned over, kissed Caitlin below the bright green leaves of a cottonwood tree.

"They finally got the last of her cancer," Caitlin said to her sister.

"Yes. Well, thank God for that."

"She still won't leave the house, Mary. The surgery left sores all over her face. She has Mrs. Litchfield picking up groceries for her from the Foodway. And even after those heal, you know there will be scarring. She is so ashamed of these things." Caitlin's voice was quivery with sympathetic pain. She had always felt the troubles of others very distinctly.

The image conjured in Mary Tower's mind by this story was a disturbing one of her mother, with surgical bandages taped up to her cheeks and to her forehead, and that red wetness of blood spreading out concentrically over the white gauze. Mary watched her mother rock herself in the living room, with all the window shades drawn, and the porch light shut off to discourage any visitors. This vision was vivid and it expressed an alienation so intense, and for a moment Mary Tower saw her own future in it.

"Oh God," she said softly. But when she said it she was no longer thinking of her mother. There were more pressing things now. She had spotted Izaak and the girl Emma. "There they are," she told Caitlin, pointing over to the far side of the river.

Izaak had his shirt off despite the brisk weather, and he was taking off his jeans as well, preparing to immerse himself into the cold water. He waved when he saw the others; then he stepped into the river quickly, only to run back onto the sand, gasping shocked breaths in and out.

"Too cold," he shouted, an inane and joyous grin on his young face. He scooped river water into his cupped hands and ran back towards Emma, heaving it at her as she ran. "Come over here, Mom, Aunt Mary," he shouted. Then Izaak crossed back to the other side of the river, hopping across a viatic group of large rocks, to show them how it was done.

"The water's low," he told them. "See the beach that we found?" He turned to his mother. "Let's eat lunch, away from everyone else. We need to do this more often," he said.

Caitlin smiled at her half-naked son. "Okay," she told him. "Let's do it."

Mary Tower looked frozen in stone by her sister's words, as if there were some witchcraft on the banks of the Kaweah River. She could not believe what she was being asked to do, and so casually. The river was dangerous, after all. This was no water park. Mary remembered the dead woman from the poster, but the woman was not pixilated black and white. Now she was burning color. Her bathing suit was bright red, but her blood was a brown sediment color where all the breakers had thrown her against the rock, and where the whirlpools had sucked her under. The woman's skin was a white the color of paste and it was loosened and waterlogged, sagging off of her destroyed bones just like boiled meat. Mary Tower felt the blood pushing at her temples and she suddenly felt very nauseous. But she would not submit to an attack here, in front of all these people, in front of her own family.

"We can't cross the river," she told Caitlin flatly. "It is too dangerous."

"The water's low," Izaak repeated. "But there's a foot-bridge a half mile up if you need it." Then he crossed back over the rocks with all the lightness and celerity of a water fowl.

"It's hardly flowing," Caitlin told her, parroting her son's insane rationale. "You guys can take the bridge and we'll wait for you." Apparently, she did not think Rick would be up to it, either, and she followed after her son, losing her balance for a moment in her excitement and letting out a quick, happy scream.

Rick's small black eyes reviewed the passage behind Caitlin with little darting movements just like a timid rodent, and Mary thought that she had at least one dependable ally for the footbridge. But when he made the decision to cross, he did not falter. He was as rigid as a beanpole, but his steps were precise. Rick high-fived with Izaak on the sand, and now Mary Tower found herself completely alone.

She could not have told anyone what it was that pushed her towards the river. She might have said that it was the last thing that she could have ever done on her own. But it was not a decision that she made—it was a kind of visceral irrationality instead which untied her, it was an anxiety that pushed her into the fire rather than away from it—it was a confusion that spun Mary Tower right in the direction of the avalanche.

The first rock that she stepped onto was smooth and flat and it was shaped like a large anvil head. Mary found no relief in this at all, in the concreteness or the easy footing on the surface of the boulder, because she only trusted the vatic certainty in her blood which told her that the single outcome of this crossing would be disaster . . . that, having stepped into the river, she had signed a contract for her own death that could not be voided. Each step she put forward seemed to have nothing at all to do with her, absolutely nothing to do with her own will or volition, and Mary stepped down onto the next rock and then the next without thinking, "I need to step here, in this manner, because this boulder is angular, or this rock is shaped like this." She could not consider that far ahead. She was trapped in the terrifying moment—a deranged Buddha clasping her pink purse in the nightmare, as isolated in the river as Gautama under the Bodhi tree.

The only certainties now were her fat pale calves below her, their disorderly purple veins crawling up to the truncated fabric of her Capris like a child's scribbled drawing, and the small white sneakers that she walked in, so absurdly disproportionate to the mass that they carried above them. Then there was the abysmal water below her rock portage, and the shadowy movement under the surface that might have been small fish, and the water-smooth granite that she stood on—these strange and clean facts of nature that were so out of place beneath the surly landscape of Mary Tower's own body. She didn't believe any of it. It was only some kind of fevered dream.

But now she heard Caitlin's voice calling her from the other side of the river, prompting her forward. It was her sister's voice that did it—her sister's voice that woke her up. Mary Tower was standing on a small, flat rock in the middle of the Kaweah River. The weight of her body pressed water from the spongy growth clinging to that limestone, and she could see that the sky above her was much darker now than

166

when she had walked with her sister, the clouds more dominant and gathering around the mountains, threatening rain. Mary did not know how long she had been standing m the river. It might have been five minutes or it might have been five days.

Her very next step put her into the water, sending great spasms of river cold swimming through Mary Tower's bloodstream. Her heart fibrillated wildly with that shock, and her tennis shoes quickly filled up with the river. Mary could feel her pants heavy and waterlogged against her clammy skin, and when she looked back at the walk now, she could see two figures staring at her from their place in the sand. The figures were dressed all in black, and their rigid bodies were straight and quiet as sentinels on that beach. In their stillness and darkness they seemed supernatural to Mary Tower, and she imagined that they were harbingers of her own death—two dead trees from the river banks that were given life only to take hers away—and with the shock of everything she thought that her heart would stop, and she began to cry. It was very quiet at first, until finally Mary was sobbing in great heaving implosions of her chest like a resuscitated patient gulping in all of the precious air.

But she was standing. Even in her delirium she could see that much. She was not being pulled downriver at all. The water moved in gentle rills around her large ham legs, and it was quiet—there was no violence of whirlpools in the water, and there were no foamy breakers crashing beside her—but still she felt the overpowering need to brace herself, so she lowered her body further into the frigid channel and she reached out for one large boulder. Now that she was immersed much deeper in the water, her bright blouse bubbled up around her just like spilled dye. She must have let her purse go when she grabbed onto the rock, but she spotted it again. It had descended just beside her, a boxy pink gem in the river silt.

When Mary Tower looked up she could see to either bank, and there were many more faces watching her now. Several people had stopped in their motoring along the walk to stare. She could no longer see that strange couple in black, and she did not like it at all that they had hidden themselves, because when they came for her at last, it was sure to be unannounced. All of the faces were still staring from the shore with the same pale sympathy that one directs at invalids, and Mary knew that she cut an absurd and boorish figure planted in the Kaweah River like some stuck buffalo. It was absolutely disgraceful. She needed

167

all of the people to go away, and to never look in her direction again. Suddenly their eyes on her were so much more terrifying than the river itself, which seemed smaller now and stripped of its power, like a kiddy pool or a calm pond. Then she understood, it was the cold and not the current that would claim her. The iciness of the river pushed through her remaining composure which she had built up so assiduously, her greatest careful construction in life, and Mary Tower wanted to scream. She wanted to pull all of her hair out and rip her hat up into shreds, but she no longer had the energy for it. She could not even make a decision to move. She could only hear her teeth chattering away in her skull like a wind-up toy. No one understood that her blood was freezing.

Then began a mild rain in the valley that upset the surface of the water around her like very small bugs landing, and Mary could see her sister standing above her now in the river. She stopped in just the right spot to shield her body from all of the downdrafts and the winds, but to allow those remaining rays of sunlight through, and Mary could smell her perfume—it was a scent that she always carried of rosewater and vanilla. Caitlin's voice was coaxing her. She was reassuring her in a very calm voice, like you might use on a child, making sure that there was no alarm in her tone, even though the situation was in all probability very alarming. Caitlin pulled her up onto her feet and she helped to steady her shivering figure, hugging her body with one dry wool sweater, and Mary thought that her sister looked so much brighter than anything else on the landscape. There was a glowing nimbus like a soft cloud that reassured her. It was a lightness that convinced her, Caitlin was here for her protection, and Mary Tower allowed herself for the first time in her adult life to be led. As she stumbled through the river and back to the shore, Mary understood that her sister was saving her. That she would have stayed in that icy water until everyone left and the stars came out and the river was dark and quiet.

# Who Will Save You from Hell?

I wake up to the scent of cocoa butter mixed with carbolic. I am not sure how long I have been here—five hours or five weeks. My grandmother and my great aunt Lucille are leaning over me with their hands clasped and their eyes closed, and they are praying the first day of Novena. Their devout heads come together above me like the apex of a holy pyramid, and smooth, flaccid skin hangs from off their necks like pouches of discarded satin.

Right now I can feel my heart pulsing through my cheek cavity with a lazy dull throb.

Out of my peripheral vision I can see the empty folding chair and a sun-faded handbag with leather tassels that cannot be mistaken. An opened pack of Merit cigarettes sticks out of the top. The purse invokes instant and sharp nostalgia. It is a cancerous reproduction of old photographs that hits me in the gut. I have not seen mom for three years.

This should be quite a reunion.

I try not to give myself away with any obvious movements from my bed. The last thing that I want right now is a series of forced and awkward exchanges with my devotional relatives above me. But I do not want to return to my dream, either.

In the dream I was walking down a narrow riverbed that was cut into a pale, green valley. The valley was very flat and continuous for as long as the eye could see—it looked like a plane of still, green water—except for one juniper snag on the horizon and then this perfect river channel that wiggled through it with symmetrical crests and troughs like the negative of a sound wave that was carved into the landscape. When I rounded a bend in the river, I saw my mother and brother resting in the silt ahead of me. But when I approached them, they bore into me with penetrating and accusing looks, like archetypal figures out of some unknown mythology. I felt afraid that, if I came any closer, they would become violent towards me in some way.

But here in my hospital bed, I can hear my grandmother's soft voice implore Saint Joseph over the beeping of monitors and the electrical hum of hospital equipment. It is like undertow, dragging me, and I let myself return to the river.

* * *

My grandmother and Lucille are gone when I wake up, but they have left index cards for me with explicit directions on how to complete the remaining eight days of Novena . . . and balloons and flowers, a turquoise-colored plastic rosary, and a sincere hope for God's grace.

I managed to stay unconscious the whole time they were here.

Mom is here with me. The skin around her eyes is raw and stretched thin like play putty from crying. Her dyed red hair is pulled back into a short ponytail with the dark roots exposed underneath, and I can see the prints from her sale-bin lipstick on two little plastic apple juice containers that are sitting on the bed stand.

Mom compulsively handles an unlit cigarette, and she keeps looking around, trying to find something on the walls that she can focus on, but the walls are only white curtains. She is past the yelling and accusing and seems unsure of her role now.

I suspect that Lester Brown, MD, PHD, has talked to mom about the yelling. He is the liaison psychiatrist assigned to my case. He has told her something like, I am in a fragile state and need compassion. I am glad that the yelling is over, but I imagine my mother is more in need of a liaison psychiatrist right now than I am. It's just that, when you make such a final and irrevocable decision, and then you fuck it up beyond all recognition, it takes everything out of you, including the ability to be angry, or even sad about it. The only thing that I can feel about life right now is dull annoyance like a mild toothache.

Mom needs to fill the quiet, so she updates me on our family members in Detroit, how many children so and so has, and how so and so is going to such and such college. She tells me how my cousin Nicky has been given mandatory drug rehabilitation; it is somewhat of a scandal, but she stops herself mid-story when she realizes how much worse her own son is. She talks about the harshness of the Michigan winter, how it has come too early this year, and how last week's ice storm left her and Phil and my brother without electricity for eight hours, and how scary that was, with Tobey's medical equipment. She laughs self-consciously, and she says that after this winter, she isn't sure that global warming is really such a bad thing.

Every comment that mom makes, she looks over at me to gauge my reaction. We don't keep eye contact for very long, but every time her eyes catch mine, she has the confused look of an animal caught in a trap, and I want to kill myself all over again.

When Dr. Tubak comes in, mom brings her hand up and combs her bangs away from her face. She rubs the dark crescents of old mascara from under her eyes with a tissue she is holding.

"How are we doing this morning?" Dr. Tubak asks me, closing the curtain behind him. He places a large, bony hand on my shoulder. Dr. Tubak is only slightly smaller than Andre the Giant, and the truncated sleeves of his white lab coat accentuate a pair of massive, rheumatoid wrists. It is hard to imagine those large hands performing delicate surgery on my face.

"I'm okay," I tell him. "Alive, anyway."

"How is the breathing?"

"Strange," I say, because it is a very unsettling sensation to have a ventilator breath for you. It breathes in and I breathe out. It will take some getting used to.

"But not *strained,*" Dr. Tubak checks.

"No, not strained."

"Good. Let's see. His eyes scan printouts and diagnostics. "I will give you a quick explanation of what we have done, and what we will be doing, and I will answer any questions that either of you may have." Then he looks expertly back and forth from mom to me.

Dr. Tubak's language is a Latin nightmare. He uses words like *maxilofacial* and *nasogastric,* and phrases like *zygomatic bone dejects.* Mom keeps interrupting for clarification. So Dr. Tubak apologizes, rephrases, expands, explains. Then mom nods, repeats back to him, understands. The surgical and post-operative aspects of my condition are things that she can wrap her head around. It seems to console her.

What it boils down to is, they performed the tracheotomy first because of severe irritation in my throat and airway caused by the aspiration of large amounts of blood coming from the floor of my mouth and my tongue. After the airway was secured, they cleaned my mouth of blood, disconnected tissue, bone fragments and uprooted teeth; and they used direct pressure to stabilize the bleeding areas. They set tubes into my nasal passages, which will be used to feed me until I can swallow again on my own.

171

On the cosmetic end, a surgical team performed skin grafts to reconstruct my skin and muscle, and stabilized what Dr. Tubak refers to as the "large bone defects" using small plates. He says that the actual bone grafting will take place during a second surgery four days from today.

(As Dr. Tubak talks, I am drooling onto a paper bib that is pinned to my paper gown. When mom notices, she wipes my mouth with her shirtsleeve, like I am an infant again. Dr Tubak looks over and he tells me that the *leakage of saliva* is due to a *lower lip inconsistency*. What he means is, I am a drooling retard with a fucked up lip. He says that he will see what can be done about that during the next surgery.)

After a functional assessment of my lower jaw and palate, Dr. Tubak tells me that a third surgery might be performed if it is deemed necessary; then it will be close to twenty days total before they remove all the hardware for my tracheotomy, and I will breathing again on my own. It will be the same amount of time before I will be swallowing and eating solid food. This is me summarizing, but according to Dr. Tubak I should be out of the hospital, and back on my feet, in just over three weeks.

I look at mom, and I think I am not sure that it is the worst alternative.

\* \* \*

I meet with Lester Brown, MD, PHD, for one hour on every Tuesday, Wednesday, and Friday. Today is our third visit. His most defining characteristic so far is that his personal color preferences are those of a teenaged female.

Today, he is wearing his hot pink dress shirt. The last time that I saw him it was a kind of pale, Easter-egg purple.

Dr. Brown becomes excited every time he interviews me. He tells me, "It is okay to let loose, Paul. It is okay to scream. It is okay to cry. It is okay to speak in tongues and shout 'Lucifer' if you want to." He waves a small notebook that he is holding in the air for emphasis.

I tell Dr. Brown I'm not sure that is the best course of action. But mainly, what I try to get across is, I do not care to scream. I do not care to cry. I am a fly on the bleached curtains. I am here, but I just don't give a fuck enough to scream or to cry.

Lester Brown prods me. "You are just not looking at it, Paul," he tells me. "Of course you care." He insists that the problem is that I care *too* much.

But what Dr. Brown doesn't know, and what I suspect, is that I have tripped some automatic function that filters passion because this body and mind will not risk extinction a second time. I think that maybe this is my punishment. From now on, I will watch romantic comedies and laugh at bad jokes. From now on, I will wear button-up dress shirts of a pale, Easter-egg purple.

Dr. Brown sets a composition notebook and a package of black number 2 pencils down in my lap. "The key to healing is narration," he tells me. "We need to *narrate*. We need to reflect in an organized fashion, we have to convert our experience into *stories*, Paul. We must supply our own meaning like a footnote, because it is *not* inherent in events."

Dr. Brown reaches over and flips through the empty pages. "Fill the whole book if you need to," he tells me. "Fill it with whatever is on the tip of your brain. We can use your writing as a springboard for our sessions." When he sits back in his chair and stretches, I can see two small circles of sweat at his flamingo armpits.

"I am a fly on the bleached curtains," he says, and winks at me.

With the blank pages in front of me, what I think about is that last night. There is a heaviness in my brain when it angles in that direction. I want to sort it out. After the first sentence, everything else comes quickly:

The small details are still here like a song that I hate that is stuck in my head. Like how Pete Pitkin told me in his droll monotone and his broken sentences like a village idiot, "Dorito truck's not coming. Broke down. Toilets backed up. Tills ready."

When the Audi pulled up there was an older woman driving. Her hair was short and it was sprayed to hold the style, and she was wearing these long, pearl earrings that would swing back and forth when she moved her head. But it was her husband who came inside, it was her husband who got his cash from the ATM machine and went to the drink cooler in the back, it was her husband who was taking his time, trying to decide. He was meticulous. I think that he must have read every label that was on every drink.

And finally the woman started to lay into the horn, but it was more than that, really. She started screaming with it, it was this long extended scream, she was putting all of her weight into it.

And I know that she could see me looking at her from behind the counter. I was stoned completely still, like some kind of dumb monument, by the violence of her reaction. It seemed desperate. It seemed to point to darker things. She kept going and her face was purple and twisted with ugliness at waiting. I remember her pearl earrings seemed to swing back and forth with the momentum of her rage.

And when the man came to the counter finally, he had decided on a bottle of vitamin water. He counted out the exact change to the penny. Everything about him was exact, from the cut of his suit to the way he laid his change down on the counter, piece by piece. He seemed calm and he did not look up at me, and the whole time there was still the steady blaring of the horn outside like a siren. I did not tell him to have a nice night.

I just thought that the noise was somehow the woman's soul, and the little piece of her soul that was left after all of the shit was screaming at itself.

It acted as some kind of catalyst. It was what set everything else in motion, like when a brilliant red flower provokes a set of memories and associations in some art-house film. But this was not nearly as nice as a red flower. I saw everything under the ugly fluorescent neon light. . . .

Dr. Brown looks over. He can see that I have filled several pages and he says, "Good. Very good, Paul. He assures me that I have started down the road to psychic well-being.

I know that what Dr. Brown means is—if I am lucky—I have started down the road that leads to something simple, to something easy, to something that I can take.

I have to admit, that wouldn't be so bad at all.

\* \* \*

After the bone-grafting operation, mom has to return to Michigan. She has been here for over a week. She has to get back to work, and she has to get back to my brother, who requires a lot of care. She talked to Phil last night and he seemed agitated and overwhelmed.

Right now, Mom is listening to Billy Sinkowitz gushing something about Ave Maria in Florida, and also something about Pope Benedict. I am not listening. I am looking at Billy's face, which is purple with acne under the fluorescent light. His eyes are close together, and his tight, slanted lips are only a shade lighter than his prune-colored face. He is holding a pamphlet that asks in heavy blocked ink, "WHO WILL SAVE YOU FROM HELL?" The answer is somewhere inside.

Before Billy, it was Sarah from the United Methodist Ministries. She offered me a cold wheat bagel as she ate her own, and as she guzzled down her Red Bull. I watched as she swallowed the contents of a little plastic bag of supplements in one heroic mouthful. She segued from her meal into her testimony with, "God wants us healthy; he wants us to take our vitamins." She wore a pink sweat suit and seemed to be in a hurry. She threw her hair into a ponytail, and she spoke quickly about salvation.

Sarah and Billy are only a few that I have talked to. Evangelism is big here. I think the angle is, the sick and invalid are more receptive to God. There is a basic formula that they all use, and I already have it down. It begins with a disappointing confession, something like, "I used to get drunk every weekend, and I didn't realize how much this affected the people I loved, and I wasn't even twenty-one." This is usually followed by an eye-opening event of hitting bottom, which is the point when they become aware of the need for Jesus in their life. This is followed by some kind of immediate return, like "I used to be scared of dying, but not after I accepted Christ into my life." Their narrative is always wrapped up with, "Do you feel like you have come to know Christ yet, Paul, or are you still on the way?" A trick question.

But I am not so easy. They are going to have to do better than that. I will take fire and brimstone, I will take Jerry Falwell, over their half-hearted testimony like a boring fuck. It makes me wish for a steadier trigger finger.

Earlier today, when I first came to after my second operation, I looked into a mirror for the first time. I used mom's little Clarion compact. She sat there, watching me, her hand to her lips. She knew how bad it was.

When I looked into that little round mirror, I saw some kind of half-formed fetal monstrosity out of a David Cronenburg film. What I saw was a big mess of seeping bandages and bleeding tissue. Then I looked at the spaced holes in my earlobes where my double-gauges used to be. I looked at my green hair, which used to be a proud Mohawk, but was unwashed and falling down now and somehow reminiscent of a deflated tire. I had to laugh. I thought, "I will never wear earrings again. I will shave my head, because it is a farce to decorate anything as ugly as this face." Then I had a quick fantasy of living the monastic life. I saw myself wearing some earthy, Franciscan robe and meditating and listening to little sparrows sing in an abbey courtyard.

But no, I reconsider, if I have to live, I damn well better be having sex. But who am I kidding? No one will fuck me with this face. I have to be honest with myself here. Sex is likely over for me.

I still have mom's compact sitting in my lap. I close it and say, "No girl will ever have me again." I am not complaining. I am just stating fact.

Mom is quiet for a minute but then she tells me, "Women are understanding, Paul, and can accept almost anything."

I hand the compact back but she says to me, "Keep it." It is an awkward gesture. The last thing that I want is to look at my face some more, but I know she is leaving and wants to give me something, so I don't say anything.

Mom says, "When you get out, you can come stay with us in Detroit. At least until you get back on your feet." Then she seems to choke something back and says, "*Goddamn* you." I guess she reconsiders because then she says deliberately, almost sternly, "Well, I love you, Paul." Now mom is looking at the curtains again, and she fingers a tiny crucifix that hangs around her neck. If she blinks, she will cry.

I tell mom that I am sorry, and I am. There is nothing more to say. I watch her fumble with the curtains on her way out, and she half-rolls an ankle from stepping funny.

\* \* \*

The days at Good Shepherd are long and full of nothing. The nothing is interrupted by calls from home, by nurses feeding me antibiotics, by lukewarm sponge baths, by pallid, unrealistic sexual fantasies starring the female staff and the Mormon missionary girl Lisey, by meetings with Lester Brown and the ACE's. (ACE is my own acronym and stands for Ambulance Chasing Evangelists.)

To get back to that night, I know that it must have been thick in that car. I watched them drive away, and I thought about when I lived in Michigan, how I asked a girl I was with where she saw herself in five years. We were lying in bed, the window wet with fog, and it was just before dawn when the black outside turns gray. This girl was ready. She told me, "head of HR at Aventis Bio Services." She asked me the question back, and what I told her was, "walking on water." I was aiming for something higher. Now, five years later,

I had to call my own bluff. The woman had been screaming for her soul, and I had to call it.

I came in here every night at eight, and I left nine hours later. I wondered about God sometimes. I had been with countless girls, and I had never loved one of them. I paid my taxes on time, and I worried about shitting in public restrooms. I had my green hair and my Indian ink tattoos like some

It wasn't enlightenment. It was something else. It was something much worse. I stumbled into the bathroom and vomited into the dirty toilet.

An old man came into the store somewhere near mid-shift. He was wearing starched pink golf shirt and a leather fedora that fell too low on his small head. I remember, his white go watch caught the light like a mirror and threw it back onto the wall in a small circle. He smelled like cologne mixed with leather preservative. I can still see the way that his pressed clothes fit his diminutive body. They hung too loose on him, like a potato sack.

All that I could think was, he was asinine, his sunken figure dolled up like that. He was a cymbal monkey wearing a band suit. I thought about how we all were. They filed in for their Ho Ho's and potato chips and malt liquor, and I felt the veins on my forehead standing out. I imagined them blue and ugly.

When I smoked my cigarette outside, my hand was shaking like palsy, and I looked back in at the chip displays and the blow-up Budweiser long neck that was the size of a child's inflated punching bag. I knew that I couldn't go back in. So I locked the front door and I just sat there in my car.

I watched as people walked up to the store. I watched them pull on the handle a few times. Then I watched them crane their necks to look inside.

A few of them saw me sitting there in my red vest and my nametag in my piece of crap. It must have been obvious that I worked there.

They said, *Hey man,* and I just shrugged my shoulders like there was nothing that I could do about it. I shrugged my shoulders like I was locked out, too. In my mind I saw a flash of gun steel at a pale temple, and an anonymous finger half squeezing a trigger, and it was gone just as quickly. I have always had these quick, violent fantasies.

But *that night* I went back to it. *That night,* I let my mind rest there. *That night,* I saw it as a possibility.

A young nurse comes into my room with a small Dixie cup that is filled one quarter with multi-colored pills. When I set my pencil down to take them, she asks me how I am feeling this afternoon. I tell her that I am feeling just fine, and I am.

It feels good to write. It feels good to try to make some kind of sense out of things, to look at the pain from a distance like someone else's car wreck. The young nurse smiles at me before she leaves and that feels good too, even though I know that it is not personal, and that she is only smiling at me because she is expected to.

I read back over my pages and I am fascinated.

Somehow, I know that the person I will become will be someone much different. He will have to be. It is a matter of self-preservation. I can see it on paper. I just looked at things too deep and ugly, and I couldn't take myself.

I would like to become like the quiet old veteran with the live bait stand near the docks on the Upper Peninsula. There is something honorable about the way he nods his head at you but does not speak. There is something honorable about the slight smile that is always resting on his lips. It hints at some existential secret.

I keep writing:

There was a voice at my car window, and I didn't look up at first. I just heard, *Hey man, I got a cigarette for you. This is for all those times you got me. I told you I'd get you back. It's Jamal, man.* I looked up at his face finally and it seemed familiar, but his eyes looked startled like a rodent's, and he kept looking back over his shoulder.

He said, *Let me get a ride up on Van Buren and Seventh; I can get you some gas money, man.*

So I took the crushed Doral, his shitty little offering. I can remember how it was sitting in the palm of his hand like a broken insect. I said, *Sure, Jamal.* And I was thinking, why the hell not. I was thinking that I would just ride the night out.

And then he was in the car and we were driving and I had the dial to KJZZ. They were playing classical. It was Beethoven, it was *Moonlight Sonata.* I was afraid that I couldn't drive. I was afraid I would have to pull over. The music was too much that night, the way that it suggested a stillness and peace and then it showed you, that was impossible.

But the quiet parts of the sonata were drowned out by the high idle of my engine, and it was broken by Jamal telling me, *Hey man, give me fifty cents.* He was drumming his fingers on the dashboard, finding a beat in the classical, a beat in Beethoven, and he kept scamming me for quarters every five minutes. I felt like my molecules were coming unglued and dispersing into black space. I

178

had to explain it to Dr. Brown, it was a feeling of *dissolution,* doctor. Not *disillusion.* I just drove Jamal around all night, with Beethoven, dissolving.

We drove through these open, dark areas in Phoenix with only a few warehouses and dusted, tired homes. We might have been in the country somewhere except for the concrete that covered everything like a hard membrane and the well-laid grid of Phoenix streets. The houses we went into had dark living rooms, and dark serious men who would talk low to Jamal in the corner. I was sized up with silent, yellow eyes.

I remember there were handguns resting on coffee tables among half-eaten sandwiches and unopened mail. But I didn't have the balls to grab one and just take care of it.

The moon was almost full. I sat on an uneven porch with peeling gray paint somewhere in Phoenix. I stared across the driveway at a malnourished horse chewing dry cheat grass. The horse was on this little fenced-in square of brown land under a large moon on the edge of Phoenix sprawl, and when he was done eating, he sniffed at a green glass bottle that had been tossed over.

I just thought that it did not make sense for him to be here. I thought he was as much of an anomaly here as I was. Then Jamal was done with me, and I was still alive.

I drove home. I didn't need to think about it. I walked out to the shed where my roommate kept his 22 long rifle, the one he used for deer season in Coconino with his folks. I took it off its rack and I just stared at it. It seemed straightforward. I wetted my fingertip and wiped a streak of dust from the barrel. I rested my chin on it experimentally.

I look up at the ceiling to search for words. I need to convey that it wasn't desperate. If I was an artist, then maybe I could paint why I did it. It would be this dark, seductive thing with a lot of empty space but as heavy as gravity tide.

My chin fit there perfectly, and the metal was warm and natal when I had expected it to be cold. When I flicked the barrel of the rifle with my fingertip, it seemed to resonate like a tuning fork. Everything felt right. . . .

* * *

I have been talking to mom most nights in Detroit. She seems to do better over the telephone. I think it's that she does not have to look at me. She does not have to see my damaged face like a train wreck.

Tonight when I called, mom asked me if I was coming home to Michigan. I know that what she wanted to know was, if I was coming back to Michigan *to stay.* I told her that I still hadn't decided yet.

But I know that Uncle Pete has a job for me if I want it: degreasing engines and running for parts. That should help.

Going back to Michigan has always been some kind of final failure in my mind, like maybe I couldn't make it on my own. But I know I am not in a place where it makes sense to think like that anymore. There are certain points you can't fall past.

I look out at my roommates. I look out at lethargic heart rates snaking their repetitive patterns across monitors. There is the low volume murmur of daytime television and the smell of antiseptic. The retirement home vibe of the room is thick. I feel cancelled here.

In only four more days, I am out of Good Shepherd. I don't have much of an idea what comes next.

I nod and I try to smile at Dolores with my eyes, and she smiles back at me in her sweet, old woman way. I can see every time she smiles how she feels sorry for me. Dolores is recovering from hip surgery. It is Paul Davis in the other bed. He was admitted to Good Shepherd for angioplasty. If he was awake right now I would say, "Hey, Paul," and Paul would say, "Well hello, *Paul,*" and then he would wink at the coincidence that we share the same name plus the same hospital room. He is snoring now with a book opened on his chest.

I am watching the clock. She is five minutes late already, which is unusual for Lisey. Suddenly I am scared that she will not show up at all. But she finally walks in, and when she does I almost lose it in my hospital gown. Lisey is wearing an outfit that I have never seen before. It is made out of some kind of silky material that clings to her slim, iris body and the color is a deep, sky blue. She appears outstanding among the insipid white walls of the recovery room, like she is sculpted out of some different element, something that glows in the dark. I have never seen her in anything other than blue jeans and a plain blouse.

I imagine for a second that she has made herself up for my benefit.

Lisey says hello to Dolores and to the other Paul, now and propped up on his elbows. He is grunting something to Dolores about being a political conservative but a social liberal, and how he believes in things like charity and community. Lisey tells them that they are both looking good—she means to say *very healthy*—and then she moves away. She is here for me.

When she makes it to my bed, Lisey does not give me an inspired retelling of Nephite extinction. She does not start out with biblical wisdom from Moroni. We are past that. Instead, she picks up the C++ text that mom sent, and she flips through the pages.

"Paul, how can you read this stuff for fun?" I can tell by the way that she asks and then keeps looking that Lisey is impressed.

I tell her, "There is nothing ambiguous about it. I like it because it is formulaic. I like it because it all fits together perfectly."

"Well, what on the earth were you doing at Circle K?" she asks me. I guess in Lisey's mind, understanding a programming language and working retail are somehow incompatible.

I tell her, "If you really want to learn something about humanity, just work graveyard shift at some shitty little convenience store in Phoenix." But I know that it was not as lofty as that, as learning something about humanity. There is no good point in building it up to be more than it was.

"You can learn something about humanity at temple, too," she teases me. "You can see how *good* people are." What I think of are eighteen-year-old boys in suits, riding their single-geared bicycles to chapel when all decent people their age are hung over in bed. But I don't argue.

Lisey looks so delicate in her outfit, just like a china doll. It is an ugly male thing to see something like that and immediately want to violate it.

She says, "Let's go down to the cafeteria and celebrate. I'll buy." She points at my throat. They have removed my trach, they have sealed everything up, and for the first time since I was admitted to Good Shepherd I am breathing again on my own.

Lisey tells me, "I'll clear it with your nurse first."

I let Lisey lead. She knows her way around Good Shepherd better than I do. We make several right turns and then a left tum down long, green hallways with track lighting. We walk down a small set of stairs, and past a little window with a serious looking black woman behind it who scowls at us through the glass, and a sign that warns us, "No Children or Specimens Allowed on Counter."

I experimentally brush my hand across Lisey's waist when we ride down in the large elevator. I am just lightly touching her shirt—the blue material is smooth and cool as water—but I know that Lisey can feel the heat of my fingers. She does not move away; she smiles just slightly at the corner of her lips, and I start to think that maybe mom was right. That maybe women *can* accept almost anything.

I know it is these little distractions and the small rituals we play that will help keep me moving. They make it seem like something is happening, that maybe there is a point. I feel all right.

The elevator stops in the shaft, and the two of us step out onto the speckled orange linoleum. A worker in a pink apron there counts down her till after we pay, and three interns eat stir-fry sitting at the table beside us. Then it is just me and Lisey. I spoon tepid soup into my mouth, and Lisey asks me, have I talked to my brother recently? She is always asking me about Tobey. I think she believes that Tobey's handicap and my suicide attempt can be woven into some kind of poignant religious parable.

I laugh and say, "You think that Tobey is the key to something, don't you?"

"No," she says, "No, I don't; I'm just interested." She touches my wrist lightly with her fingertips and then draws them away. "I can tell that you really care about him, Paul. That's all."

I like the way that Lisey always says my name in sentences, and I like the way her eyes narrow in concentration every time I speak. I like the way she makes small noises with her mouth when it is quiet. They are little smacking sounds and small sighs. Suddenly, it becomes overwhelming.

I know it is unfeasible, but I reach across the table, and I grab Linsey's hand. I slide my fingers into hers, steeple style.

She looks everywhere but at my face. The seconds seem drawn out. She says, "I don't mind, as long as you know. . . ."

"Okay," I interrupt. I won't make her finish.

We are alone and it is very quiet and I am still holding Lisey's hand. The interns are gone now. It is just a young girl with pink barrettes wiping down the tables. I want to fill the quiet. I look out through the window at a crowded parking lot. I think about how a lot of people are dying.

I say out loud, "I drove myself here. I walked in on my own two feet with a dishtowel taped to the side of my face, blood-soaked gauze shoved up each nostril, and more gauze wrapped around my head like Jacob Marley on Christmas Eve, to keep my mouth and jaw from falling open. I was swallowing my own blood. I kept tasting charcoal."

Now Lisey is paying attention. Now she is looking at my wrecked face. A long strand of hair falls forward, and it clings to the moisture on her plum lips. I can feel a quick, stabbing desperation, like the shipwrecked when I stare at her, and I want to ingest Lisey, to possess her somehow, to have her for myself. But she is sitting there unattainable like the Holy Grail. It is maddening.

I look at her and I think, "Not this time around." This time, I will have to find different things to hold me up. This time, I will have to find other things that can make it breathable.

When Lisey finally pulls her fingers out from mine, she is scared of overwhelming me, like she knows that a faster separation would be somehow vulgar.

Over her shoulder, framed by the window and the sky, I can see the sun-baked red cliffs in the distance, and I know that I will be going home to Michigan. I will be going home to family outings and Sunday Mass and meatloaf dinners. Mom will want me to check in on most nights. That will be okay for a while. Me and Tobey can listen to the new Clutch album on his computer, and I'll help uncle Pete around the shop. I'll put money away when I can.

What it is, I will have to learn to crawl, and then I can learn to walk, and finally, I will burn the crutches. In five years I might not be walking on water, but maybe I will be able to see a point in time when I might be.

# Red Wolf

The Shaman held a mirror for Katsumi as they stood inside the bamboo chapel. It was the first time she had gazed into her own wolf eyes—they were fierce, visceral, yellow lights. Katsumi inherited the wolf gene from her mother's family, but the gene had lain dormant in her blood, triggered just that night by the shaman's potion. She watched as the red wolf took over, and her hair became thick, rough, and coarsened. She watched as her body was overcome by a red pelt, and encrusted with salt and dirt. She ran her pink tongue across bone-crushing sterling white fangs, then bolted into the streets beneath a lunatic moon.

Katsumi felt her body come alive in the brisk air. She lost her mind. It was invigorating. All ideas fled. The night flooded in. The night was movement. She saw each juniper, each sparrow hawk, each blade of grass, each of those spidery, crystalline filaments, inter-weaving into a canvas of purple night like delicate clasping fingers. Katsumi's own filaments reached out and joined them in perfect, pre-datory cohesion. She felt her canine heart pumping, arterial streams which warmed her hindquarters as she pushed off over the rim and into the wild.

Katsumi moved agilely through the thick vegetation, guided by her heightened wolf sensibilities. She threaded the underbrush with spontaneous grace. It was a night of great good fortune, because she came upon an unguarded nest of whole snake eggs, which she ravaged joyfully before continuing through the forest, her face dripping with delirious, nutritive yoke.

When she came to the end of the woods, Katsumi found herself on the far side of town. Residents still walked the charcoal streets. The humans were different from the other creatures. She saw that their fields did not connect to one another. They traveled solitary, magnetic fortresses. Most impressively, Katsumi saw the incendiary halos which surrounded their skulls like blazing furnaces. It was only here that their filaments reached out, and their mind-fingers scorched the night, like blowtorches.

Katsumi saw an old woman sitting on the bench of the quiet plaza. She wore a conical rice-farmer's hat. Her skin was as thin as paper, and her opaque eyes were dulled by pain. Katsumi sat in front of the woman, who only stared at the ground, her eyes never meeting Katsumi's gaze. This was wrong, Katsumi knew. She whimpered and trotted away, but came back again and again, over and over in a kind of restless, vital agitation. But the woman couldn't see. She was occluded by some inner torment.

If she could have spoken then, Katsumi would have yelled, "Look! Look at me! I am the Red Wolf, and the world is a brilliant night!"

# Everything Is More Beautiful Here

Kathy Warren stared out at the avenues from the passenger seat of the Buick sedan. A sickening vibration had tormented her body for the past week, as heavy and constant as a limb. She accepted the anxiety, simply, as a new expression of her genes. Her husband did not appear to notice. He whistled the Andy Griffith theme song as they turned down Gomez Street.

Kathy saw the coyote again. Their headlights grazed its ocher eyes. The beast weaved in and out through tufts of rabbit brush. It trotted beside their vehicle, through the pebbled lawns, keeping pace and escorting like a loyal dog. Then the creature darted towards the Gonzales house, and Kathy lost sight of it in the chemise.

The Gonzales boy, José, was washing dishes at his sink, framed by lit glass.

Kathy Warren hated him, fully and mechanically. She knew what he had done to her son. What they had done together.

They pulled into the driveway, and Kathy stared at José while the car idled.

She said, "He took the bike, Rick, I'm sure of it."

"I don't know," he said. "Well, we can't prove it, Kathy."

Almost a year ago someone had stolen the bike from their Sangre ski-cabin. The thief had smashed through the glass panel of their door with a bottle of children's cough medicine, leaving behind a tread print in their mudroom the color of green apples.

"And he never goes to class," she said. "I've seen him at the café on the plaza, smoking cigarettes and reading D.H. Lawrence."

"Well, it doesn't sound like he would have much use for a bike, then. He isn't very physical, is he?"

"He would sell it, Rick," Kathy said.

They walked the flagstones.

A large Hunter's Moon dominated the horizon. The highlands beyond the asphalt conducted their strident score of birth and predation. Kathy had never, and would never, love that land. She loved the well-laid streets of their subdivision. She loved the perfect, terracotta houses. But in twenty years, she had never felt one ounce of love for the fatal desert, and did not understand those who called it beautiful.

Something raked the dry grass beside her, and Kathy jumped back with a scream and launched her handbag. Her attack sent a small rodent scurrying beneath the portico.

"It's nothing," Rick said. "A prairie dog."

He was surprised at her outburst but left it alone. Kathy did not like him to ask after her condition. She considered it fawning.

"It's so dry here," Kathy said. "You can hear everything. It's ridiculous." Then she straightened her blouse, retrieved the handbag and climbed the front porch.

When she finally fell asleep that night, Kathy Warren dreamed she was being crushed beneath a gigantic mill-wheel.

* * *

She woke up late morning. The sun had passed her casement hours ago, and the bedroom was dark. The harsh red digits of her alarm clock blinked at her. Kathy lay in bed listening to the empty house.

She flipped on the bathroom light, while talk radio played. The mirror reflected her ruined image back at her—the powder-blue walls of the room were riven by it. She had aged. It was mostly her eyes. They looked small and starved, and she was shocked by them, the way you are sometimes shocked by a friend who removes her glasses—you did not expect their expression to look so violent, or innocent, or dull.

Kathy combed her dark hair. It was cut short in an executive style with one hard jet of gray. Her skin was olive-toned and her lips a watercolor shade of hibiscus. Clients trusted her instinctively. She imagined it was because she radiated a tough, yet feminine strength.

"Things are fine," she assured her reflection.

On her way down the stairs she stopped at the landing, disrupted by the memory that, as children, José and Atticus had been bitten by the same dog. Her head was split by the image of the rabid canine. Was that the reason? But no, it was too impractical. She was still running on dream logic, she told herself. She just needed her coffee. She did not understand that these convulsions of late were her mind's attempts to stabilize a deep contradiction within her, and that caffeine would never fix it.

187

She measured six scoops of grounds and poured water into the top of the machine. An opened box of applejacks rested on the counter. It was her daughter Anne-Marie's breakfast of choice. Kathy put the box away and peeled slick bits of arugula off the formica while her coffee percolated and steamed.

The arugula was Atticus. Her son had eaten salad for breakfast every morning for as long as she could remember. He once explained to her that the human body was a delicate machine and should be run on high octane. They had been standing in the kitchen when he said it, and to prove his point, he set his forearms on the counter top and raised his muscled legs parallel to the ground, then easily up past the crown of his head.

The human body was his main, creative interest, and Atticus inhabited it with the intention of an artist. He seemed to be constantly aligning with invisible forces, allowing his weight to fall into his feet, pivoting always on the ball-bearing of his center, falling easily into balance with the gravity and dimensions of whatever space he moved through. He flowed like water. And he was beautiful. Kathy noticed how all eyes followed him filled with light. It had been a source of great pride for her. But he had ruined it. Shamefully.

She remembered the day she had discovered the truth about him. A fine rain had been falling from the tinted October sky. She was back to grab her planner, and caught sight of him in an upstairs bedroom of the Gonzales house. He gazed out, bare-chested and tousle-haired, at the coal-colored mountains to the north. José was behind him. He rested his chin on her son's naked shoulder and kissed his neck gently. If they had looked down, they would have seen her frozen there.

Kathy had hurried away like a thief. She sat down on her couch and inexplicably removed all her jewelry as her heart jackhammered. She rummaged through her purse searching for her phone to call him, but what would she say? She could not think. Her thoughts had devolved into a weather pattern of reaching and cross-hatched association. His delicate manner of talking. His lack of girlfriends. All the time spent with José. As a child Atticus had danced with pink flowers in his hair. At four, he cried inconsolably when she slaughtered the June Bug. Sensitive boy. . . .

The violent sound of air brakes outside had woken her, and Kathy rose from the couch and stumbled next door like a concussion victim. She was certain that she had been separated from her son in a final and irrevocable way, and the realization aroused in her sudden, titanic anger. She smacked at the oak panel of the door with her open palm and kneed the lock rail, injuring herself. She was maddened, disoriented, on the verge of something, she did not know what. Of course, no one had answered her clamoring.

Since that day, Kathy had not seen her son during the daylight hours. When she went down to the basement (for meat from the chest-freezer, or to gather laundry from the dryer) she half-expected to find him in a dark corner, as though he were some new breed of vampire who could no longer coexist with the sun. She had never confronted Atticus, or outlined her requirements. And she had not told Rick of her discovery. Her mother, dead now fifteen years, would have used the word ineffectual to describe her handling of the situation. It was only because she could not see a way through that would definitely end in her favor.

The shame of it ate at her.

Kathy drank the strong coffee and agonized.

When the doorbell rang it was May Demming. She stood on the porch in her prune-colored corduroys and a baggy white sweat shirt. The shirt had an airbrushed pastel of a wolf and a sunset.

"I'm early," May said. "I know." She held a stack of clipped articles in one shy hand, and a plastic grocery bag in the other.

"Early."

"Yes. For our lunch date. "

"Yes," Kathy said, "Come in, May."

It was not that she had forgotten the meeting. Instead she thought it was likely, when they made the plans, that May would not keep them. May Deming was a recluse by most standards. She had news and groceries delivered to her place on Gomez street. She often worked in her herb garden, rarely leaving her plot of ground.

May sat down in the dining room and Kathy brought in a thermos of coffee and two porcelain mugs. She sat beside May at the table, but then felt a certain resistance to speech, as though her ability to make small conversation had atrophied. It seemed that it required too much effort.

May untied the grocery bag and spread the top, revealing airy clusters of light green leaves. It's lemon balm," she said. "You can use it as a garnish, like mint. It's native to Southern Europe.

189

May grabbed the stack of articles from the table beside her and shuffled through them lovingly, like they were archives of great importance. She had brought them for Kathy. On top was a glossy photograph of a coiled rattle snake. The photo was surrounded by the microscopic print of a technical journal.

Kathy could not imagine why May thought she would be interested in such things. It showed a certain disconnect to the pulse of others.

"I have an idea," Kathy said, taking the papers from her, "Let's have lunch on the plaza instead, at Diego's. And I'll look at these tonight, if you leave them."

"Snakes," May said, "can see your body heat, Kathy. Actually see it as if you are a map laid out for them."

"Tell me about it," Kathy said, "over warm food. It is good for you to get out, May. The world is not so scary."

The woman nodded. Her translucent face shone with the fatigued innocence of a sick child. And like a child, she trusted Kathy Warren beyond reason. It was because Kathy had helped her after the long summer of fires and floods.

For the life of her, Kathy Warren had not seen this relationship coming. It was almost a month ago that she first knocked on May's door. She had been walking home from church, and a single blue flower caught her eye, curving up towards the sky from the oaken window planter. The flower was stunning and intense—its petals the clean, drenched blue of a mountain lake. Kathy had knocked to pay May her compliment, and to ask about the exotic plant.

There was no answer. The front door was open, though, so she had walked inside, calling her name. Something fine and sharp in the air had sent her immediately into a coughing fit.

The whole place was humid, and patches of soft-white fungus clung to a flood damaged rug. Two mollusks resided in the damp corner, fat and nourished on the scum.

Kathy had gasped as though struck from behind, paralytic in her Sunday clothes. It was unfathomable to her that these conditions existed on their clean and quiet street. She felt indignant, and something started to grow inside of her. Something like a sense of justice. So she had organized the neighborhood and they had pulled the carpet up, they pumped the crawlspace, they did a million small things and made the house livable once again, and Kathy Warren was respected in their community for spearheading this charity. She was known by all to be a woman of grit and volition. A woman who acted, who set things right.

So even as her mind fractured, Kathy marshaled her energy to maintain this reputation of strength. She was committed to May Demming. Kathy said, "We will beat the crowds, and get the best table." Her authority over the woman reassured her. She felt the fog in her mind burning off.

\* \* \*

They drove the tortuous streets towards downtown. May stared out the window, tongue-tied by the pulsing activity as they drove the main artery.

They parked at Diego's, and May asked, "Has Atticus decided on a school yet? I'm sure he is scholarship material. He gets his brains from his mother, of course." She smiled.

"Atticus is a junior, May. He still has one year left."

"I'm sorry," she said. "I knew that. This is somewhat nerve-racking for me."

At the mention of her son, Kathy Warren became locked into a delicate, frozen terror. She felt that she was made of glass, and that any sudden movement might shatter her silicate heart. His name—Atticus—the word *Atticus* set firmly in her mind, eliminating all reason and sense. She could not get away from it. It launched her tired body into an unchecked red-zone. It was the same sickening vibration of seeing him in the window. She thought she might throw up. She walked automatically in the direction of the restaurant. She commanded herself: Stay together.

Two bearded vultures circled the parking lot. It seemed to Kathy they were zeroing in on her from above.

The two women climbed the stairs, and the young host led them to a table of distressed wood and handed over the calfskin menu. It was illuminated with black buffalo and tiny, brick-red labyrinths.

The walls of the restaurant were sea-green, riven by murals of large white peacocks. Kathy remembered thinking the design very chic on her previous visits. Now the pattern was strange and offensive, and the garish white birds overwhelmed her senses.

May ran her finger over the raised ink of the menu and said, "Oh, this is lovely. This is too much, Kathy."

"Nonsense," Kathy said. "You have to treat yourself." She was swooning, yet managed to sit up fully in the rustic chair. She clucked her tongue and scanned the room, relieved to find no familiar faces. She caught a grossly transfigured glimpse of herself in one mirrored-wall, her face drained and bloodless, her small eyes scared back into her skull like some caricature.

May unfolded the plied napkin and lay it down on her lap. She beamed as though she were the guest of royalty. It was a strange reversal, Kathy thought, that she should feel so crippled, as May lightly hummed her tune.

And it seemed her neighbor had emerged from her hermitage with a tidal flood of speech. As they ate, May thanked Kathy for saving her, and spoke of her dream the previous night, in which the two of them flew over vast dark oceans, diving with white birds beneath the oiled waves. She told her—Kathy was not certain she had heard this right—that she had woken on her couch just the other morning to find the image of Jesus Christ burned onto her plasma TV screen. "It was unmistakable," she said. "It was Him. This was significant," May insisted; "don't you agree with that?"

To all this, Kathy Warren nodded and interjected at the correct points, with a tone of mild condescension which maintained the hierarchy between them. The interaction was skillful, considering Kathy was in fact feverish and very weak. Too weak, almost, to handle her ice water. It seemed that her once-powerful limbs had deossified beneath her skin, and that she was now some soft-boned creature, meant for the dark ocean bottom.

They finished lunch and walked together towards the center of town and the central shops. The sun beat down on Kathy audaciously. She felt exposed by the light, and filled with terror by her son.

\* \* \*

Nadine Parker stood just ahead of the women near the entrance to the office park, working her weekends, Kathy realized, as usual. She was the top broker at R. R. Hart, and Kathy the second, which roiled her blood. She watched Nadine set her attaché case down on the bench and spring the gold buckles, then begin searching through her documents self-importantly. Her coworker was predatory and intelligent. Kathy knew that Nadine would smell her hidden shame, like a dog sniffing cancer, and revel in it.

Kathy quickly turned onto the footpath before the woman could spot her. The path was sheltered with the bright yellow litter of cottonwoods and aspens. It followed a wash that ran strong from the recent rains.

"Water," May clapped. "Oh, how beautiful." As though she had forgotten that such things flowed.

"We should do this more often," she went on. "Every Tuesday."

Kathy resented the pluck in May's voice. Kathy watched May wander down to the water, then kneel beside a cottonwood tree and dip her hand into the frigid shoal. The roots of the cottonwood overhung the muddy bank like large wooden knees.

That was when Kathy spotted it.

A coyote watched the women from the opposite shore. It held a small, mangled finch in its jaws. Kathy watched with horror as the bird thrashed one useless wing. The canine's casual posture as it shook its meal communicated both impish disregard and superiority. It was her coyote, yet now the sunlight revealed huge swaths of inflamed mange covering its body like scabrous continents. The canine pranced across the water and trotted down the chip-seal, glancing back at Kathy with a muzzle full of squawking feathers.

Kathy whispered, "Wait here, May. I have one quick errand." She spoke hypnotically. She was being lured by the beast despite her revulsion.

She followed it down the path where, at pavement's end, the coyote darted away through a bosque. Kathy lost sight of it in the mesquite, and found herself alone beside the cemetery gate. The small pitched roof of the entrance and the ponderous cross were familiar. The creature had delivered her here.

Kathy grabbed the iron bars of the gate and stared through to a sea of grass and headstones.

Her son lounged with his lover at the opposite end of the yard. They sat beneath a thick-trunked elm tree. Even from such a distance, she recognized his flaxen hair, the feline attitude of his body, the salmon-colored sweatshirt which he wore much too often.

She was aware of her role as voyeur and this thrilled Kathy, and also had the effect of calming her, so that she was able to watch the young men from a quiet psychological space. She felt still for the first time that day, and awaited her revelation.

The boy José rose and walked to a stone outbuilding where he filled his jug with water from the spigot. When he was back, he dug into his pack and retrieved a loaf of bread, which he passed to Atticus, and the boys ate their bread and drank their water under the canopy like two pilgrims.

When José stood again, he held a large book open in his hands. He paced the ground in front of Atticus, and his voice soared with fiery verse. He might have been ministering to the interred souls, or mocking them with his raucous health. Atticus listened with an ear turned to his companion, and when José was finished, he leapt from his spot and held his arms wide open to the sky, then howled a yelping war-cry at the sun the moon and the stars above him. José joined in, intoxicated—and Kathy watched in stunned fascination as they barked their primitive sun-salutations to a cathedral of sky. She felt a flame of tenderness burning within her as she watched the ritual, although its heat was dulled by ice and the fuel decadent and impoverished. Still, the warmth was there, and it burned as she watched her son's vital movements, watched his golden hair blazing like a sunburst. He shone with the exacting brilliance of cut quartz. She could not remember a time in her life when she had ever felt so young, or inspired. She did not know how long it was that she watched them.

The young men made their way out finally, pausing as they went to read the heavy stones, and to marvel at the sea-green copper of the saint's statue. She lost sight of them in a stand of trees.

When they were gone, Kathy felt thoroughly exhausted. She rested against the gate and looked at her watch. It was only one-thirty. How was the day still so young?

When May found her, she lay asleep in the dirt below a giant wooden cross.

\* \* \*

Kathy added lemon to the preparation of glaze as Barbara Streisand played through a single speaker on the cabinet radio. It was Rick's birthday, and it was important to her that things should go perfectly for her husband. Their family had not dined together in some time.

In the two weeks since the cemetery, Kathy had returned to work and had resumed her duties as head of the Warren household. She paid the bills, enforced curfews, kept up with housework, and got on, more or less, normally. But the shadowy presence of a monstrous shame haunted her body—it hid out in a slim cavity, nestled between a jigsaw of organs, ready to blossom at the slightest touch like oil in a gulf. She had been holding her breath for two weeks.

When she was through preparing the meal, Kathy brought the serving dishes into the dining room and arranged them on the sideboard. She sat and watched the clock impatiently. Rick relaxed at the opposite end of the table with the paper and his Earl Grey. He set his article down, sensing this was appropriate.

The long table left a chasm between the couple. The time was past when they had anything of interest to say to one another. It was the horror in domesticity. They awaited the children.

Kathy attempted to conjure a feeling of warmth. She smiled and told Rick, "Well, everything is set."

"It looks perfect," he said. "It smells unbelievable."

Kathy surveyed her spread. She had set the table with the company dishes. The plates were painted with dark red birds in the style of a woodcut, and the tablecloth she chose was deep red, matching the birds. The hibiscus-colored walls of the room, she imagined, gave its inhabitants a sensation of wine.

A large portrait of her mother hung from one wall. Kathy revered the woman beyond reason. More in death, even, than in life. The widow had raised Kathy alone.

The Victorian proportions of the giant frame dominated the room, and her mother's dark hair was pulled back tightly from an angular face toughened by weather. Her hard eyes watched the dining area with an expression both grounded and righteous. Her severity gave the photograph historical presence, as if it had been culled from some frontier archive, and restored to color by the magic of modern technology.

Anne-Marie tromped down the stairs loudly in her combat boots and slunk into her chair. It was exactly seven, so she had arrived on time, if resentfully.

"Happy Birthday," Anne-Marie said to her father. "Where's Atticus? He has to be here for this."

The girl had dark, literal eyes which resembled her mother's, only Anne-Marie's were sharper, and clinical. The cable-knit sweater she wore matched her coal black hair.

Atticus breezed in through the front, as if in answer to his sister. The boy was covered in red dirt. It shaded the hollows of his eyes. It darkened the folds of his skin. It dusted his clothes, and was caked thickly under his nails.

"Perfect," Anne-Marie laughed.

"I'll wash up," Atticus shouted. "Back in two." He took the stairs in bounds.

Before he returned he had cleaned himself over the sink and quickly changed his shirt. The new threads were Indian blue with two solid, yellow lines at the center. Kathy thought the symbol looked familiar.

Atticus held a rough stone in his hand. "I found this in an arroyo," he said. He tapped the rind against the table. The stone clacked hollowly. "There's quartz inside. Don't worry, dad. It's not your main present."

"And now that we are all here, we can start." Kathy stood and went to the sideboard and started to chain dishes clockwise around the long table.

There was the scraping of silverware, and the clearing of throats as they ate. A bird's eye view of the room would show four bodies, placed equally around one central table, with the portrait of the deceased matriarch lording over the setting, and the whole scene wooden if not for one glowing young man. And Atticus understood his role in these situations—it was to break the pack ice. It was to warm the blood of the others and to share his oxygen.

"Las Conchas is different now," he said. "It looks like the moon. Even the rocks are charred."

"Well, I hope you were careful," Kathy said.

"I won't mention the slab I was scaling, then. And trees falling left and right. I'm alive, though."

Kathy watched the tendons of his neck hammer smoothly as he chewed. The fabric of his shirt clung thinly to the curves of his back like a second skin. He was beautiful. Perfect. She didn't understand how it could be  . . .

Kathy sensed the cliff's edge, and turned back.

Atticus spoke to Anne-Marie. "I broke my egg, Anne. Day one."

"And how should I interpret that absurd statement?" she asked.

"Our psych assignment? Caring for an egg like it's our kid, supposed to teach us to be parents? "

"Boil it," she said. "Harder to break."

"And now it's smithereens?" Rick asked him.

"It was José's idea to take it. Said it would make the climb interesting. Now we have one egg left between us. That little guy is so precious."

"Why don't we just talk about something else, other than eggs," Kathy blurted. The idea of her son and José caring for an egg together like their doll-child was too much. She drained her wine.

"Okay . . . " Atticus said.

"Family values are a sham, anyway," Anne-Marie intoned. "The family unit promotes tribalism and factions. It's all, take care of your own and exclude others." She looked hard at her mother. "Of course, the Warrens fail there too, fail even as a tribe. We're hobble-footed and crippled."

"Hey, let's calm down, everyone," Rick suggested.

"You talk like a book," Kathy fired. "A ridiculous book. No one even knows what any of that means."

"No one? You mean you don't know . . . . "

"It's almost time for dessert," Rick said. "Who's ready for cake?" He raised his hand.

Kathy turned to Atticus. He was the one who always kept her from sinking. "Now, what is that on your shirt?" she asked him, civilly. "Is it some kind of ancient Chinese symbol?"

"Not exactly," he told her. "It stands for marriage equality."

And in one protracted moment, Kathy Warren felt her resolve leave completely. It was a sensation of tumblers unlocking, and it was also a great relief, as though she had decided, finally, to stop swimming upstream and to let the tide take her, even though it could break her against the rocks.

"Marriage equality," Anne-Marie hissed. "That symbol is every-where. You don't have your finger on the pulse of anything, do you? Besides property values."

Kathy sat quietly in her seat and trembled like a leaf.

"Anne-Marie, the ice-cream is in the chest-freezer," Rick said. "Go get it."

"That's in the basement."

"Go get it," he said, more pointedly. "Take your time."

"That's just Anne-Marie," Rick told his wife once the girl had left. Kathy didn't speak. Her eyes were locked on the portrait.

Atticus went to her. He laid his hand gently over Kathy's. When he did, she relaxed her grip on her fork, which she had been clutching unconsciously as if a weapon.

"Mom, you're purple. I want you to say something to me so I know you're breathing."

"I'm breathing," she whispered.

"I want you to drink this." He slid his water over.

"No," she said, "this is what I need." She lifted her wine by the stem and drained it, then refilled it to a rich, red globe.

Just then, the portrait of her mother began to breathe.

Kathy's own breathing fell into step with the respirations; both chests rose and fell evenly. Kathy was certain that in order for the transformations to continue, she needed to keep these developments to herself.

"I understand it's just Anne-Marie," she lied. "Thank you," she added, sipping the water, "I'm feeling much better now." Her voice roared in her skull like an ocean.

Then Anne-Marie was back, and there was cake, and Rick opened his gifts, while the portrait gained dimension. The gray hairs strayed from the widow's temples like live wires. Her skin took on a nutritive luster. Her clean eyes surveyed the dinner party with the moral certainty of a woman who knew exactly where she stood on her grandson's issue. Everything else was distant.

"It's my first published story. 'Death and Ice.' I signed it for you."

"That's wonderful, hon. I love it."

"It's a skinny tie, dad. It's a much better look for you. Trust me."

Kathy watched the surface of the portrait pulse in a kind of wave-like algorithm. It wavered with the sensitive modulations of nerve endings. She was not alarmed, though. She felt silvery and smooth. She was possessed of a supernatural sangfroid, borrowed from her mother.

The widow's lips parted and she moved her imaged hand, but when her limb broke through the glass it became a web-like organ at once organic and mineral, casting a net of soft living vessels sheathed in fine exoskeleton. The whole room was overtaken by the feather-light anatomy, and it had the effect of hushing the scene. The widow's voice was transubstantiated to blood and protein. She spoke with her daughter genetically, delivering an age-old and undeniable message— love was between a man and a woman. Anything else was dangerous, an unnatural perversion.

And Kathy knew this to be correct. Her shame dissolved. The salt it left behind was pure righteousness.

She turned to Atticus. She spoke her words clearly, so as not to be misunderstood. "You are not welcome in this house any longer. You *queer*," she added.

Her eyes fastened on her son's in a silent locking of horns.

Anne-Marie stood from her seat suddenly, rattling the table.

"Now hold on, what the hell is this, Kathy?" Rick demanded.

Atticus searched for some sign of softness in the woman's hard eyes. He found none. His mother could not hear an echo of love over the din of hard values. Her mold had, in fact, been cast long ago.

There was nothing to say to it. He was driven out. Atticus looked quickly at his father. It was an admission of guilt, and the father buckled to see his son so shamed. Atticus stumbled towards the front door of the house and he walked into the night.

Kathy looked to her husband, "I have the evidence to support my claims. Your son and José are lovers. Atticus is no longer welcome in this home. Not one more day."

"That's not your decision, Kathy," Rick said. He scrutinized her with brutal condescension, as though he had woken to find her subhuman. "I'm bringing him back tonight. If he can stand it." He left the table, followed by his daughter. Kathy heard the front door slam after them.

When they were gone she sat alone at the dinner table, staring at the festive crumpled paper, and at the small plates of melting ice cream. The portrait was quiet now. The widow had done her work. Kathy Warren felt made of stone.

\* \* \*

She did not know how long it was that she sat in the empty house. When Kathy finally stood up, she walked outdoors. Checked the mailbox. Swept the porch and shook out the mat. Atticus' running shoes sat off to the side, caked with drying mud, and Kathy slammed the soles together and put them away inside. Then she put on her parka, grabbed a fresh bottle of Bordeaux, and left

She drifted through the familiar neighborhood streets and made her turns thoughtlessly. Right on Cactus. Left on Dome. Right on Canyon. A parcel of birds flew in strict formation above her, and an albino squirrel skittered past her numb feet, its ghostly coat matched by the fat, white moon on the horizon. Kathy followed the footpath through Church Park and stopped to rest on the weathered bench. Her chest felt molded from broken concrete, and her head jackhammered, sending sharp, cold pain shooting through her skull.

Had her husband found Atticus, she wondered? Were they back at the house, right this moment, preparing for bed? Had her authority been completely overruled? Kathy started to piece the night together in her mind. The memories were dream images, changing shape and refusing to come into focus.

Kathy went for her bottle of Bordeaux, but brought up an empty hand. When she tried again, it was the same bizarre outcome. Each time she commanded her body, it responded with the mirror image. This confused her, yet she felt no strong emotion toward it, as it was somehow in keeping with the rest of her evening.

It is amazing, she thought, the endurance required to live.

She watched a young woman angling through the park with her canine. The mutt jerked the girl along as it probed each ash tree. Kathy thought of calling out to the stranger, but at the last moment lost her nerve, and the pair plodded by silently with a jaunty rattle of dog tags.

She felt that if she stood from the bench and attempted to walk, she would likely find herself in the dirt, as she no longer had good reason to trust her body. It was apparent by now that it was not her servant. Her body was her brutal master. She was, quite simply, stuck, and Kathy considered for the first time that she might be in real danger.

She tried the wine again. This time her hand obeyed, although it had been transfigured into something monstrous. Volcanic, ridge-like tendons snaked down her arms towards the tips of her fingers. Both hands were claw-like and reptilian, hooking into rigid half-fists. Kathy dropped the wine bottle, and it shattered at her feet. Her head hammered wildly. The pain was excruciating.

A voice told her, "We have a serious problem."

It said, "This is a stroke."

It told her, "You need to call Rick."

She had experienced transient attacks before. This was much worse.

Kathy reached into her pocket and by some miracle retrieved her phone. The light from the screen burned her retinas like wildfire, and it took incredible concentration to remember her husband's number, and all of her ambition to press the keys in the proper order.

Then something shut off. It was clean—like a circuit breaking—and in an instant Kathy Warren was gone from the world of Church Park, and the world of her phone, and the world of calling Rick. She was still conscious: in the way that an unfurling leaf is conscious of the sun. She no longer had the faculty to organize, to plan, or make sense of things. There was no telling where her body ended, or where the cracked timbers of her seat picked up. She dissolved and vibrated in accord with some universal electricity.

It was fantastic.

Then the circuit reopened, and she found herself back at the small wooden bench, clutching a phone in her hand.

The numbers on her screen had changed to irrational hieroglyphs. She did not remember where she had left off dialing. She reset the screen, and through some conditioned knowledge, managed to push the first three numbers in the proper order.

A diesel engine gunned on the road parallel, throwing out a jet of black exhaust. When Kathy looked up, she saw the pack of wild, ocher eyes staring out at her from the chemise. A pair of eyes rose towards the sky, as if a beast was climbing to a standing position. As its shadow came towards her, Kathy felt the same shift coming on; it was heralded by a vibrating of molecules, a dense tingling at her fingertips. She kept her finger resting on the last number, so that when and if she returned, she would know where she had left off dialing. It wasn't much, but it was the only plan she had.

The space that she went to was one of connectivity. Thought and concept and memory did not exist in any conventional sense. There was a certain order to everything which she felt essentially—certain distilled patterns in the thrilling textures of the early winter evening. The wind howled through the park formulated by light. It parted the darkness like a biblical sea, and the mass of the moonlit air settled on her warmly like cotton, and the trilling of the insects was wintery-toned. Forty-three years of emotional baggage seemed to steam from her skin in a palpable, warm fog.

Everything is more beautiful here.

She thought that, and also thought of her son. Rather, she conjured him through some faculty more subtle than thought. She felt him as a tremor of contracting muscles, as an electrical storm bulleting down her spine that projected outward to the tips of her fingers and toes. She felt him as a molten arrow through her heart.

She saw Atticus as a child, chevrons of war paint decorating his cheeks as he ran through the tortuous streets of the old neighborhood after the monsoons passed, collecting frogs in his small, cupped hands. He thought that the frogs had rained down from the sky.

She also saw him as the young man that he was now, eating bread in the graveyard under the shadow of saints, saluting the burning sun boldly as his oldest and most divine friend. The good flame within Kathy burned and grew. As it expanded, her whole body was swallowed in blue ambiance.

Kathy understood everything, but could fix nothing.

When Kathy came back to the matchstick world of park, of bench, of phone, of her plan, it was no longer good enough. It seemed much too thin. She needed to get up. She needed to make it home. She needed to start her vehicle, and would not rest until she had found her son. It was all that mattered.

Kathy moved from the bench. Her body would not listen and she found herself in the dirt, with her limbs jerking rudely. Her phone had fallen just out of reach.

She stared at the device as though she could will it into her hands. As she did, Kathy thought, "I need to call Atticus and let him know I am leaving the porch light on. I will remind him the key is still under the mat."

# A Brand New Saint

Dear Mother,

    I hope this letter will not cause you anxiety or suffering. I know that if father gets to it first, these pages will end up as thin paper streamers in the office shredder and never find their way to you at all. Please let me know, by responding, that you have received them. My commissary is empty again, but that is how I prefer it now. Do not make any more deposits on my behalf. You should understand that I no longer have any material requirements. I am past that. What I am aiming for is simple. I wish to show you what I have become. I am not at all certain it will make you proud.

    I need to tell you that I miss you deeply, Mother. I have built up an image of you during my years at Wanatchee, resting hours on each detail, like the straight beeline of your lips which you always held closed so tightly over your teeth, the shape of your eyes like small ash leaves, the sleepy half-moons of your lids, the white scar on your chin in the shape of a lightning strike, with your stern body below like the rod conducting it. Because I built it myself, piece by piece, this image is much more special to me than any truer memory or photograph.

    I talk with you and father each day of my imprisonment. In your absence from me I must address you both as ghosts. Your ghosts watch over me in this place from an absolute perspective as from an afterlife, and from that absolute perspective you both understand without judgment and I am not vile to you.

    The guards here worry that I might find some way to off myself, so they have given me half dull pencils for writing this, and they keep an eye on me through a closed circuit television system. My image is broadcast to a remote viewing room where they can watch the live feed. The viewing room is stacked up from floor to ceiling with salvaged video monitors. There are cracks in the convex screens that fragment my pale image into jagged halves, and an electron hum of static electricity that stands the CO's neck hairs on end. They will watch me in shifts—all night long and into tomorrow—until I am through writing this.

Sometimes, I imagine the prison officials let you in, Mother, to show you by those screens that I am still alive . . . that secretly, you check up on me here. But that is beside the point.

The inmates of my wing are not allowed any interaction. We are the demons and the murderers. We are allowed out of our boxes for one hour each week, and for the remaining time they keep us sealed off in our hermetic cells like pinned butterflies, or the beasts of some exotic collector.

What I have instead of fellowship is four walls and a concrete floor. A wire cage like a catcher's mask on the ceiling protects a naked bulb that glows like a white-hot ember. There is a soundproofed door. There is sink and a toilet and a showerhead. There is a small, metal grated drain situated beside one thin squatter's mattress, and a camera angled down from the ceiling like an unflinching eye. Half-frozen meals in small tin boxes are shoved through the chuckhole at meal times. I wait for their noisy delivery three times a day when the food carrier slams into my cell like dynamite, the racket quickly absorbed by the silence of this place.

When I first came here I realized, this must be the clean and quiet architecture of Hell. I realized that Hell was this scrubbed box without distraction. Of course I was sent here with the other damned souls. There was nothing to wrap my thoughts around, Mother. There was absolutely nothing to fix them on. My mind became a jigsaw of words and images as illogical as any dream. You cannot understand the magnitude of that ugliness or what it did to me. I sought out forms of physical pain as a type of buoy. The pain became the one thing that kept me grounded.

Near the beginning I broke my fists into the walls until I could no longer close them. I broke them until they became purple, swollen mittens. I remember holding them out in front of me in the silence, trying to calculate some kind of significance. They seemed like two horrible trophies, destroyed completely like that.

When my cell door opened that night, five men stood behind it. The man at the front of the gang switched off his small Motorola radio. He had a thick-boned face with a Neanderthal skull and deep-set eyes that burned green like just out of the fire. When he holstered the radio, he looked at the red walls and then at my destroyed fists and he told me, "We could have saved you all that trouble."

I suspected the guard would be vicious, Mother, but he watched with his hands held together in a steeple formation as the others beat me down. Before I went unconscious, he bent over me and crooned, "When you act up here, you have to take The Treatment." His voice purred with arousal, and I understood that it made sense for the men in charge to hire such demons to police us. The other COs called him Lieutenant Swain.

You learn to sleep in a sitting position when you have broken ribs. Some fractures heal in strange patterns of raised bone like thick mineral sutures. I no longer think anything of my own body, Mother. There is no power in it now. I move around this small cell to the shower and to the head and then back to my mattress like a corpse that has just broke through the soil. When I leave my cell for that single hour each week it is in a wheelchair with "Property of DOC" stenciled in slanted white letters on the back of it.

I am not complaining, Mother, or looking for sympathy from you. I just want you to know, despite my physical condition, it is not over for me here. I am making my mark, like I always told you I would. I understand now that I had to come to this gimp state before I could envision something so much greater.

Well over a year ago now I began to immerse myself in the spiritual texts of humanity. What resonated with me most of all were the narratives of Shamanism. The Native American Shamans were artists and priests not imprisoned by the constructs of ordinary perception as most of us are. Of course I felt immediately connected to that lineage. I read about the ritual of Vision Quest, where the supplicants deprive their mind of all stimulation, and deprive their body of all sustenance. Once they prove themselves to be intent and worthy through their denials and meditations, then the divine comes through and fills that newly opened space. The divine comes through to transform and sustain and evolve those who prove devoted. I think you will be convinced by the end of this letter. I will make it clear to you.

The Great Spirit reaches you incarnate. It can come as a caribou, an antelope, a feral hunting dog in the amplitudes of an outside wilderness. Of course I understood that some creativity would be needed to reach me here in Wenatchee, through all of the thick concrete and the razor wire. Still, I never doubted, Mother, from that moment forward. Not even for one second.

205

In fact, if I had not known better, this cell might have been designed with the purpose of Vision Quest in mind. It was not a cage to me any longer but a monk's solitary. There are just certain points where everything aligns. This was looking up from the Money section of the Sunday paper and realizing that I was surrounded by snow-tipped mountains and cerulean lakes. This box came alive then. It was hued and electric and young. It was coiled with energy. Even my body, when I looked down at it, seemed to glow with a soft white radiance, somehow stronger. All of this, and I had not even started on my Vision Quest yet. That power was sprung by my decision alone.

Swain's jurisdiction seemed so much smaller after that. I knew that he could never keep me from this. I wanted messianic awareness through Vision Quest, and I was certain that I would have it as a true acquisition even in this lockdown.

The fast is step one of Vision Quest. The point of the fast is body purification.

I learned from my studies that if you wish to approach the divine—or what the Lipan Indians call Great Spirit—it has to be with the clean-blooded physiology of a gazelle or a forest creature. The fast is there to carve you down into something that is basic. It is there to whittle you down into something that is elemental and pure. But that transformation is not easy, Mother.

The hunger was brutal. It was a killing pain that radiated from my center in large and vicious waves. The hunger pain was so great I believed I was dying. Then after several days into my fast, the pain calmed, and it was a drugged dizziness swimming in my bloodstream that ran my thoughts together into blurred sequences, like the theta trance you hit right before falling into sleep. I would wake up in a sweat every morning, pulling out of dreams with sweet, sugary fruits and pints of cold buttermilk. I would wake up with phantom tastes in my mouth of thick, warm breads and rich custards.

That is only describing the first stage. If I was a poet, I know that I could communicate it better. (But like you, Mother, although a fan of poetry, I have always been so analytic and literal.)

Only nine days into my fast, those hunger pains disappeared for me altogether. The dizziness that I initially felt turned into a physical lightness of being, so that I never seemed to fully touch the ground below me. With that rebirth, every riveted stick of furniture in this cage became fantastic. Every hard edge was just one small piece in a brilliant aesthetic. I was an astronaut in zero gravity, looking down at a perfect and geometric earth.

There was also a sharp-edged lucidity, Mother, at a level I had never experienced before. That lucidity, like looking at every object in its blueprint, was seeing all of the dimensions and geometry there, and knowing that somewhere in that math was meaning and essence waiting to be uncovered—a riddle planted by God for me to find.

Of course, I cannot lie to you. That purification left a mark on me that you would find distasteful. I became anemic and slat-ribbed, and my belly was distended like a refugee's. But I understood that I would never break, no matter how desiccated. My body and soul were an indestructible alloy, and I could cull the very air for nutrients.

Wanatchee is a brutal environment. Other inmates here study law books and compose long, handwritten letters to the state. They shout about the eighth amendment, and they point at arthritis and diabetes. They point at heart disease and hallucination. They point at any chronic condition as evidence of cruel punishment, and they angle hard for their way out. I do not blame them. I know I am different to not care about these things. It is important to realize, Mother, that the world is full of political types angling for loopholes, but there are too few prophets. I have always known that I was meant for something extraordinary.

Every week I left this cell with a pair of COs for that sacred hour of "free-time." I heard lazy dialogues above me of baseball and pussy and wives as they wheeled me through the empty corridors, my diminutive form hunched over and perfectly still in my wheelchair, without spit mask or padded helmet or cuffs or chains, since I had long ago been crushed into submission. They would smack me on the shoulder and tell me I was alright. They'd tell me that soon I would have radio privileges. They said they could get me right with Lieutenant Swain. My role changed over into the three-legged pet once I was a gimp.

The recreation area where they left me each week was enormous. It was high-ceilinged, with an oblong pit at the center like a drained swimming pool. I sat alone for my sixty minutes in that vast warehouse right at the bull's-eye and took deep breaths in the larger air. I watched the dust settling in the window light and listened to the distant sound of vehicles on the state route outside, and on lucky days I could even smell rain. I felt revitalized by that thin life spilling its way in through the cracks and filling the vacuum. I know that it does not sound like much to you, but to me it was leaving the closet. The warehouse was my wide world and my Sinai vista, and I felt I could think in even greater terms there.

Every single night before lights out, I would kneel down naked in my box, my knees bruised by the concrete below me, and run my fingers along my slatted rib cage. I would stare at the distorted flesh reflected in the steel toilet. By my reflection, I looked like a dying supplicant who was begging for the miracle of bread. Then an angry voice would come over the speaker, and I would have to put my clothes back on. One leg and then the other. One arm and then the other. Losing my balance and then regaining it. Watching my skin disappear under cloth.

There are simple forms of deception in the prison universe that echo back to childhood and adolescence. There are simple forms of deception that echo back to tricking the parents. I just sat on my mattress at mealtimes, and shoveled forkfuls of nothing into my salivating mouth, then mashed the contents of my meal box as well as I could into a type of pig swill for flushing. Three times a day I poured the gruel into the head right before box collection, when I knew that the COs were making their rounds.

It wasn't until the forty-third day of my fast that I woke up to five of them standing in my cage. Lieutenant Swain was at the front of the pack. The other guards cornered me and tied me down to my mattress using restraints that tore into my flesh, and they fed me opaque liquid nourishment from a skinny IV stand that was wheeled in. The feeding itself was handled efficiently by a dark-skinned technician wearing a bleached lab coat. He had on orthopedic shoes that were wet with white polish, and his face had a purple sheen to it under the light of my box that was iridescent, like insect wings. First he touched me gently on the shoulder as if to reassure me in that nightmare. Then he stuck the needle in. The solution sent long spasms of river cold winding throughout my entire bloodstream.

Lieutenant Swain stood over me the whole time. He bit off the tips of his short nails as he watched us, and he spat them like husks onto the ground. Then he stuck two fingers into the back of his mouth, and he picked old dinner from out of his cavities, and he chewed on the loosened cud while he watched us.

He breathed, "Every day for the next two weeks."

The straps were unnecessary, Mother. I was no more of a threat than a Ken Doll lying there. But the terror that I felt was more fantastic

208

than anything that I had ever experienced. Imagine a devout pilgrim in the Gobi or Kalahari Desert who is subjected to such a surrealistic feeding. Then you might understand me. Imagine a pilgrim searching for divinity and purity in the desert solitude, but then the demon Swain emerges from a sand trap and spits his dirty fingernails at you. My heartbeat became arrhythmic. I couldn't breathe properly. I believed I was dying.

But I came back to consciousness finally—a broken heap on top of the starched bed sheets—with dark bruises all along my wrecked body where the guards had ratcheted me down. There was no memory at first, only the certainty that something brutal had just taken place. That a stampede had just passed through. I could still feel the dust settling.

Everything in my cell was dead again. Everything had returned to ordinary matter: hard and bromidic and gray. I felt certain that Swain had somehow pulled this switch on me. I crawled over to the toilet and I vomited up a whitish fluid. I could feel the thin crescents of his discarded nails digging into my cheek when I lay on the ground afterwards. I might have stayed in that spot for eternity, Mother. There was no ambition to even move. But one sound brought me back to my purpose here.

My heart began beating so much faster, and I could hear it clearly. There was a buzzing in my cage—a background vibration like electricity that would be so easy to ignore in any world with movement or noise. But that buzzing was dominant in this stone quiet. I had never heard anything so beautiful, Mother. To me it was the sound of life in a dead-zone.

I rolled over onto my back, and when I looked up at the ceiling I could see it—taking off and touching down on the bulb casing. Alighting then landing, over and over again in fuzzy micro-bursts of static. I was transfixed, absorbed to the core by the clumsy dance of a house fly. Can you understand me, Mother? It was amazing to me, the way that one small piece of life had found its way into such a fortress.

That's when it sliced through me. I knew it like Abraham. This house fly was my Spirit Guide, here to teach me because I had proven myself worthy.

House Fly whirred down from off of the bulb casing and then He settled onto my naked stomach. Even that small movement seemed like a miracle to me. That heat attraction of life to life. I reached down to touch Him. I reached down to stroke Him with my quaking fingertip.

209

But He flew away, hovered, and then landed again. He stared right at me with lidless eyes. Those blind eyes were fixed on me without color or emotion like porous bulbs. Like honeycombs. Like an equation. Like fractals repeating themselves over and over again into infinity.

House Fly was intent and waiting.

The Lipan and the Yaqui shamans, lying on the dark earth, had no doubt inspired more impressive spirit hosts. It was not Coyote Spirit or Mescalito who had found me, Mother. But who was I to question the delivery? Swain might have ended my fast in his ugly manner, but now I knew with certainty that he had come with his punches too late. Perhaps it was not so surprising. I had forty-three days of fasting on him, after everything was said and done.

Christ, if you can remember, did only forty.

Everything in this box came back to life with perfect intensity. I stood within a city that had been frozen in stone, but was released from that witchcraft. This cold broom closet was breathing again. The walls were flowing arabesques. The walls were detailed scrimshaws, caroming and rebounding in the wide open space of this cage like great swales of land. If I was a painter, I know that I could put it down for you on canvas. Everything here was interaction and connection. Everything—interlocking meshes of dancing energy. The walls exhaled, and when I touched them, they recoiled gently, with the sensitive modulations of nerve endings. It was alive, and I could see it. The whole idea of fixity and separation was the worst, graceless sham. The pieces were coming together. House Fly would show me. . . .

Just when it had all started to unwind, something in this box shifted again. The shifting was a heavy movement of underground plates, disrupting, and then locking back hard into place like the rough end of a carnival ride. A voice came over the speaker in this cage. But it was not the voice that I was used to. It was not any voice of authority, Mother. The new voice talked to me, very gently.

It told me, "Lights out, Number 27671."

It was a considerate but inhuman voice, like HAL from the Kubrick film, pre-recorded for an automated system. When it cut out everything here went deep black. I imagined whole city blocks going out along with the light in my cell like a great smothered flame.

On reflection I reconsidered. The voice that had called me was not really gentle at all, as I had first thought, but mildly chiding, like just barely keeping back laughter. They had never told me that before. They had never told me, "Lights Out."

It was easy to see it now. This was a type of subtle game that they were throwing at me. Swain was hoping to break me in a final way. After that, he would discard me like medical waste at the bottom of his backwoods trash-heap. Did he really think he could fool me so easily? You might already know, I have always seen quickly to the heart of any situation involving angles.

I could remember the needle now in the darkness—glinting like a polished blade—and everything inside my cell flooding. I could feel the wet air all around me, Mother. It was moist, like the back of eye-lids, the way that it glistened. I clutched the sides of my small mattress, cramping my fingers with the exertion, and biting in the best I could with my short nails. Everything here was in motion, oceans without Dramamine. I could hear the clicking sound of crustaceans or beetles scuttling around me, trying to escape from the rising tide. I understood that if I fell asleep, I would drown here before the morning, thrown right over the bow. But I knew somehow that if I could make it through the night, when the lights came back on, and when prison routine came back to illuminate this small cloister like a rising sun, they would never be able to touch me. I knew that after that, they would never be able to take me down.

And I made it, Mother. Somehow, I did.

Now I am something new. I am something that you have never seen before. I feel myself blend in to the gray composite of the walls, and my anatomy bends in hard right angles like the cold metal of the riveted furniture. I am an animal of this particular environment. Moreso than any native on any vision quest who hugs the earth and speaks its language. I feel the muscles of my back blending with the stone wall as I lean back into it. The wall opens up to take me in, cradling, and then it closes gently around me, the way that a baby's gums close around a mother's finger. There is an umbilical chord that attaches me here and nourishes me on fine bits of stone ore. But I am not trapped. My arms and legs can still move freely. I can get up when I please. The wall releases me with a schlupping sound.

I know that I could hide here if I willed it, Mother, in this mostly empty space. I am a brand new kind of chameleon. An old man sits in the viewing room and he strokes his tabby cat as he watches me on the closed circuits. To him, it looks as if I have simply vanished. He sets his

211

soda pop down and puts the cat off of his lap. He scratches at his liver-spotted head, and then hits the monitor on its side, three times, like a broken television set. . . .

I will admit to you, Mother, that I do not have all of the answers yet. At times, it is hard to process all that I can see now. Sometimes, it is much worse than others. The Gods give me glimpses, but of course it is all in cipher. There is a needling voice in the back of my head, daring me to take things to the next level, but I am not sure what they expect from me. I am only certain that I am being tested again in some way. It exhausts me, and on most days it is easier just to sleep.

House Fly has still not returned, Mother. He has left no clues for me that might suggest how I am supposed to take all of this. He has left no clues to suggest exactly what all of this is supposed to mean.

I have searched every square inch of this box for any signs of His small, insect corpse. I have gotten down on my knees. I have slithered on my stomach like a snake. I have climbed the walls like a spider. I have seen his track on the light cage, Mother, where he first landed on a thin blanket of dust. I have combed this box with the slow deliberation of a police force, dragging some District lake for the body of a missing senator.

It seems that He is gone without one trace.

Despite all of this, things are not as bad as you might imagine these days at Wenatchee. Swain has left for an assistant warden position in Florence, Arizona, and they now allow me small amenities that make things livable. For example, I have access to the prison library again. I can order a book, and the guards will bring it here to me in my cell, where I can read it comfortably, and safe. If they do not have it on the shelves at Wenatchee, they will order it in for me, on loan from the county library.

So maybe you can tell that there is some amount of freedom here with Swain gone.

Now I am breaking up this writing to you by speaking passages from a slim volume of illustrated poetry that I have on loan from the county. The volume was written by an anonymous Sufi mystic. The acoustics in this box are perfect for verse, and the words wash over me from the air just like cool river water. It is a comfortable feeling like sinking, or like closing your eyes.

These passages make me think of you, and how you enjoyed Pablo Neruda.

Do you still read his poetry?

When I open to page twenty-three, there is a beautiful white flower with brick red veins like delivering heart-blood. It is framed by an intricate and illuminated border. But the flower is not there as part of the illustration, Mother. The petals are thin and pressed into a soft, satiny skein, and the perfume has long ago expired, replaced by an attic smell of old paper. Still, I can imagine the sugary scent. I have to wonder how far this flower has travelled to end up at such an unlikely spot. I have to wonder, considering everything that has come before, did House Fly place this between the pages for me to find?

I can remember strange things when I stare at it, things that I might have ignored at one time. They were discarded details, but are resurrected now from deep inside of my consciousness.

I can see a dominant sky that threatens rain and wildfire. It is framed and viewed from out of a moving car window. When the engine is turned off, I can hear the sudden whine of cicadas, singing like chalk out of a muggy quiet. Now I see two small wrens hopping towards me as I sit cross-legged on the sidewalk, holding a piece of green chalk in between my fingers. They stop short to fly up and perch gently on shallow grooves in the rough oak bark. And there are orange, leached ores that dribble rusty puddles into the dry creek bed on Grandpa's farm in West Virginia, and that foul smell of compost. I am seven years old again running in pollen-smeared jeans, stained bright yellow from those large fields of grasses and wildflowers. You watch me the whole time from the doorway, Mother. Your face is tight and expressionless. You are holding a sweating glass of sweet tea in your hands.

And now I see myself from a distance, as if through a distorted glass window, being pushed along by gorilla guards to the Warehouse, my greatest freedom here at Wenatchee. My diminutive form is hunched over and still in my wheelchair, without spit mask or padded helmet or cuffs or chains. I am a brand new kind of monstrous saint.